BLOOD ON THE BRAIN

a novel

ESINAM BEDIAKO

Red Hen Press | *Pasadena, CA*

Book design by Mark E. Cull.

Library of Congress Cataloging-in-Publication Data

Names: Bediako, Esinam, 1983– author.
Title: Blood on the brain: a novel / Esinam Bediako.
Description: First edition. | Pasadena, CA: Red Hen Press, 2024.
Identifiers: LCCN 2024005997 (print) | LCCN 2024005998 (ebook) | ISBN
   9781636281803 (paperback) | ISBN 9781636281810 (ebook)
Subjects: LCGFT: Bildungsromans. | Novels.
Classification: LCC PS3602.E34128 B58 2024 (print) | LCC PS3602.E34128
   (ebook) | DDC 813/.6—dc23/eng/20240208
LC record available at https://lccn.loc.gov/2024005997
LC ebook record available at https://lccn.loc.gov/2024005998

The National Endowment for the Arts, the Los Angeles County Arts Commission, the Ahmanson Foundation, the Dwight Stuart Youth Fund, the Max Factor Family Foundation, the Pasadena Tournament of Roses Foundation, the Pasadena Arts & Culture Commission and the City of Pasadena Cultural Affairs Division, the City of Los Angeles Department of Cultural Affairs, the Audrey & Sydney Irmas Charitable Foundation, the Meta & George Rosenberg Foundation, the Albert and Elaine Borchard Foundation, the Adams Family Foundation, Amazon Literary Partnership, the Sam Francis Foundation, and the Mara W. Breech Foundation partially support Red Hen Press.

First Edition
Published by Red Hen Press
www.redhen.org

BLOOD ON THE BRAIN

For my mother, Patience, my sister, Kafui,
and my Uncle Souley—
for heaps upon heaps of belief

BLOOD ON THE BRAIN

1

I linger at the information desk, running my fingers along the faux wood panel, sliding them up to the plastic placard on which the Department of Housing engraved his name: Daniel Cobblah. The same last name as one of my cousins on my mom's side. I fleetingly remember the story my mom once told me about a Ghanaian guy and girl who met in the States, fell in love, married, and moved back to Ghana, only to discover from some great-aunt who kept track of the family tree that they were actually related. But I'm not marrying Daniel, just asking him out, and besides, the guy and girl of that old wives' tale always stay together. After all, whether he's a distant cousin or a stranger, a husband is the same kind of burden, or so my mom jokes.

As usual, I'm thinking of my mom when I shouldn't.

"Hi, Pete," I say to the middle-aged white guy at the desk. Pete often greets Daniel with an awkward fist bump and a "what up, dawg," not noticing Daniel's discomfort.

"Hi, Sue," he says, calling me by the Americanized, bastardized version of my name. Appropriately, as I fit both of those descriptors. "Looking for Daniel? He's out in the field. Freshman got locked out of her room. Dan had to bring her a key because she was in nothing but a towel. Quite the opportunity for a lady's man like Dan."

Pete grins and licks his chapped lips, which I know are rubbery and salty from the time he kissed me at the Housing, Facilities, and General Staff Christmas party. He doesn't have to mention that the call to the field is one he wishes he'd gotten instead of Daniel. Pete's perviness is so pervasive that he couldn't even guess that I was the one who anonymously reported him to our supervisors; he has a long list of other women he's harassed.

The phone at the front desk rings and Pete tells me, "Dan asked if you'd wait for him. He'll be back from the field soon," before answering it.

"The field" is a smattering of dormitories on a compact yet architecturally alluring college campus in New York City. Two years ago, I finished undergrad here; six years ago, I started a work-study job in the library and didn't expect that, after graduation, I'd still be working in the same department and be buddy-buddy with all the staff who once ran around unlocking doors and fixing clogged showers for my classmates and me. Nor did I expect that I'd be asking out Daniel Cobblah, Housing Department Staff Level II. Once a week for three months, since I started working the late shift at the library on Sundays, I've been meeting him at his desk and talking to him during the last half hour of his shift, after which he walks me halfway to my apartment before saying good night. He's my lifeboat. I know that sounds intense, like I'm getting carried away over some guy, but I'm not. Lately, I've been feeling more and more adrift, and my weekly talks with Daniel have kept me from giving up and going under.

"Akosua."

There it is, his rumbling voice with that accented, authentic way of saying my name.

"Daniel, hello."

He stands perhaps two heads taller than me. I move closer to him without meaning to, and now he's standing so close I can touch him if I want to. I don't touch him, willing him to do it first: pat my arm, hold my elbow as he greets me, take my hand, and ask me out so I don't have to do the dirty work.

Instead, he retreats behind the desk, sits in the chair next to Pete. I step back over to the desk. Now I'm taller than him, but I don't feel like this gives me any advantage.

"How are you, Akosua?" He's always this formal; it's like I'm speaking to one of my aunties at a Ghanaian get-together. Disconcerting from someone my age, yet familiar in a way that warms me.

"I'm fine, and you?"

"Well, I don't really enjoy running to unlock doors for careless students," he says jovially. "I never locked myself out of my room when I was an undergrad . . ."

Here he goes. This is what he does. Always the same format when I ask him how he's doing: first he says how much he doesn't enjoy whatever housing-related task he's wrapped up in, and then he discusses how he's never been so irresponsible as to engage in X careless coed behavior (get locked out of his room, set a fire while merely boiling water, clog a toilet with tampons and paper towels, and so forth). Then follows a rapid downward spiral into reminiscing about our days as undergrads here and how special we are now that we're graduate students and employees. We're not special; we're pathetic. Stagnant. Reliving the same moments again and again. But I don't want to burst his lovely, chocolate-skinned, well-muscled, bright-futured bubble. He is a catch, and, for once, I'm ready to do what it takes to reel one in.

". . . always had my keys on a shoelace, which I put around my neck . . ."

This is the problem: he is the most gorgeous thing walking, but he's from the country or something, from some remote village in Ghana whose name my mother laughed at when she heard it. "Good luck getting anywhere with him," she said yesterday when I told her I was going to ask him out. He wears his keys on a shoelace. He carries a pocket protector. His nerdiness is endearing, but at the same time, it makes things difficult because he doesn't seem to pick up or send out any of the signals a young, minimally hip person might know. Things that even someone like me, who still says "hip," would understand.

A gaggle of girls approaches the desk. They need the key to the fifth-floor lounge to rehearse their hip-hop dance. Pete clasps his hands together, a little too joyous. "Daniel, you finish talking to Sue there and cover the desk. I'll be right back."

As Pete follows the girls, I know I have it. My chance. I'll ask him now, force him to stop talking about boring stuff and just say yes to me.

"Daniel, I've been meaning to ask you—"

"Yes?"

"Um, we only really see each other every Sunday, here, but I think we're getting to know each other pretty well, so—"

"Yes?" He cuts me off.

"I was wondering if I could ask you—"

"Yes?"

"Ugh!" I slam my open palms down on the surface of the desk, upsetting his name plate. I give a smile. "Sorry. I just . . . you're making it hard for me to talk to you right now."

"Oh. I always find it very easy for us to talk."

"Well, me too, which is why I'm trying to ask you—"

"If you don't mind, I've been waiting all week to tell you something myself." Daniel takes hold of my hand over the desk. A first. In three months of this Sunday night ritual, he has never held my hand. "I have spoken to my cousin about you."

"Oh? Why?" Because Daniel's interested and needs advice on how to romance me? It can't be anything but that, unless he's trying to pimp me out to his cousin. "Your cousin . . ."

"Kwesi Cobblah; he is a doctoral student. Not here, but in Brooklyn."

"What exactly were you telling him about little old me?" That question is an error, a grave mistake. In an attempt to sound like some kind of sex kitten, I come off as wheedling and self-conscious.

"Just naming some of the Ghanaian girls around. He was very interested to hear your name." Daniel grins as he says it. "Mercy Akosua Agbe. It is not so common to find an Agbe in New York City. In fact, aside from you, I've never met an *Agbe* in all my *life*."

Now his voice cracks into a cackle, for he has made a joke. My surname, Agbe, means *life* in Ewe, our language and ethnic group.

"You get it? I've never in my *life* met an *Agbe*?"

"I get it; I get it." I can't help but laugh with him; there is something sweet about the cheesy things he says, perhaps because he says them in such earnestness.

But while I am laughing at his joke, glad to be with him in this warm, shared moment, he says, "So anyway, my cousin Kwesi knows an Agbe. Kofi Agbe. Your father."

"How do you know that that particular Kofi Agbe is my father?" I ask, but I know right away it must be. After all, like Daniel said, it is not so common to find an Agbe in New York City. Plus, my mother and I have already heard through the Ghanaian grapevine that he has moved to New York and is teaching here.

"Because Kwesi asked if he has a daughter by your name, and he does. I know that after so many years of his absence, you are probably interested in seeing him. I could get his phone number for you—"

My hand that he's been holding is sopping wet now. The thoughts inside my head feel waterlogged, too. His words have opened a door in my brain, triggered a flood of thoughts and emotions that do not fit this situation. I am asking a guy out on a date. I am not asking to hear about my father. It's not news that my father has returned from a long stint in Ghana and now lives in New York, but it's news that my crush could have any connection to him. I don't want to have to think of my father during a moment like this. If I can't control the way my father moves in and out of my life, at least I deserve to have control over when I think of him, right?

I pull my hand from Daniel's, wipe it on my jeans as discreetly as I can. "I don't talk to my father. I haven't in years, and he didn't try to contact me or anything when he moved back to the States. So tell your cousin no thank you."

"I know you haven't spoken to him. But this might be a good thing. My cousin says your father is a very nice man." Daniel speaks as

though he's telling me what he ate for lunch. "Just take your time
and think about it, and maybe—"

"No." I reach both hands out to grab one of his, the closest we've
ever come to an embrace. I smile, lean across the desk and talk directly into his ear. "I don't care about my father. I care about you going
out with me. On a date."

He squeezes my hands, his face falls. He plasters on a pleasant,
avuncular expression. "Oh. Sue. Thank you, really. I'm flattered. But
I'm horribly busy. Maybe next semester?"

Oh.

I tear off my gloves, hat, and winter coat, throwing them around the
room piece by piece as I press the phone to my ear, listening to my
mother attempt to placate me in her perpetually amused voice.

"So the engineer turned you down for a date, eh? He says he is
too busy? Well, it is possible. He is an engineering graduate student.
Very, very serious with his pocket protector and protractor." She lets
out a giggle. I can picture her slapping her knee, swiveling in her favorite chair at the kitchen counter in her condo. "Trust me, I know
that type of man. You are better without him."

"But Mom . . ."

"You don't even like him that much, anyway. Every weekend you
talk to him. He's nice. He's smart. He's an engineer like your father.
But that doesn't mean he is worth all this effort."

"This has nothing to do with Daddy," I mumble. I don't tell her that
Daniel actually brought up my father before rejecting me; I don't
want to think about my father at all.

She snorts. "Funny that three months ago is when you started
stalking this boy, and three months ago is when we heard that your
father had come back to the US."

What she doesn't know is that three months ago is also when I
broke up with Wisdom. Then again, she doesn't really know that
Wisdom and I were together in the first place.

"Whenever we hear news about your father, you start running toward anything Ghanaian," she says.

Whenever we hear news about my father, my mother starts running away from anything Ghanaian. When I was seven and he left us, she stopped going to Ghanaian Bible Study. When she heard he was divorcing his second wife, Mom moved us from my childhood home in Detroit—the house she and my dad bought together—to an apartment miles away in West Bloomfield. Then, when the gossip among the Ghanaian community in Michigan got too thick (will Enyo get back together with Kofi, does she know how many other children he has, will Akosua be a good girl and seek out her father), she moved across the border to Windsor, Canada, where she now lives in a condo community with a mix of elderly people and young families. No one there knows or cares about her love life. They just like that she smiles and waves and gives out whole candy bars to their kids at Halloween.

"Mom, I don't want to talk about Dad. I want to talk about why I'm a prime target for rejection. Why don't guys like me?"

"The question you should be asking is why you like men. Name one that has done something good for you." She laughs wildly; the sound always reminds me of a spooked flock of birds, a flutter of wings escaping to the sky.

"Mom, you always say that love is important, that I should go for it, blah blah blah . . ."

"Well, you should go for it, I suppose. That's what people do in life. But I'll tell you, you shouldn't expect to enjoy it. Because it has to do with men, and that can't bring you much good."

I am crying. I've been crying without realizing it. Who is Daniel Cobblah? He is an objectively handsome man whose Ghanaian accent and rumbling voice evoke a pallid pleasure. He is someone to talk to once a week, about nothing, a diversion at best. Why am I crying over him?

Luckily my mother stops cackling in that way that makes me feel like she is lonelier than I am. And she speaks in the sweet, buttery tone she saves for when I really need it:

"The only good thing any man has brought me was you."

∽○∾

The last time I saw my father I was seven, and I don't remember much about his leaving. But I do remember the last time I heard from him. Sweet sixteen, or close to it. A week before my birthday, I found out my prep school friends were throwing a surprise party for me; I accidentally overheard the girls discussing the ideal time to call my mom to coordinate the details. My best friend Nisha, whose mom worked as a doctor at the same hospital where my mom was a nutritionist, knew my family better than the rest of my buddies and was the only one who'd been to the birthday parties my mom usually threw for me. My mom's parties were huge events that involved Ghanaian aunties and uncles and cousins, in addition to other family friends who weren't Ghanaian but close enough—perhaps Caribbean or Indian or Filipino. The ticket was that you had to be an immigrant, not for any reason other than that many of the adults had been drawn to the familiarity of each others' otherness.

"All we have to do," Nisha said to the other girls from their place a few spots in front of me in the lunch line, "is get Akosua's mom to trick her into thinking that she's planned a big Ghanaian party or something—make Akosua think she's going to a sweet sixteen family affair at one of her aunties' houses, but then—surprise!—her mom actually drives her to my house and we'll have everything set up, and she'll be so freaked to have a real party for once without adults around."

I had to clasp my hands over my mouth to keep from shouting out my friends' names and running over to hug them right away. I loved them for planning something for me, but most of all I loved Nisha for understanding that it wasn't the Ghanaianness of the parties I'd grown tired of; I loved the smells of kenkey and jollof rice cooking, the bright colors of my aunties' dresses, the smattering of pidgin and Ewe and Twi mixed in with English. I just wanted to feel like a teenager, to have a celebration that did not include a bunch of adults to whom I had to bow my head and speak my polite yet halting Ewe.

To give my friends the space to continue to plan my party, I decided to leave the lunch line and hang out in the computer lab. I logged into my account, not expecting to find anything other than junk mail in my late-nineties, newly-minted Netscape inbox. Instead of junk mail, I discovered a message with the title, "HAPPY BDAY, AKOSUA" from a sender called Agbe.

I assumed it was a family member from Ghana, that maybe my mother had given out my email address to a cousin or some other relative I barely knew. But then I clicked on the message.

Dear daughter, I hope you are well and that your mommy is well.
I understand you are celebrating a birthday this month and wish
you a fine day. Your daddy.

I started to shake so much that the kid next to me asked if I was okay. My leg would not receive the message my brain tried to send it to stop rattling the computer table. I closed the email and nodded, crossing my legs to keep them still. The trembling that remained was mostly on the inside, where no one could see it. In the first couple of years after my father had left us, my mother purchased birthday and Christmas gifts and told me he'd sent them, but she stopped the charade when I grew old enough to know that his never calling, writing, or visiting pretty much invalidated any gifts he could send me. He never contacted me or sent me so much as a birthday card. He never tried.

And now I was glad he never had. "Celebrating a birthday this month," he'd typed, as if he didn't know which birthday I was celebrating or on what day. Imagine if every year I'd received such a half-assed effort?

I told myself it was good that he'd made a clean break. I deleted the message without replying, and whenever I found my thoughts drifting to him, I swiftly reigned them in. It was easy, the promise of my upcoming sweet sixteen the perfect distraction. A week later, at my birthday party, I feigned surprise when I arrived at Nisha's house, and really *was* surprised when I discovered that half of the kids in our grade were there. I played the role, laughing at jokes I didn't get, dancing to music I didn't like, flirting with boys I knew didn't like me, all the while wondering how Nisha had bribed this many people to show up for me. *Nisha has the nicest mansion in our grade. That's why they're here.* Some girl I barely knew passed me a tiny bottle of vodka. "I've already had too much," I lied. I was a fraud, sober and lame, but she seemed not to notice. No one ever did. On the outside, I know I looked calm, sedate even, but on the inside, I could always feel the blood rushing through me. I wondered if I'd always feel that way.

Tonight, even after speaking to my mother on the phone, I am not calm on the outside. I am hot and restless, unclean and slick with sweat. Living in this city, I sweat. In the summer, in the subways, I sweat. Now it is nearly winter, and my walk from the Housing Department to my graduate apartment five blocks away made me sweat, even though it was cold outside. Perhaps it is because I ran more than I walked; perhaps it is because, even after speaking to my mother, I cannot shake this shakiness in my gut. In the Midwest, where I lived until I came East for school six years ago, I drove everywhere. You didn't have to run, so you didn't have to feel sweat trickling down your back. Or maybe I didn't sweat because I was younger then and had nothing to be in a hurry about. Or nothing to run from. All I know is that I need a shower now, like I always need a shower, like I can never get clean in this city.

In the bathroom, in the mirror, I'm disturbed. Not because of what I see, but because of what I can't see. I've taken off my contacts but my glasses are in the other room on my dresser. Didn't I stop going to my annual eye doctor's appointments to avoid yet another stronger prescription for these myopic eyes? I figure if I don't let my eyes get used to the idea of seeing better, they won't get any worse. Yet here I stand, my reflection mottled, like someone spilled acetone all over a painting of me and the colors have run together. I can't see myself clearly anymore, even though I'm just a few feet in front of me.

But I know that the 20/20 view isn't great, though it's not bad. Actually, it's nice: I'm naked. Not that I am so comfortable looking at myself naked, but the fact remains that I look okay undressed. I raise my arms perpendicular to my body, palms facing down. Though I can barely see them now because of my terrible eyesight, I know they're there: trim upper arms. But if I turn one palm up to face the ceiling and use the other to jiggle the arm fat, the fat will oblige. And the belly points toward the mirror, slightly rounded, unnoticeable beneath a T-shirt or even a reasonably tight sweater, but I know it's there. Wisdom started noticing it months ago, teasing, poking, pinching. I promised him I'd lose it, but I only ended up gaining a little more, even after I cut back on stress-eating chocolate. In truth, my arms and stomach don't offend my sensibilities much; I have other assets, I suppose. Height, hips, bust, wide black eyes, a white smile. And legs that get whistles on the few occasions I wear skirts or dresses, legs that feel like jelly right now from all the running they've just done to help me escape my thoughts. Plus the important assets, the ones I've lived my whole life striving toward, the nebulous qualities of my mind and heart. Right?

I attempt to slip into the shower without touching the mildewy shower curtain, an art form I've perfected in the three months since I've washed it, but my trembling body is not so agile right now. *I'm trembling because of all that running I did*, I tell myself. *Not because of him. Not Wisdom, not Daniel. Not my father.*

But it doesn't matter why I'm shaking. I just am, so much that my legs give and I slip and fall in the tub. I hit the back of my head on the edge of the tub so hard that when I try to sit up, I feel the urge to vomit. Each hair on my body stands on end; all the blood in my body courses toward the back of my head. I lie back down and close my eyes and watch stars dance against my eyelids.

I don't know how much time passes before I haul myself up and stumble to my bed. I am not in good shape. All I want to do is sleep, but soap operas and medical dramas have taught me that's the last thing I should do. I reach over to my bedside table for my glasses and my cell phone, and I start to call my mom, but that makes no sense. She is hundreds of miles away and I don't want to hear her laugh at me, however gently, for falling.

I consider Daniel for a moment. But not for long. I see red smudges and feel sharp pain behind my eyes when I hear Daniel's words. *My cousin says your father is a very nice man.* Because nice men leave their wives and children and never look back? If I'd said yes to Daniel's offer to give me my father's phone number, would I be calling my father for help right now? Maybe hitting my head is enough of an emergency to transcend years of abandonment and neglect.

But probably not. I call my friend Ella, who doesn't pick up, so I leave her an incoherent message. And then, because he's the only other person I don't mind seeing me naked, I call Wisdom, who says he's coming over, already breathless because he's rushing out the door to me. For me.

Wisdom is an Ewe, like me (though, unlike me, he was actually raised in Ghana, is authentic in every aspect that matters). There are many ways to tell this, but the fastest way is his name. Wisdom has an Ewe name (Selom), an Ewe day name (Yao, which means he was born on a Thursday), speaks Ewe (with a waning accent). He has doe-like eyes that make him look innocent rather than wise. But his parents had already named their firstborn daughter Innocent, and somehow when they looked at his baby face they had reason to believe he'd someday be wise.

Wisdom still has a key to my apartment and barges right in, his eyes huge behind his black-framed glasses. He looks intelligent in them: fitting, since he is intelligent. He doesn't have the muscles Daniel has, but his arms are the only ones whose feeling I've memorized. As he lifts me from the edge of my bed to reposition me in the center of it, I think that he is the kindest person, man or not, that I have ever known.

"Daniel Cobblah and I are dating," I find myself telling Wisdom as his arms surround me.

He covers me with my bed sheet, pushes all my junk off the bed. "Are you cold? Let me stay with you."

"Daniel from Housing. Daniel from the Volta Region."

"Well, where is he now?" Wisdom checks the back of my head, touches the pain gathering at my skull, and his hands come back clean. No blood. He takes off his pants and climbs in bed with me, wearing boxers and his blue Oxford dress shirt.

"What are you doing?"

"Let me stay with you. I know what I'm doing, remember?"

Wisdom is in med school. His long lashes brush against my cheek and he pulls the blankets over us. He hums me to sleep. It doesn't seem particularly medical, but it is good, and I close my eyes and fade away knowing it is safe to do so.

∞

After nearly two years of dating, it took only a day for Wisdom and me to break up, just as quick and strange as us getting together in the first place. We'd met at a New Year's party held by a mutual friend in the business school; Wisdom had mistaken me for an American, which I technically am.

"I'm Akosua."

"*Really*?" He rubbed his hands together, an expectant grin on his face, like he expected me, with my American accent and Ghanaian name, to be clueless about who I am. "And do you know what your name means?"

Like I wouldn't know.

"Born on Sunday."

"Ah, I see. And your last name?"

"Agbe. I'm Mercy Akosua Agbe."

"What is an Ewe doing with an Akan day name and an Ewe surname?"

"My dad's mom was Akan. My dad wanted me to be Akosua in her honor. Or so I'm told."

"Or so you're told?" he asked. "Have you been to Ghana? Have you met your father's family?"

"If you keep trying to test me, I'll make sure I'm standing next to someone else at midnight." I said this with confidence, maybe a bit of sass, and after a couple hours of talking, I knew he was as pleased as I was that we were still standing together at midnight. But also—who was that person who had all but promised him a kiss at midnight? Surely not me, the girl who never went around kissing people she had just met. As the clock struck twelve and his face leaned toward mine, I felt my head turning to the side so that instead of a kiss, his nose brushed against my temple. He cracked up, a laugh I can only describe as joyful, his eyes squinting into half-moons. My whole face burned. I left the party so fast, he had to ask around for my phone number. I ignored his messages for a week, but, once I got up my nerve, I called him back and never stopped.

∽o∽

The glaring sun interrupts, wakes me up to my headache. It's morning and Wisdom sits on the edge of my bed, reading my copy of the text for the ancient Japanese history course I dropped out of back in September. Wisdom doesn't know that, soon after we broke up, I dropped from fifteen credits down to two and became the only history grad student in the history of grad students to be registered for just a Spanish conversation class. Despite the pain, I snatch the book from his hands.

"I'm not taking this class anymore."

"Oh? It sounds so interesting."

I can't tell whether he's mocking me or not. This is one of the reasons why we're only friends now, if that.

"I am interested in all kinds of history," I say.

"Are you really?" He smirks. Or smiles. I don't know. My head pounds. "Are you taking any Ghanaian history this term? Or any other African history classes?"

"Get out, now. I mean, thank you for coming, but please get out before my head explodes."

The smile slides right off his face, and my chest feels hollow. He never understands why and how he hurts me. Hell if I'll cry again. I try to channel my mother. *Laugh, damn it; laugh. Brush him off like it's nothing.*

"I didn't mean it like that," he starts saying.

But before he can say anything else, there's pounding at my door, and a voice calling, "Hellooo, Akosua! Let me in! Are you alive?"

Enter my friend Ella. She's Jamaican, and probably the most beautiful woman I've ever seen, aside from my mother. The most sophisticated, too, yet she always wears this homely red scarf she knitted for herself. She's all lanky arms and legs as she flies into the room once Wisdom opens the door for her.

"Are you okay? Your message said you'd cracked your skull, girl, but you look fine to me . . ." She purses her lips, indicates my bare arms and calves; though sheets and blankets cover the rest of me, the situation seems pretty clear to her. "Are you with this fool again?"

"Yes. But it's not what it looks like; I fell in the shower and hit my head and called you both. He came over first."

Wisdom's voice comes an octave higher than usual. "What do you mean, 'yes'? I thought you're dating Daniel Cobblah?"

"I meant 'yes,' I'm okay, not 'yes,' I'm with you."

I will Wisdom not to leave. But I know he wants to. It is awkward. Since college, Ella has been the best friend who picks up the pieces when Wisdom or any other man or beast breaks me. It is a horrible part to play, I'm sure. She probably hates Wisdom, just from hearing tales of our relationship and, of course, the night we broke up. He feels guilty because he knows she must know all the bad parts of him and not the good. He feels ashamed and wants to leave. I need to make him stay.

"Guys, I need to ask your advice on something," I blurt. "I want to call my father, but I'm not sure . . . I need your advice . . ."

"Why don't you ask Daniel Cobblah for his advice?"

The bitterness in Wisdom's voice lets me know I've won a small victory but makes me fear he might still leave, now out of jealousy at my new imaginary boyfriend.

"Daniel is the one who is encouraging me to talk to my father. His cousin can get my dad's phone number for me," I say, even though I could get it elsewhere because someone, anyone in the Ghanaian network—except my mom and me—knows someone who knows him. Maybe not so, but that's how it feels, that everyone seems to know something we don't, that we're on the outside. "But Daniel doesn't know me as well as you two do. And I just need your advice."

Maybe it's working. Wisdom sits on the edge of the bed, Ella at my desk. It'd work better if Ella would leave. I love her, I do, but I miss Wisdom . . . I don't really want to discuss my father, I want Wisdom to stay, and I'm hoping Wisdom won't see right through me.

"You haven't seen him in—what—sixteen years?" Ella asks.

"Seventeen," Wisdom and I say in unison, and I add, "and I haven't talked to him in eight years, not since high school, and, even then, it was just an email."

"Why now? Because he's in the country?" Ella sounds dubious.

"Well, it is convenient that he's in New York now. Now you have no excuse." Wisdom takes my hand. I think of Daniel. I ready myself for the blow because no one holds my hand unless they're going to say something horrible. "You've hidden from him enough. He's your father. You're not an American girl; family should matter more to you. Don't you think the respectful thing to do would be to reconnect with him again?"

There it is. The refrain I've heard from family back in Ghana as well as our family friends in Michigan. Most people minded their own business, but a disconcerting number of people in our lives had at some point or another implied or stated outright that my father deserved forgiveness, that I should never turn my back on my blood. Never mind that he cheated on my mom for years. Never mind that after he left us, she tried to divorce him *in absentia* and learned that he had been legally married to another woman during their whole relationship, voiding my parents' marriage in the eyes of the US court system, voiding my legitimacy. Never mind that my father had married a third wife after leaving us and supposedly cheated on that one, too, and had a colony of illegitimate children running around. Despite all of that damning evidence, the respectful thing for a good Ghanaian girl to do would be to reconnect with him, simply because he's my father. And now the same mantra from Wisdom.

After nearly two years of dating, it took just a day for Wisdom and me to break up. Our last day together as a couple, strangely, smacked of the same vibe as the day we met, the same vibe that had lingered throughout all our days together but that I'd tried hard to ignore. Every day, this man I loved enough to let my guard down seemed to question my authenticity, asking me over and over and over, "And do you know what your name means?"

We're standing in the street outside of his apartment, and he's dressed to the nines, new jeans, suede shoes, ready to hang out with his crew. His friends Kwame and Rebecca, a couple, and another girl, sometimes Marie, sometimes Sedi, are waiting for him in Times Square or someplace, ready to drink, to club, but I am not invited, not after the last time, which was the first time, a fluke, a freak accident that he wants never to repeat.

"Please let me come."

"No."

"Just this once."

"No, baby. You came last week, you don't have to come again."

"I promise, it's not that I want to always come, or cramp your style, I know you need friends other than me, but—"

"No, Akosua, no. Now I have to go. I'm going to be late."

"—but I just want to get to know them better. And last time wasn't that bad. Please?"

Back and forth, please and no. But this time, I do something I've never done before. I refuse to go home. I tell him I'm coming with him. I feel daring. I feel bold and powerful. He cannot escape me. I don't have to will him to stay or to want me around because I refuse to let him do anything else.

At first, he laughs. I'm standing in front of him with my shoulders squared and feet planted; it's ridiculous. I laugh, too. But then it's not funny anymore; it's no joke. When he takes steps toward the subway station, I follow. He stops; I stop. I tell him that I'm coming and that he can't prevent me.

"*Tso*! Don't be annoying. You can't come. You just don't fit with them, okay? You embarrass me, how American you try to be."

I fall down in the street, backward, on my ass, inexplicably. He doesn't help me up, just turns and strides down the street, down the subway steps. I scramble to my feet, not knowing how I fell in the first place, but feeling the weight of it, the weight of how much I don't add up to anything, just a question mark identity, and, suddenly, I know how I ended up down on the ground. His words hit me square in the chest. He might as well have punched me in the sternum.

This is a story that runs through my head nearly every time I've seen Wisdom since then, even though he's apologized repeatedly, and it's beating in my heart now as I lay naked in bed, my head nothing but a dull ache.

I ask him to leave and mean it, at least for today. Ella slaps me a high five as if to say, "You go, girl," but she doesn't say it. She is too cool for that, and she knows he'll probably be back.

2

I'm in the tiny park near the Cathedral of St. John the Divine, sitting on a concrete bench with Ella at my side. We used to come here all the time in college when we wanted a break from campus—I swear I'd know nothing about this city without Ella encouraging me to venture out of my head and into the streets—and there's something comforting about the aggressively verdant shrubs surrounding us. It's like we're in the park that autumn forgot, and I try to delude myself into thinking it's actually spring. I'm clutching a lukewarm cup of tea and a congealed breakfast sandwich that turns my stomach. Ella took part of the morning off work to meet me, but I overslept and arrived an hour late, so I can't exactly complain that the food she brought me has gone cold.

Ella ate her breakfast while waiting for me, so she's knitting while we talk.

"You promise your head's feeling okay?" she asks for the third or fourth time in ten minutes.

"Yes," I say, even though I'm not really sure. It's Tuesday morning—the first time I've left my apartment since I hit my head Sunday night. Pain still gnaws at my skull, a constant reminder of my embarrassing fall. "I'm sorry you even had to come out to my apartment yesterday. I overreacted. There was no need to worry you. Or to bring Wisdom into the situation."

"Mmm-hmm . . ." Ella doesn't look up from her knitting, but she purses her lips like she's trying to lock words away.

"What?"

"You bring Wisdom into every situation."

"No, no, I don't. Well, I did call him. But only out of an old, dying habit. We're done."

"Okay."

"No, really. I'm the one who broke up with him, remember?"

"Yeah, girl, I said 'okay.'" Her voice remains mild, but I know it won't if I keep going down this track.

I wave my hand in the air, swiping away all talk of Wisdom. "How's work?" I ask.

She smiles, and now she's looking at me rather than the patch of forest green yarn blooming from her fingers. "Pretty good, actually. The interior designer liked my pitch, so it's looking like I finally get to take the lead with a client."

"Interior designer . . . ?" I say this before I have a moment to think. Should I have known about this?

But if Ella's annoyed, she doesn't show it. She tells me all about her new client, an up-and-coming, eco-conscious, Nigerian-American woman interior designer whose future success could translate into a promotion and big fat raise for Ella. I'm trying to listen, but it's hard when all I can hear is how much Ella is thriving, which naturally leads me to start thinking about all the ways I am not. I'm floundering in grad school, in my love life, in my family life. Meanwhile, Ella's PR job is her dream job. Her boyfriend Roger is her dream man. Ella sends part of her paycheck to her parents each month to help them build a house back in Jamaica, so I'm sure they brag nonstop about their generous, competent daughter. When Ella introduces me to people, she says we met as awkward freshmen during college orientation, but that's a half-truth. Only I was awkward. She was as confident and open and charming then as she is now. Even her falling apart looks put together; when her first boyfriend cheated on her during our sophomore year, she skipped classes for a couple of days, splurged on a plane ticket to Miami, and, after an impromptu beach vacation with her sister, returned to campus, sun-kissed and beaming. That's probably the most in crisis I've ever seen her. Of course I don't want to see her in crisis, and of course I'm happy she's doing well. At the same time, looking at her is like holding up a mirror to my own failure.

Suddenly Ella's standing up, tucking her yarn and needles into her shoulder bag. "All right, girlie. Let's get out of here. I gotta get to work."

I scramble for something to say to show that I'm happy for her and finally land on, "I'm happy for you."

When I try to stand up, I stagger a little, and right away, Ella's reaching for my arm. She loops hers in mine, and we walk out of the park together. She makes me promise that I'll leave campus early if I have a headache or feel dizzy. I don't tell her that I already have a headache and feel dizzy.

When we reach the point where we'll need to part ways, she stops. "Hey, I almost forgot. Have you given any more thought to that little bomb you dropped on Wisdom and me yesterday?"

"About dating Daniel Cobblah?"

"*No.* About your father, silly. Are you going to get his contact information?"

"No." A breeze picks up and I shudder, tucking my hands in my coat pockets. "What makes you think I'd want to do that?"

"Because you asked for our advice about it?"

"Oh, I didn't mean it. I only asked because I knew talking about my father would make Wisdom stay."

She tilts her head at me, arms across her chest. "Woman, you should hear yourself sometimes."

I want to tell her that all I do is hear myself, all these thoughts running through my head and crowding out any kind of quiet. But before I can get the words out, she's hugging me goodbye, and we're walking off in opposite directions.

On campus, I dawdle. Unlike Ella, I have nothing of consequence to rush to, just Spanish conversation class and then a shift at the library. I hesitate before entering the hall where my only class is held, because today we're supposed to talk in the *pluscuamperfecto*, and I don't understand what that means. More than perfect. The past perfect tense describes an event that has completed before another past action. *I had been a mess before I hit my head. I had started missing my father long before he left us.* I understand the grammatical constructions in English, but I don't understand the Spanish conjugations. More than that, I don't understand the concept because no event in my life ever seems completed. There are no past actions. Everything keeps happening and happening.

Take Daniel Cobblah. Here he comes up College Walk, and it's like he's rejecting me all over again because there's a girl by his side: Aku Aggrey. She's a sophomore who moved here from Ghana at the beginning of the semester. I know of her through the African grapevine on campus, plus I gave her a day pass at the library when she forgot to bring her ID card. Surely that must be how Daniel knows her, too: he probably helped her at the housing desk. Surely they're not dating; he's got to be at least seven years older than her. Not that I care about dating him anymore. I see now that I got carried away by the idea of him. I just want him to know that I know that his schedule didn't magically clear up in less than two days.

But instead of saying anything smart-ass to him, I smile and wave as they amble down the tree-lined cobblestone path that winds through campus. A golden canopy of leaves frames Daniel and Aku in autumnal perfection as they walk together, close but not close enough for me to tell what they mean to each other. In their cable-knit sweaters and impractically draped scarves, they're the portrait of elite collegiate life, right out of the admissions catalog. I pull the hood of my tattered coat over my head, knowing I look like I rolled out of bed, because that's exactly what I did.

I stand outside the building where my class will begin shortly. Then I wander to a nearby courtyard to sit on a bench and hide with my nose pressed to my Spanish book, trying to work out the grammar enough to be able to speak two sentences if I'm called upon. Pigeons and people flit around me. My head pounds; it's like someone has put his hand on the back of my head to comfort me but decides instead to thump me, continually, as if burping a baby too hard.

"Hey, Akosua."

I turn my head too fast. Behind me stands Alan, my coworker, one of the few non-Ghanaian people who calls me by my full name. He's thirty-five and a full-time regular employee, though you'd mistake him for a grad student, since he makes use of the free credits the university extends to its employees. He's taken everything from a Chaucer seminar to Women's Studies to Physics for Poets. Now he's all gung-ho seeing me cramming for Spanish class, since he's under the impression that I'm a model student. Little does he know that he's probably enrolled in more classes than I am.

"What up, what up, my little scholar from the D?" He's from Trinidad-via-Bed Stuy, Brooklyn, and for a long time he thought that, because I was born in Detroit, I have some street cred. Over the years he has realized how truly wrong his assumption is: I'm a run-of-the-mill suburban girl. "I'm on my fifteen-minute break and I gotta get back. I'll see you in the office at four, right?"

"Yeah, yeah. I have this Spanish class . . ."

"Right, right, your Spanish class. You're always studying. I wanna hear stories of you having fun in the city, you know?" He laughs. "The undergrads have more fun than you and they're not even legal."

We work with a bunch of undergrads who show off pictures of their wild parties on every social media app you can imagine.

"I went out on a date this weekend," I lie, but I have to think for a moment about what's more plausible. Daniel or Wisdom. Instead, I blurt, "I'll tell you about it at work, okay?" and jump to my feet because I'm going to be late and also because I'm at a loss for something good to say to Alan about my nonexistent social life. As soon as I stand, my legs feel like they're melting.

"Whoa, whoa." Alan grabs hold of my arm, guides me so that when I sink to a sitting position, I'll land on the bench again instead of the pavement. The whole world feels like liquid; people rushing past us look like smears across my eyes.

"I just stood up too fast."

Alan stands in front of me, patting my shoulder awkwardly. "Did you eat and stuff?" He thinks every sick woman or girl is starving herself.

"I did eat. I hit my head in the shower the other day. Sunday. But it's okay. A doctor checked it out."

Alan bends down, squinting at me. This is not his territory. He knows library policies, not medical diagnoses. "You can call in sick if you want. You might as well tell me now so we can get a cover for you."

"No, no, no. I'm fine. I just got up too fast." I'm already barely doing grad school. If I can't even drag my sad ass to my part-time desk job, I'm on the slippery slope to nowhere.

"Okay. If you say so." Alan shrugs, looking huge and powerful in his oversized down coat. I'd like to ask him to carry me to class because my legs feel wobbly, and I can't imagine myself walking up any stairs. "See you later; I gotta get back to the office."

I watch him trot across campus to the main library. As he leaves, his figure broadens for a moment, until he's two Alans. I wave at both and the curtain draws shut.

Intermission. Now we can rest our eyes and brains which have been racing for hours around and around the same point, which is those men and my father . . . well, let's not get to the point, that's the entire problem, that's how we ended up so tired right now, our brain so throbbing and full of hurt, all because we were focused too much on the point, when, really, isn't life all about the grand, disastrous journey?

For a journey, you need a mode of transportation, and when you're seven, that's a bike. I wanted one for my birthday so I could cruise the sidewalks of Detroit, Michigan, rocking a ten-speed and a bright red helmet. Picture the streets of Detroit. No, minus the abandoned buildings and rundown yards you're probably imagining. That's not even how it was. More like sprawling green lawns in neat yards lined with shrubs. Cute elderly people sitting out on their front porches, waving good morning, saying hello to Akosua, the little African girl with the name they have to struggle to get off their tongues until they settle for the path of least resistance: Sue. Sue runs everywhere because she doesn't know how to ride a bike. She doesn't know how to ride her bike because, of course, her parents never learned how, having grown up, well, in Africa.

That's what Akosua assumes others assume about her. In truth, the situation has nothing to do with Africa. What's really happening is that little Sue's mother can't afford the bike, and her father, in the process of abandoning his young family for a new one he's started on the sly, cannot afford the financial strain of a new bicycle or the time it'll take to teach his daughter how to ride. Instead, he buys her purple roller skates from Montgomery Ward, not even for Christmas or a birthday or anything, just one Saturday in late October when it's starting to get too cold to skate outside.

All through breakfast, she imagines her father has gotten his own pair of matching skates, and she smiles to herself at the image of him tripping in them. She's seen him do graceful things before: he runs all the way to the State Fair Grounds every other morning before work; he lifts thirty-five pound barbells in the basement; he dances to West African highlife music during parties, wiggling his hips to the music, smiling and raising his eyebrow in a way that makes Mommy put her hands over her dimples and makes all the aunties tease, "Enyo, your man is hot stuff!" But roller skating would be new to Sue's father. He would trip, his gangly legs in the way, his handsome face contorted in comic, cartoonish fear. In her daydream, Sue saves him, grabs his arm to steady him so that he doesn't fall.

She's a naturally skilled roller skater. But only in her imagination. In reality, she's never skated before.

Rapt in her daydream, Sue barely notices that her mother eats over the stove, not joining Sue and Daddy at the table, or that Daddy shovels food into his mouth as fast as he can, then leaves the table without a word.

Sue sneaks outside in long johns and a winter coat, deciding to skate in circles in the driveway. Though it takes a long time to lace up the skates, Sue doesn't mind. She won't need to run anymore; she can skate everywhere. She'll skate to the store when Mom forgets to buy the orange juice Daddy likes with breakfast. She'll skate to the playground whenever she feels like escaping from her home.

Surprised that neither parent has come out to scold her for going outside without supervision, Sue rises to shaky feet and thinks of figure skaters on TV. Surya Bonaly. Yuka Sato. And now Mercy Akosua Agbe. She tries to spin, making a perfect arc above her head with her stick-skinny arms. She pushes off with her feet and falls, an instant puddle in the driveway.

Poor Sue, the onlookers probably say. They perch on their porches or peek out their windows, the perfect theater seats to view this perfect failure of a family. Sue lies for a while in the driveway, waiting for her father or mother to find her sprawled on the pavement. But her parents are inside their bedroom now, her father's voice booming, her mother's replies quick and sharp. This isn't the norm; usually, her parents save their arguments for nighttime, when they think Sue is sleeping. But right now, she's wide awake, and everything's clear: this fight will change her life. Her world, which had firmly consisted of Mommy, Daddy, and Akosua, is now unsteady. She can feel this new uncertainty as sure as she feels the ground beneath her body. She shuts her eyes against this new knowledge.

She hears scuffling sounds and opens her eyes. Boot-clad feet shuffle toward her; the neighbor from across the street—an older woman in curlers and a quilted housecoat—approaches her, lays a hand on her shoulder. The woman helps Sue scramble to her feet.

"Never seen you in these skates before, Sue. You just trying to keep yourself entertained while your parents are busy?"

Sue says nothing, wondering whether this woman can hear her parents fighting.

The woman goes on in her wrinkly voice, saying how she's watched Sue through all the seasons: reading books on the porch during springtime, running barefoot through the sprinkler on the front lawn during muggy summer afternoons, gathering autumn leaves into large piles and jumping in. Making a solitary angel in the snow.

Sue doesn't know where this conversation is going, but she lets the woman keep talking; a good Ghanaian girl always listens to her elders, even if the elders don't seem to be making sense.

"It's good you know how to keep yourself entertained," the neighbor says before shuffling back to her own home, leaving Sue alone. "Everybody needs a nice diversion once in a while."

Is it really curtains for good? The world shifts, and the bench tilts, dumping me out of my childhood memory and onto the herringbone brick walkway outside my Spanish conversation class. All I feel is my pulsing head and a rush of nausea. Alan's zooming over from the direction of the library, and for a moment, I swear he's wearing roller skates. He waves his arms and shouts my name. His movements somehow make a hollow sound, an echo in my head. He disappears as my eyes close.

"Sue. Sue." Someone with a voice I don't recognize tugs on the sleeve of my coat.

"Akosua. Call her that. That is her name, she'll answer to that," came the accented voice, gravelly and grave now, Daniel Cobblah, Housing Department Staff Level II.

"Should we carry her to her dorm?"

"Sue's in a graduate dorm, not nearby. And she doesn't look very light." Daniel sucks his teeth. "I once had to carry an undergrad who had passed out from alcohol poisoning . . ."

"You shouldn't do that, it's against protocol." A snicker. "Unless you plan on carrying her back to your place."

Oh, the unrecognizable voice from before: Pete the Housing Perv. Why is it that these are the people God recruited to save me?

"And I could tell," Daniel continues, "that other girl looked easy to lift. But Akosua . . ."

I think my eyes are open, but I can't see anything. I try to open my mouth: *Do you have to insult me even when I'm dying?* I want to say to Daniel, which will surprise him, since we've never said anything to each other that isn't cordial. I'm sure he doesn't even consider his comment about my weight to be an insult.

"I don't know Akosua that well, but we are countrymen, you know. She doesn't seem the kind to drink in the middle of the day. But I guess you never can tell."

At some point, my eyes open and I can see. Alan has returned, not wearing the skates of my daydream. He's wearing white sneakers and the most serious look I've ever seen on his face. He peers down at me but doesn't say much.

"Ambulance is on its way."

∽○∽

When I wake up, I find I've draped one arm over my face, veiling my eyes from the light. The fluorescent glow worsens my headache and dizziness, and when the nurse enters, she dims the overhead lamp.

Her long colorless hair brushes against my shoulder as she leans over me to check a beeping monitor at my side. "You're looking more alert."

Her face turns upward as she works a machine behind my head. She smiles, revealing wrinkles around her eyes and mouth. She could be somebody's grandmother, but her long hair made me believe she was younger. I'm delighted that she's older. She's so close to me, I almost want to hug her. I think of Wisdom's arms around me the day before as he positioned me in my bed, of the paramedic's grip on me as he hoisted me on the stretcher in the middle of campus.

The nurse gently takes hold of my arm and repositions it on the bed. Then she proceeds to poke at each and every vein in my arm until I bruise.

"You're so dehydrated," she says. "You sure you hit your head just a couple days ago? It's as if you've been sick for a while." I don't know how to answer her.

Finally, she pushes the needle through a vein on the back of my hand. I watch the saline flow into me until I fall into a dreamless sleep.

After what feels like hours of unconsciousness, my legs itch with the desire to get out of this uncomfortable bed. Aside from a headache and nausea, I feel fine. Actually, I don't feel anything at all.

"Hey, um . . . Ak . . . A-su-ko . . ." A new nurse, a young man this time, pushes aside one of the curtains and strides into the ER cubicle.

"Ah-KOH-soo-ah." Speaking makes my head vibrate.

"Right, yes. Sorry 'bout that, hi. If you're feeling all right, you've got some visitors who'd like to see you."

"Visitors? Can't I just leave?"

"We have to run some other tests, but for now, there's a group of men dying to see you." The nurse nods, plastering an eager expression on his face.

As soon as he leaves, I tuck my hair behind my ears, patting it down as best I can, knowing it always sticks up on top. So just because I'm a basket case, I don't deserve the human dignity of a mirror in which to see myself?

As I'm wiping my lips, which I realize are crusted with dried drool, footsteps approach the room and the sound bounces around in my skull. I squint my eyes against the pain, and, once I open them, I'm greeted by Alan and Pete's scared faces, and the eternally serene face of Daniel Cobblah.

I crane my head to look behind Daniel, the tallest person in the room, but there's no one else behind him.

"Ooh, not lookin' so hot, Sue." Pete puts his hands on his hips, shaking his head as he stares at me.

"Thanks a lot," I start, but I change course because sarcasm and anger will require too much energy. "For coming. Thanks."

The men have crowded around my bed, and they look down at me with critical eyes. I am covered to my neck in a hospital sheet, and beneath I'm dressed in one of those embarrassing hospital gowns. Hurriedly, I finish wiping the crust off my face. Pete points at a monitor at the right of my head, next to the IV bag.

"What's goin' on with that? Heart's okay, right?"

"This has nothing to do with my heart," I tell him. "I hit my head against my tub on Sunday."

"Aww, see, I told them." Alan looks too animated as he transfers his weight from foot to foot. "Pete and Dan here thought you had alcohol poisoning or something."

"Just 'cause that's what most of the college kids go to the emergency room for," Pete explains.

I glance at Daniel looming silently, farthest from me. If he steps back, he'll vanish through the curtain. During our Sunday visits, we talked enough for him to know I have too much pride, or shame, to get fall-down drunk in the middle of the campus in the middle of the day.

"I remembered earlier, when I ran into you, you said something about hitting your head, so I told the EMTs," Alan continues. "Otherwise, they might've pumped your stomach, who knows. But it looks like when you hit your head, you probably knocked it worse than you thought. Probably should've come to the hospital when it happened."

"I'm not a college kid," is all I manage to say, still looking at Daniel.

Pete clears his throat. "I gotta get back to the housing desk. Just wanted to make sure you're okay, Sue."

Finally Daniel speaks. "Fortunately, my shift ended just as Alan came to the desk and told us of your predicament. It seems you had been unconscious in Courtyard East for several minutes."

Pete backs out of the curtain with barely a wave.

"Guy hates hospitals," Alan says. "He was squirming the whole time in the waiting room."

When I ask for the time, Alan steps close to me, puts his wrist in my face and announces what the hands of his watch say: four o'clock. I remember I sat on that campus bench around noon. How many minutes of life did I lose lying unconscious? I know all the emergency room waiting and sleeping and being poked and prodded must have taken time, but I didn't realize how much had passed.

"It's time for me to be at work," I say, attempting a smile, and Alan smiles back and tells me that a trio of work-study students have taken over at the library until he can get back, which he assumes might be right about now, since he knows I'm all right.

But am I all right? No doctor has spoken to me. I know I am dehydrated, that I probably have a concussion, but why am I still here? Suddenly I'm aware that my feet are cold, that I'm shivering inside, that I haven't felt right in my head since the fall. I feel distant from myself.

But my hospital guests don't notice. Alan tips an imaginary hat to me and strides out of the room, somewhat less rushed than Pete.

"I'm not a college kid," I say as soon as I face Daniel alone.

"Yes, I am aware."

"Yeah, but you assumed I was drunk on campus, and I wasn't. You should know me better by now."

He nods blankly, his lips still pleasantly upturned despite the silence. He always looks this way. It occurs to me suddenly that I don't want him to see me lying on my back like this, in such a vulnerable position. He's acting as if we are standing with the housing desk between us, chatting about something mundane. Should he get less "busy" this semester and allow me the pleasure of his company, he would look like this on our date; he would look like this if I tried to kiss him. I doubt anything could knock that polite expression off his face, but, for some reason, I want to make it my mission to try.

Just as I'm considering pushing aside my hospital sheet and flashing him, his face does change, only because he opens his mouth and says,

"The doctors think you will need supervision while you recover, so I have contacted my cousin who will let your father know about your accident."

"You've got to be kidding me." I sit up too abruptly, but the vibrations in my head pale in comparison to the feeling of the wind being knocked out of me. It's like Daniel has reached inside my chest, grabbed my heart, and jerked me to an upright position.

"Well, you did tell me your mother lives in Canada, so I figured since your father is close by—"

"Tell your cousin to nix those plans. Call him right now and tell him not to tell my father anything."

"But—"

I try to keep my voice calm. "I've told you before, my father left us. I haven't seen him since I was a kid. He's not who I would call for help."

Daniel presses his hands together beneath his chest as if he is praying, a thing I've seen several of my uncles in Ghana do. "But he is family. Who else would you call?"

At this point I'm almost off the hospital bed, I've inched forward, I'm teetering on the edge. "Nobody. I'd call nobody before I'd call my father who I don't even know. Do you know how many bones I've broken, how many times I've cut myself or gotten sick? Countless times. And my father didn't need to be alerted. We got on fine without him."

"I was not aware that the situation was as such."

"I've told you he left us and that we haven't talked in years. I told you he lied to my mother, had an entire secret wife and family. Does that sound like someone who deserves my familial loyalty?"

He shrugs his shoulders slightly, hands hanging like question marks in the air.

"You are *insane*. You have no normal parameters for life operation. You know, you can't just smile politely and thus get away with rude stuff."

Still, he's looking handsome and gracious, though he's posed his hands in another typical Ghanaian gesture of pleading forgiveness, palms up, arms outstretched toward me, the back of one hand clapping against the palm of another, a motion that I thought of as backward applause when I was a child. "I beg; I beg. I didn't know, o."

"Just like you didn't know I'd figure out that your rude, stupid way of rejecting me was actual rejection? Who says they're busy *until next semester*? You know, it's your fault that I hit my head, anyway, because you were rude to me Sunday, and I was upset and I wasn't concentrating so I slipped in the shower, and you're the jerk who—"

My nurse yanks open the curtain. "Excuse me, miss," he says, no longer bothering to mispronounce my name. "You're being disruptive to the patients around you. Are you okay?" He looks at Daniel, but not for long; the nurse rushes toward my bed, fiddling with my IV line, which I'd nearly pulled from my hand without realizing. A few spots of blood dot my hospital gown. "Is she okay? Are you upsetting her? They're ready for you in radiology. Do we need to sedate you?"

I hesitate before answering. It might be nice . . . "Sure, why not?"

"All right. So you're fine." The nurse grins now, relieved. "A little too much excitement for a concussion victim. Let's go get your head examined, young lady."

3

The doctor clasps a medical chart behind his back like a gift he's waiting to surprise me with and announces, sure enough, "Surprise. Your neurological tests all came back normal."

At this point in the evening, I've already been transferred from my temporary curtained cubicle to a real room with walls, a TV mounted to the ceiling, a relatively comfortable bed whose position I can adjust using a switch within arm's reach. My own private bathroom and air that smells of pine, of vigorous disinfection, of the infinite battle between purity and contamination.

The doctor shifts, planting his feet wider like he's going to stay awhile. "Let's say someone's in a car accident. She passes out, she fractures her skull, she's unconscious for days, and then she wakes up. Everyone expects a long recovery and anticipates that time and special care are necessary, right?"

"Right," I say, thinking of the countless soap opera characters I've seen with white bandages wrapped around their heads, wearing brave smiles as they're told that it'll be months before they get their memories back/walk again/regain the dexterity needed to resume their lives as world-renowned surgeons.

"Well, what people don't realize is that with mild head injuries like yours, it's not unusual to experience lingering symptoms, too. Not every blow to the head will do this, but if you hit your head at just the right angle, at just the right speed, you can cause injury to just the right vulnerable portions of white matter in your brain. It seems you did that."

"So I'm lucky is what you're saying," I try to chuckle, to see if this is a chuckling situation.

Maybe. The doctor smiles and brings forth my medical chart, onto which he has clipped a drawing of the human brain. He points out the lobes, throws out words like parietal, occipital, white matter, gray. He flips to an actual image of my brain, showing how it's clear of any visible trouble spots, no blood, no bruises. Then he's back to the original drawing, and, with a pencil, he sketches little flecks of pain in the white matter, areas injured from shearing against each other when my head hit the edge of the tub.

He mentions possible headaches, sensitivity to noise or light, nausea, double vision.

"Have you ever suffered migraines?"

"No."

"Well, you might begin to experience some migraines."

He describes other potential symptoms: ringing in the ears, fatigue, insomnia, inability to concentrate, mood swings, depression.

The more he speaks, the more I feel muscles in the back of my neck tightening. "So I fell down in the shower and now I'm going to be a total wreck?"

"Not necessarily. Nothing is certain. You could suffer from one or more of these for a few days, or a couple of weeks, or more."

"Or less."

"Or less."

"Or not at all."

"Perhaps."

What he's given me isn't a diagnosis but a cluster of bad things that might or might not happen, for however long or however short a period of time. I wipe my sweaty hands on the bed sheets. "So anything's possible."

"Exactly."

"I'm confused."

The doctor smiles, touches his silver mustache. "Of course you are, you've hit your head."

Everything I had with me when I collapsed in the middle of campus—my backpack with Spanish books, my purse, my coat, boots, sweater, and jeans—is in a white plastic bag with PERSONAL BELONGINGS printed across the front. Someone, a nurse maybe, or an orderly, put the bag on one of three chairs lining the wall by the door, should I have any visitors. I need to get to that bag, to get out my phone. It's evening now, around the time that I call my mother every night, and she'll wonder where I am. And maybe I should call other people. Ella, Wisdom . . . he will kick himself for letting me get hospitalized under his charge, I know, and I am reluctant to call him, but I know that someone out there besides Pete, Alan, and Daniel Cobblah needs to know I am in the hospital.

I consider pressing the nurse call button for help but decide against it. My mother has always taught me that wellness is a state of mind; I've got to get out of the bed myself and make the short walk to the chair, because pretending I'm okay will make it so.

I haven't been on my feet since this morning when I walked from my apartment to loiter outside my classroom building, and at first it's not difficult at all. Careful not to pull out my IV line, I make the three steps necessary to get to my bag of PERSONAL BELONGINGS, but settling back onto the bed is what jolts my head. The room spins as I hoist myself; again, I shiver and feel my skin prickle. I've never stayed overnight in the hospital, never been sick with anything as nebulous as this. At ten, I fell out of a tree I'd been climbing. At eight, I caught a fever that wouldn't break. Each time a doctor had given a clear diagnosis: two broken bones in the ankle, pneumonia. Now, I am shaking and dizzy in a New York hospital, my mother in another country that's neither hers nor mine, and I'm feeling beside myself. Literally so: I feel like I'm lying next to myself on the bed, watching my own helplessness unfold.

As I pull my phone out of my bag, I begin to wonder what the harm would be if Daniel really did tell my father about my accident, if my father calls me and comes to take care of me in my hour of greatest need. Doesn't he owe me this at least? It would be odd, surreal; he'd have no reason to recognize me, nearly two decades later. If I call my mother, she will try to help, but she's so far away.

From New York to Windsor seems closer than from anywhere to my father, so I call the number listed under HOME, because even though I've never lived full-time in her Windsor condo, wherever Mom is still feels like home.

The busy signal I get almost crushes me, but then the phone at my bedside rings, and I know that somehow she found out.

"Hello? Mommy?"

A weak chuckle on the other end lets me know it's her. "So you're alive."

"Of course I am; don't say that."

"*Tso*! My only daughter, collapsing in the middle of campus, hurt without me to care for her. How?" Her accent always comes out the strongest when she's scolding me. I won't be surprised if she begins to spew out words in Ewe, despite the fact that I can barely understand the language.

"How did you find out?"

"How could you not tell me that you hit your head, hmm? And to have Auntie and Uncle Fergie call me first?"

"But I didn't—"

"Your auntie and uncle told me you had an accident. They told me what hospital you got sent to. They helped me find the phone number. You did not even let me know that you hit your head. So disrespectful."

I let a breath out, holding the phone away from my mouth so she won't hear my sigh and call that disrespectful too. Some of the shivers in my body subside as she talks on and on. I know exactly what she's most likely to say and how she'll say it. Even though I don't love that she's angry, the familiarity of her cadence hugs me like a blanket.

"I knew it, I knew it, yesterday evening when I called you and you only spoke for a minute, saying you were busy. I had a feeling you were not well, o. That something was wrong. But I thought it might be about that Cobblah boy. I didn't want to invade your privacy, you always tell me not to invade your privacy, so I didn't ask. But now I see. You wanted to keep your pain a secret from me."

"Not a *secret*," I say, "I hit my head on Sunday, I thought I'd just sleep it off. Besides, I'm not a kid anymore. I don't need to tell you about every bump and bruise."

"You don't sleep things like that off! Such a thing is an emergency, a very serious situation. Haven't I taught you better?"

"Mom . . ."

"Well, at least tell me how you feel. Can you at least tell me that? How long have we been on the phone, and you can't even tell your own mother how you're doing? Start talking."

"I—"

"Don't you owe me at least that little bit of respect? I'm waiting."

"I'm trying. You breathe while I talk." I can't help but laugh a little, and she laughs, too, quietly, not her usual wild one. I tell her about the dizziness, the coldness, the blurry vision, the hollow feeling that permeates my body. The ache in my head. As she coos and comforts me, I imagine her palm on my forehead.

"It's not a big deal," I say eventually. "I'm sure I just need to rest for a couple of days. I'll stay with a friend of mine until I'm okay." If Mom asks who, I'll name Ella, though I don't intend to do anything but go home to my apartment once they release me from the hospital.

"What? What are you thinking? Akosua, we will stay with Auntie and Uncle Fergie. I booked a flight for tomorrow morning."

"But the money . . ."

"Don't worry about money, o. I am a grown woman; you don't need to worry about my affairs." She chuckles, but with effort. "What friend were you planning to stay with anyway?"

"My friend Ella," I say, too quickly, and my mother clucks her tongue.

She doesn't buy it, but what she says next is not what I expected. "You don't have to lie to me. Who you talk to, where you stay, who you decide to trust. All of these things are your own decision."

"Who I decide to trust?"

"Never mind. As long as you are okay, that is all that matters. Let us not worry about any other people or things."

She gives me her flight information, we say goodbye, hang up. Something inside me feels deflated, but I'm not sure why. My mother gets mad when I'm sick or hurt or sad, and she definitely gets mad when I don't tell her when I'm sick or hurt or sad. But something in the tone of her voice changed at the end of the phone conversation. What wasn't she saying? And how did Auntie and Uncle Fergie, who live in Jersey City and whom I rarely see, know I was in the hospital? For a moment, I'm almost angry that Mom thinks I would have called them first, or at all. As if there's any need for her to question my loyalty to her, given that she's all the real family I have.

When I was younger, I spent many weekend afternoons poring through the stacks and stacks of photo albums that my mom had compiled over the years. To me, it seemed there were so many pictures, some still in their envelopes, some black and white and yellowed with age, that I would never get through them all. I don't know if I realized it at the time, but I was looking for clues in the pictures, hints that would fill in the gaps of my parents' life together. Wedding pictures, photos from dates or parties or trips. But instead, I found pictures of myself as a chubby toddler, hanging onto my father's legs, or as Akosua the baby, splashing in the bath.

"Is there anything older, from before I was born?" I asked my mother once when I felt brave, when my father had been gone for about a year. She'd never before sat down with me to look at the pictures, claiming to be busy. But for the first time, I actually asked her a question about the photos, and she set down the laundry basket she'd been carrying and strode over to where I sat buried in old memories.

"Your Mommy really used to party," she said, her chin dimpling, and she pulled out an album I'd never seen.

I instantly recognized Auntie Irina and Uncle Ossei, who still lived in Michigan but in Ann Arbor, too far from Detroit for us to see them often. I barely remembered Auntie Grace, Irina's younger sister. She had married a General Motors engineer and moved to a mansion in Beverly Hills, Michigan.

My mother pointed to a picture of two Afro-sporting, mini-dress-wearing young women in platform heels. "Look at me and your Auntie Yaa. She used to put me in these ridiculous outfits. Your father didn't know whether to love them because they looked good on me or hate them because they attracted the attention of other men."

I glanced up at her, my mouth opening to ask more, but my mother looked down at the album and smiled.

"Yes, Auntie Yaa, she was like a sister to me. Now she's as far away as my real brothers and sisters." Auntie Yaa had moved back to Ghana with her husband. My mother sighed, brushing back hair that was already smooth. "This life, hmm? Everybody leaving, living far apart."

My mother flipped the page of the album to reveal a picture I'll never forget: a portrait of my parents and Auntie Gifty and Uncle Akrofi. They stand in a row, shoulders touching, each wife holding the hand of her husband. My mother and Auntie Gifty wear fashionable kaba and slits, and my father and Uncle Akrofi wear strip-woven shirts and trousers.

"Our dear friends. They are the ones who took care of us all," my mother pronounced proudly. I already knew that Auntie Gifty and Uncle Akrofi had been the first of our family friends to come to the States and that they threw many of the parties that Detroit-area Ghanaians attended. They continued to hold get-togethers as I grew up, even though my mother and I stopped going. They hosted welcome parties for everyone from Ghana and adjacent countries:

newly-arrived university students, visa lottery winners, engineers and businessmen who had moved from England or other parts of the US to work in the auto industry in Detroit. Somehow, word had spread through the grapevine: if you're new to Michigan, contact Dr. and Mrs. Akrofi Edwards.

I loved Uncle Akrofi with a fierceness akin to the love a daughter feels for her father, perhaps because he was like a father, or, specifically, like my father. In photos and my memories, they often dress the same, Ghanaian shirts with American department store jeans or dress pants. They wear the same slight smile, though Uncle Akrofi's would eventually burst into something wilder.

"Your Uncle Akrofi was the life of the party," my mother said, startling me out of my thoughts. "Everyone thought your father was the quiet, straight-laced one. But I suppose looks can be deceiving."

I wanted to ask more, but something about her voice told me not to. We still saw Uncle Akrofi and Auntie Gifty often, at that time, probably the most of any of our family friends, and I couldn't help but grin whenever my uncle was around. I liked the way he called his wife "Gifty, my love" all the time, as if it were her name. When I hugged Uncle Akrofi, he smelled like my father because they wore the same spicy aftershave. I loved Uncle Akrofi before my father left, mostly because of the way my father seemed to idolize him. After my dad left, my love for Uncle Akrofi only increased, though, when I saw him, I felt a tug in my chest, a desire to run into his lap like I was one of his children, or at least his real niece, but of course I wasn't his real blood relative. Most of my blood relatives were people who barely knew me, whom I rarely got to see. When I went to Ghana for the wedding of my mother's younger sister, I met aunts and uncles and cousins, scores of them, some who even had my face. Four girl cousins were exactly my age; we spent every moment of the trip together, shared jokes and secrets and clothes, the way I imagined sisters would. On the airplane ride back home, I clutched a notebook filled with each of their addresses, but I already felt a gulf of loss widening between us. No matter how many letters we exchanged, I would always be this foreign appendage, never part of the whole.

At home in the States, all I could do was cling to my mother, and she to me, especially when the crowd of Detroit family friends thinned out as the years wore on.

"Ah," my mother said as we looked at the pictures. "Everybody is living everywhere now. Who made us believe that our homeland was not enough?" She closed the album, stood up, and walked away.

Auntie and Uncle Fergie, the relatives who somehow found out about my head injury and told my mother, aren't in many of those old photos. They'd moved to the East Coast after only one year of living in Detroit because Uncle Fergie had gotten a teaching position at a college in New Jersey, a job he still has. I mostly knew them from my mother's stories of them: "Uncle Fergie helped your father get the job at Wayne State University. You know, it was Auntie Fergie who referred us to the real estate agent who sold us our family home." And it was understood that I owed them my eternal gratitude for all the ways they'd helped my parents before I was born. I actually found them creepy as a kid, even though I only met them every couple of years or so when they would come to visit Michigan. Their matching names irked me. Though they aren't related by blood in any discernible way, Auntie's maiden name is Ferguson just like her husband's surname, and people teasingly call them by the same name, Fergie. They even look alike and speak in unison sometimes (when Auntie hasn't taken command of the entire conversation), and whenever I talk to them on the phone (usually because my mother has firmly urged me to check up on them like a good niece should), they insist on speaking in Twi half the time, even though they know that I am Ewe and that I don't even understand my own language, let alone Twi.

That my mother, who should know me, believes I called them before calling her hurts more than my headache. I want to call her back to explain, but the truth is, even though my mom sometimes treats me like a sister, I'm her daughter, and she's my elder. To question her would elicit accusations of disrespect, and I don't have the where-withal for more guilt. Just as I'm trying to figure out how the Fergies found out about my hospitalization in the first place—perhaps they're listed as my emergency contact on my university forms, that is possible—there's a knock on my opened door, and I turn my head slightly to discover Ella and Wisdom in the doorway, standing side by side.

I gasp, because, at first, it seems eerie: Ella and Wisdom make an attractive couple. She's taller than him, a good few inches since she's wearing high-heeled boots, but somehow this looks and feels right, as if his presence in the room would be too large without her physical height to subdue it. And is it possible that Ella looks even more attractive than she did this morning? Her skirt suit hugs her hips; her microbraids, pulled back in a neat-but-just-messy-enough high ponytail, cascade down her shoulders. Her hair always looks good, whether it's braided or pressed or fluffed into a curly halo around her head. I'm too tenderheaded for braids, too lazy for natural hair upkeep. Right now, it's pressed straight, falling below my chin in layers that only look good when I first comb it in the morning.

I didn't even comb it this morning. I press down my hair and attempt a smile. But it must come off as a smirk, because Wisdom immediately says, "All right, all right, Akosua, I didn't know you really had a concussion."

His thick brow is creased, his hands stuffed in the pockets of the black corduroy pants I love on him. He's wearing only a thin pullover sweater and a black jacket, which looks good on him but worries me. I can never get him to dress warmly enough.

"I know you didn't know. Of course you would have brought me to the hospital if you'd known," I say. "Wisdom, you were great to me that night."

I'm trying not to sulk at how put together they look in the door frame, their shoulders touching. Then Ella steps into the room, her heels clicking against the floor. She unwraps her scarlet scarf, loosening its loop around her neck.

"Oh *God*. Please spare me from hearing about whatever kinky shit went on when you busted your head."

"There was no kinky shit," Wisdom replies, and follows her into the room, though he comes straight for the bed and holds my hand, massaging the mid-digit area of my middle finger as if this is the most natural thing to do. Three months ago, this was the most natural thing to do. "Poor sweetie. So sorry I didn't take better care of you."

Ella strides toward the other side of my bed, pats my other hand. "Visiting hours are almost over, but we heard about your accident and we wanted to at least say hello. And I wanted to let you know that you can stay with me for a few days while you recover."

"Aw, thanks, but my mom is coming tomorrow morning. She booked a flight as soon as she heard, of course. She'll take good care of me." I feel good, both of my hands in someone else's, like I'm five years old and skipping down the street with my neighborhood friends, or with my parents.

"Honey. You need to take better care of yourself." Ella sucks her teeth. "When's the last time you've cooked for yourself? Or eaten a vegetable? Always cramped up in your room doing who knows what."

"I don't know what any of that has to do with how I fell," I reply, stifling a yawn. "Except I guess that I should learn to be more graceful so I avoid slips in the shower."

Wisdom and Ella both chuckle. I don't quite understand it, since nothing I said strikes me as particularly funny. Still, I'm pleased, because I don't want them to worry. I want them to see this as a quirky incident, not the potentially serious injury my doctor had discussed.

An awkward silence follows the laughter. I pull the sheets tighter around my body, not because I'm cold, but for need of something to do. But I immediately regret it, because it'd be childish and weird if I tucked my hands back into theirs again. Right?

"It's almost nine thirty," Ella announces. "The nurse will probably kick us out soon, and you should rest."

Wisdom steps away from my bed, so fast I feel myself about to panic, but he just heads to the bathroom, excusing himself for a moment.

Ella leans toward me, struggling to keep her voice hushed. "That boy has been driving me crazy. He's sick with worry over you. I guess I'm glad he's your emergency contact, because I wouldn't have known that you were the mystery person who passed out on campus if he hadn't called to tell me."

She tells me that "the whole campus knows," that even if people don't necessarily know who had gotten rushed away by ambulance, everyone at least knows that *someone* had. Though Ella started her PR job immediately after graduation, she remains relatively involved in campus gossip at our alma mater, since she'd once been the social butterfly, fluttering between all the different clubs, the African, Caribbean, and Black Student Organizations, Salsa Club, even Knitting Club where she made that scarf she always wears that reminds me she's a siren, though a down-to-earth one. Now she's vice president of the Black Alumni Organization and head of a mentorship program. Despite her Jamaicanness, she seems better connected to the Ghanaians here—undergraduate and graduate students—than I've ever been. Thinking of the web of people out there who could know about my embarrassing fall makes me want to stay in this hospital room for years and years. Or move to Windsor.

"I made Wisdom wait for me before he came to your hospital room. I didn't want him bothering you too much while you're sick," she whispers, a triumphant smile on her face.

"Oh, I'm not sick," I say.

"You are so vulnerable to him, even when you haven't busted your skull in, girl. You think I'm gonna leave you alone with him? Next thing I know you two will end up in the maternity ward."

"Ella, please. You can be friends with an ex. It's totally possible."

"Mmm-hmm. Maybe if he's really an ex."

"Well, he is. We're done."

"Just like how you and Daniel Cobblah are supposedly dating, huh?" Ella pokes me in the rib, and it tickles more than it hurts.

"That was the concussion talking," I try, but she only shakes her head.

Wisdom returns from the bathroom now, his eyebrows knitting upward. "So do you need something, Akosua? Are you craving anything? Maybe peanut butter cups?"

I rub the fingers on my own hand, taking over where he left off. His forehead has that vertical crease in it, the I-love-you line, the I'm-worried-about-you wrinkle. The most adorable wrinkle in the world.

I'm coughing, catching my breath that I didn't know I'd lost.

"You're being too nice." I tear my eyes from him, glance at Ella. "Both of you. You both have things to do in the morning. Go on; go home. I'm fine. You guys always help me out, last night and now, just by coming to see me and cheer me up."

"I know I'm awesome." Ella nods cockily, feigning self-importance, but when she leans over to kiss me on the forehead, she whispers, "Everything's going to be all right. Rest your head, girl," and her kindness almost makes me cry. Wisdom manages to convince Ella with a series of pointed glances that it's okay for her to leave him alone in the room with me.

When Ella leaves, my composure does, too.

"Hey, hey." Wisdom wipes my cheeks with the heel of his hand. "There's nothing to worry about. You only need to rest for a couple of days. This is more serious than I thought, but it's not so serious that you should worry. You'll probably have some headaches for a few days, a couple weeks at most."

"Maybe you shouldn't make any more diagnoses," I reply, but it doesn't come out right, and he looks guilty again.

"I really am sorry that I didn't take better care of you," he says again, after a minute of listening to hospital sounds, the drip of my IV, voices in the hall, the buzz of machines throughout the building.

"You're not a doctor yet. I won't sue."

"I don't mean just your head. I mean everything. You know, us."

"Um, I don't think it was a matter of taking care of me so much as not being an insensitive asshole," but then I feel guilty, so I add, "but don't worry, water under the bridge, it's all good."

"No, it's not all good. We should talk about this. I don't agree with what happened. It all happened too fast. You got so mad about that night when I should have just let you come out with me. You have every right to be pissed at me. I was being an insecure jerk. But we had been together for so long at that point. We were so happy. Doesn't that count for anything?"

"I'm not sure that anything counts for anything." I am speaking too loudly. I am saying something that means nothing. Because I miss him, even though he's right here. I miss him, even though I want him to go away.

He clears his throat, cracks his knuckles. There's a remote control for the TV at the side of my bed, at my fingertips. I want to watch soaps, cartoons, old movies, anything. I want Ella back in the room, right away. I don't quite understand the kind of attention I want from Wisdom, what I want at all.

"Let me pick your mother up from the airport," he offers. I remind him that he's not my boyfriend and owes me nothing, that my mother doesn't know we were ever a serious couple, but he insists. "It's the respectful thing to do when an auntie comes to town. She needs to be greeted."

I give him the flight information. At least I don't have to warn him about what things he should and shouldn't say to a Ghanaian mother. Matt, my high school sort-of-boyfriend whom my mother permitted me to see as long as we a) attended only school events together and b) never actually called ourselves boyfriend and girlfriend in her presence, used to mistake my mother's friendliness for an invitation to actually be friends, and he'd make little jokes with her that had to do with how cute my button nose was, or how clammy my hand had been when he held it on our first date. As if she really wanted to hear those types of details. Talking in general terms about boys was one thing, but hearing boys talk about her daughter was another thing altogether.

Also, Wisdom will recognize my mother, not just from meeting her briefly when she came to New York last Easter or from seeing her photos in my room, but also from the way she carries herself, the roundness of her face, the sweep of her high cheekbones and unnameable something in her eyes. The thing that makes one Ghanaian recognize another without any words being spoken.

"I don't try to be American. I *am* American. You ass."

The words come out of my mouth as if they've been waiting three months to be said. As if I'm still standing on my feet outside his apartment because I never fell down, I never allowed his words to knock me down or take my breath away. As if all the time that's passed between him insulting me in the street and now was just a dream.

Wisdom blinks. He holds up his phone, on which he's stored my mother's flight information, on which he's scheduled most of his life. "I got it. I'm all set."

But he doesn't speak these words so much as he mouths them. And I feel guilty now, for guilting him, for making him back out of the room as he's doing right now, waving his gangly, brown-palmed hands at me in a white flag surrender.

4

My mother's real greeting does not begin until we're alone, standing outside the hospital on Amsterdam Avenue, the cold morning air cutting into our faces.

"You are well, *dzinam*." She kisses my cheek, and we embrace. *My heart*, she calls me in Ewe, and her words melt me to the core.

I cling to her now, unsteady on my feet after only one night in the hospital, and she lets me. I inhale her sharp, floral scent and picture the pear-shaped glass bottle of perfume I bought her one Mother's Day nearly a decade ago, which she loved so much that she's requested it for every Mother's Day since. I breathe in again and exhale, the tension draining from me. I am back in the familiar place that is my mother.

"Are you okay standing up?" she asks, and steps toward the curb, ready to hail a cab.

I pull her back. My apartment is fewer than ten blocks away. She puts one arm around me and we walk. It's easier than I thought it'd be: perhaps because my mother's presence makes me feel healthier, or maybe all my banged up head needed was sleep and whatever magic had been in that IV drip.

As we walk, my mother hums a spiritual. Since I haven't been a regular churchgoer in almost two decades, I have no idea what the song is, but since the only music my mother sings is church hymns and easy listening favorites and this doesn't sound like a Neil Diamond hit, I know it must be something about Jesus.

I don't know the words; I can't participate in thanking God with her. I change the tune to an Ewe song she taught me when I was younger, the only song in her language that I can sing.

Akpe, akpe, akpe, akpe, akpe na dzinyelawo . . .

My mother smiles, her arm tightens around me. "You're welcome, you're welcome," and then she's quiet, listening to me sing in my best imitation of a sweet child's voice, *thanks, thanks, thanks, thanks, thank you to my parents.* When I get to the part that thanks parents for sending their kids to school, she lets loose her wild laughter.

"What's so funny?"

"You're welcome for the schooling, but, at some point, a parent wants her child to get into graduate school or else get a good job."

"I *am* in graduate school." But for a moment I panic that somehow my mom found out that I'm not taking a graduate course load anymore. Was there a Ghanaian spy in the registrar's office? Perhaps the same one who'd informed Auntie and Uncle Fergie about my trip to the emergency room? (Because I won't submit to that one impossible possibility, that Daniel has really opened up a connection, because that couldn't have happened, right?)

"Yes, but something more practical, something prestigious. Something more . . ."

"Something spelled P-H-D, right?"

My mother laughs again, nudges me with her elbow. "Now you got it."

I want to tell her that a PhD in the humanities is probably not as practical as she imagines, but I'm feeling good and don't want to diverge from the path we're on. I keep humming, my insides finally thawing out. I've been feeling frozen ever since I hit my head. Numb, detached from myself. Or had the detachment happened after my botched evening at Daniel Cobblah's housing desk? His rejection. His stupid assumption that my family life is his business. Let me keep singing; I do it loud enough that I startle a passing street vendor.

"Akosua, *mede kuku, la.* Please, don't be singing so loud in the street." My mother shakes her head once, and that's enough to silence me. After a moment, she continues in a gentler voice, "Your friend is very nice. Wisdom. I was surprised. I don't know how much I liked him when I met him last Easter."

"Why not?"

"He was too nervous then, and he kept looking at my child like she was a woman instead of my child. I didn't like it, o, not one bit." She smirks. I've missed seeing this mischievous glint in my mother's eyes. "Today he was very nice, very respectful. And less nervous."

When my mom arrived earlier this morning, I was deliriously sleepy, and my first sight of her face looked smudgy and unreal. I sensed Wisdom's presence, too, but when I awakened an hour or so later, only my mother sat at my bedside holding my hand and sipping from a plastic cup of apple juice. All I know is what my mother told me before the doctor interrupted us: that Wisdom and my mother found each other easily in LaGuardia, that they caught a cab quickly, that during the cab ride he told her I seemed the same as usual, only a little quieter, a little scared. A hard bump to the noggin, he'd diagnosed, and she'd asked him how med school was going. And that's where he went after leading her to my hospital room, to Clinical Anatomy up on the Washington Heights campus.

"You never talk about Wisdom the way you do Ella. You and Wisdom must be good friends if he offered to pick me up. Why don't you ever mention him?"

What I won't say is that I stopped mentioning him because early on, I felt certain of nearly everything about him, except whether or not it was proper for me to be in love without my mom's permission. It's one thing to talk to my mother about a crush, but Wisdom meant too much for me to risk exposing our relationship to her withering judgments.

Luckily, we have broken up and none of this matters anymore.

Because my mother's carrying a small but heavy suitcase on wheels, we take the elevator to my third-floor apartment instead of the stairs.

"Would you mind waiting in the lobby while I straighten up a little?" I ask before we step into the elevator. I can't remember the state of my room.

But my mother laughs and clasps her hands together delightedly. "Oh no, you think I will miss this opportunity to watch you squirm? Come, let's go up. I want to see how my child is living."

On occasion, beer cans and food wrappers litter the hallways and elevator, especially on weekend mornings after the guys down the hall throw parties that sound, look, and smell like an unfortunate throwback to college days. When my mom last visited, we spotted an unwrapped condom and a couple of cigarette butts in the elevator. She didn't comment, but her glare of disgust spoke volumes. I kept having to remind myself that the mess wasn't mine and I had nothing to feel guilty about.

This morning, though, the elevator and hallway are clear of debris and odors, and I'm grateful for the dim hallway light; though the light usually annoys me because of the seedy atmosphere it invokes, right now, brighter lights would disturb my sensitive head.

But as soon as I unlock my door, sunbeams cut through the window across the room, nearly blinding me so that I stagger back and cover my eyes. I could stand to plug my nose, too . . .

"What is *this*?" My mother's not laughing anymore. I am glad I can't see for the moment because the expression on her face, given the tone of her voice, cannot be very happy to behold.

"*Tso*! Do you ever clean in here? What have I raised? This girl who used to make her bed without prompt has now become a slob? A messy woman? Akosua. Am I talking to myself?"

"Mom, the light is too much." I've still got my hands over my eyes and am just standing in the doorway, facing the room I refuse to see.

I hear the sound of her moving toward the window and fiddling with the blinds. Then I uncover my eyes and let them adjust to the light, I look around and pronounce, "It's horrible, Mom, I'm sorry," though I'm actually breathing a sigh of relief because it's not that bad.

My bed, directly across from the door and beneath the window, is unmade, the sheets and comforter in a pile on the foot of the bed. A tangle of sweaters I tried on yesterday morning before attempting to go to class spills from the mattress to the floor. Books for the courses I'm supposed to be taking line the side of the bed against the wall, the place where Wisdom slept Sunday night after I bumped my head. Their spines must have poked his all night.

On the table in the center of the room lies a sin: a box of opened cereal, a couple of milk-stained bowls and spoons. A five-dollar bill and a handful of change. Leaving food out is unclean; leaving money lying around is careless. My stomach drops, and I'm a kid again, waiting to get scolded.

"You bumped your head on Sunday. It is Wednesday. That's no excuse for this place."

At least the nook that holds the fridge, stove, and microwave is clean, but that's because I don't have any food, unless you count the wasted food I can smell rotting in the kitchen garbage. Bare cupboards are almost as bad as food and money lying around.

"Why?" My mother asks, her face contorted in a way that I find a little dramatic for the situation but that pains my chest nonetheless. I know in her mind she's picturing my bedroom in our old Detroit house, books lined alphabetically on the shelf, bed made up each morning, clothes hung up and arranged by color, style, and season of the year. She's picturing this same apartment a few months ago, adorned with flowers for her arrival, swept and orderly. Viewing the room with her eyes, I know that, though it's not bad in general, it's bad for me.

"Akosua, when did you stop taking care of yourself?"

But the real question she should ask is when, if ever, did I start; I'm not certain that my need to be immaculate, developed at a young age but abandoned in my past few months of rudderless living, was ever a virtue in the first place.

Imagine me, Akosua Mercy, nearly eight years old and skating on the pale-yellow linoleum floor of the kitchen as I know I shouldn't. But my mother's out in the yard raking leaves, and I am supposed to do as many indoor chores as I can, sweeping the kitchen and basement floors, wiping down the counters, tidying my room.

As long as my mother isn't around, I clean the house wearing roller skates, the ones my father gave me the day before he walked out on us. I wear them with intention; I want to think of him because I don't think I think of him enough. I want to pick the scab, watch an old wound bleed. Because I'm ashamed that I don't miss him every day. Maybe I've gotten used to his absence, even more comfortable with him gone. My mother's laugh has grown unruly and sometimes bitter, but she plays with me more and I don't have to see her sad eyes or wake to sounds of arguing from behind her bedroom door. Instead, I awaken to the sound of my mother singing hymns, to the smell of scrambled eggs and bacon on weekend mornings.

So I skate to remember. The motion of gliding recalls his smile as he watched me open the box of skates, his rough stubble against my cheek as I hugged and thanked him. The motion of gliding—especially when I come to a sudden halt—helps me to remember falling on my butt all alone on the pavement.

Also, my father probably would have scolded me for skating in the house if he were here. I've taken to imagining him doing it, wagging his finger (which is not something I've ever witnessed him doing, but I imagine it nonetheless) and saying sternly, "Mercy Akosua," over and over.

On this particular Sunday morning, while my mom tends to those orange and gold but mostly brown leaves in the yard, I picture him sitting at the kitchen table, gazing at me with large, disdainful eyes.

"Mercy Akosua!" he snaps, and at first he is immaterial, nothing but a voice and a mouth and a pair of eyes behind glasses. "What are you doing?"

And then, because in my daydreams I'm a lot sassier than in real life, I reply, "What does it look like I'm doing?" and whiz right past him on my purple skates, hands flailing in the air.

He reaches out, trying to grab hold of my arm: now, at least, he has a hand, too. But he misses because I am too fast for him. "Mercy Akosua, what are the rules of this house?"

As I skate in a line back and forth from the sink to the kitchen doorway, I tick off the rules on my fingers. "No talking back to Mommy. No shouting. No swearing. No TV after 8:30. No running—"

"No talking back to Mommy or Daddy," he corrects.

"No talking back to Mommy," I insist. "Daddy is gone, remember?"

"I'm here right now," he says, and bangs his hand against his knee, which suddenly materializes.

"No, you're not. And none of the rules ever say there's no skating in the kitchen if Mommy's not around to see."

"*Tso*! Disrespectful girl. If you can't run in the house, what makes you think you can skate in the house?"

"You tell me. What makes me think that?" And I stop skating only inches from where he sits; I consider climbing in his lap.

Instead, I reach for the handle to the freezer door, pull as hard as I can, and take out a carton of mint chocolate chip ice cream.

"Mmm, my favorite," I say, and skate to the drawer for a spoon. I eat right out of the carton.

"That's not how I raised you," my father says, the intensity rising in his voice, and now he's not just eyes, mouth, hands, and knees, he's also a furrowed forehead, and I know he's not angry but is confused to see his good little girl breaking so many rules.

"Did you raise me?" I ask, sucking on the spoon as I begin to skate lines across the linoleum again. "Are you really done? When I'm grown up, there's not gonna be a Daddy who raised me. Just Mommy. I won't even remember you."

Now, I think to myself as I roll faster from one end of our short kitchen to the other, I have really done it. Now he will become, in addition to all the bits of him collecting in the kitchen chair, a puddle of tears. Because I am torturing him. I continue to skate, waiting, watching his almost-face for signs that it's about to crack. Heart pounding, I slowly glide closer to his chair, place the carton of ice cream on the table, peer into his eyes, so brown they are black, like mine, like looking into a mirror. I stare for so long, I feel my neck growing stiff.

But the mirror blinks, and a hand reaches out and gently flicks a finger against my forehead.

"Boo!" snaps my father's voice, and I flinch and land in a heap on the floor; my roller skates failed me. "See? If you forget about me, when I come back, I will only scare you."

I shake my head to clear it; in an attempt to hurt my father, I've hurt no one but myself. My butt hurts from landing on it, and I also startled myself so much that I almost soiled my pants like a baby. I put away the ice cream, wash the spoon, sweep and mop the kitchen floor. Then I retreat to my room to clean, not only clean but organize, not only organize but optimize all the space and make the room as neat and efficient as possible, all as penance for speaking to my imaginary father as only a bad girl would.

I vacuum the carpet, first sprinkling it with a powdery carpet cleaner as my mother usually does before company comes. I arrange my stuffed animals in two neat rows along the side of my hospital corner-made bed (though my mother taught me how to make hospital corners, until now, I've never done it unless she asks me to). I arrange my books in alphabetical order as if I am the library, hang my clothes up so they drape just so, fold my t-shirts and underwear and place them neatly in my drawers. I create a place for each possession and vow to ensure once a week that each belonging finds its way back to that place.

When my mother returns from her yard work, wiping a muddy hand across her sweaty brow, she stops at the door to my room and finds me shining the windows I've already washed.

She smiles. "All right! What a good girl! Let's see how long you can keep it this way."

And until this day that she's in my dorm room surveying this relatively disastrous area, I have kept my room—if not my life, at the very least my room—exactly that neat. But now, in real time, my mother buckles down and gets to business. In less than an hour-and-a-half the room surpasses my mother's standards and meets my own, that is, before I became a slob, a messy woman. My mom is much more jovial than she'd been before.

"You called me a messy woman. You might as well have said 'loose woman,' the way you said it."

She shakes her head. "One is no better than the other. To live like some American bachelor—it is no good! Don't do that anymore, okay?"

"Yes, Mom. But also, I'm only twenty-four. Can't you think of it as a transitory phase right now, where I'm not necessarily going to be the neatest, most responsible person all the time?"

"At twenty-four I was married and pregnant with you." She finishes wiping dust off my window, sits on the windowsill and laughs. The sun backlights her, shadows obscuring her facial expression. "Or, at least, I *thought* I was married."

"You *were* married." I know where she's going. She does this all the time, bringing up this terrible distinction.

"No, I wasn't. Because your father was married to someone else at the same time he was married to me. So, my dear, the law says I was not married."

I know this already. Why bring this up? I'm standing in the kitchen area, leaning against the wall, trying to look at her without catching the glare of the sun through the window. I'm clinging to the door frame for dear life. I'm wondering what my mom might think about Daniel's offer to help me reconnect with my father. I'm hungry.

"All I'm saying, Mommy, is that you and Daddy did have a marriage, even if it wasn't legal. Know what I mean?"

"Yes, I *know what you mean*." She imitates my tone of voice, mocking my Midwest accent, and I realize I provoked her, though I don't know how. "You mean to stand there and defend your father. And that is fine with me. I just hope you know what you're getting involved in."

"What I'm getting involved in? Mom, what are you talking about?"

My mother remains silent, though, turning back to face the window, wiping it again even though it probably can't get any cleaner. Her ponytail whips against the back of her neck as she works. There was a time when we both used to wear the same ponytail, but in high school I tried out different styles, trying to look more mature. My mother would smile, even encourage me, each time I went to a salon for a new haircut or perm or braids, but she's never changed her hairstyle, getting it straightened every other Saturday and pulling it back each morning with multicolored twist ties and occasionally barrettes, many of them the same ones I used to wear when I was little. Other than her hairdresser, a Nigerian teacher who runs a hair salon out of her basement on weekends, my mom allows only me to touch her hair, to braid, curl, or straighten it, creating styles she will never wear in public.

"Mommy . . . will you let me try twisting your hair? Ella taught me. It'll look cute."

"Looking cute is not my priority. Your well-being is."

She snaps the blinds shut, climbs down from the windowsill, moving away from my bed. Her eyes burn into me for a moment, then she turns on heel and strides toward the bathroom. She comes back in seconds, her hands empty of the cleaner and rag she was using to eliminate nonexistent streaks on my window.

"Let us focus on the task at hand. I need to do some food shopping. Auntie and Uncle Fergie are coming here to pick us up soon.

We need to have something to offer them. I will have to go to the supermarket, hmm?"

"Mom, why are you so mad?"

"Never mind," she says, and asks how to get to the supermarket. I hold my tongue and don't say anything snide about how she'll have to go back to the suburbs for a supermarket. I offer to go with her, but she says I need to rest. I can tell by her tone of voice, by the way she won't look me in the eye, that she is angry and doesn't want my company right now, so I direct her to the nearest grocery store and watch her put her coat on, grab her purse, and leave. Before she leaves, though, she tucks me into bed, under the comforter and sheet. I lean my head against the pillow and exhale because I am tired, I do need to rest, and I feel guilty for something I didn't even do yet. It's almost as if she knows that Daniel has planted this idea in my head about my father, as if she's forgotten that I don't want anything to do with him.

I refuse to consider it now. Sleep is the best idea.

A gauzy second blanket covers me. I'm sinking into the softness of my mattress, melting into the fabric deodorizer she sprayed all over my pillows, fitted sheets, bed sheets, every piece of fabric in my room, everything suddenly softer because she's here. My mother. Angry, yes, but all mine. Later, I'm sure, she'll come back and find me sleeping and she'll forget her anger about my messy apartment. She'll comfort me as she used to when I was a child. I imagine her smooth palm on my forehead, the scent of pear and bergamot on her wrists.

A phone ring wakes me up right before I fall into that comfy part of sleep.

I scan the room and reorient myself. Not seven years old. Not in Detroit. Just twenty-four, concussed, and it's the campus landline that's ringing, not my cell phone. Odd.

Reaching toward my bedside table, I grab the phone, thinking that it must be Alan from the library or my boss calling to check up on me. Unless someone else has obtained my campus number, like my father. I ready myself for his voice, a voice I may or may not recognize.

"Is this Akos ... Asuka ... "

The Spanish word *azucar* comes to mind. Sugar. What if my name were *sugar* instead of *born on Sunday*, something sweet, instead of something strange on American tongues? I deflate; the voice on the phone belongs to a woman.

"Ah-KOH-soo-ah," I sound it out for her. "Yes, this is she."

"This is Dean Jervis's assistant. She'd like to schedule an appointment with you before Friday if possible, to discuss your academic status."

"Oh."

"Um ... do you have a day that you prefer?"

"Well ... I'll call back and let you know, but right now I'm, like, I'm ..." I want to delay this until my Mom's out of town. She hasn't told me when she's leaving, though, and, at the moment, I don't even remember what day of the week it is.

"We've sent you an email about the situation. We tried to contact you yesterday."

"I was in the hospital."

"Oh, I see. Sorry to hear that." The woman pauses, and I hear the clicking of nails against a keyboard. "How about we set a tentative appointment for Friday afternoon and if you can't make it ..."

"Sure, sure, good." I like the word tentative. I pretend I am making note of the appointment somewhere and am insulted when she actually asks me if I've written it down, as if I'm some child who needs to be checked up on. But I guess that's what this meeting is about anyway: the dean wants to check up on me. Or kick me out of grad school.

"What exactly is there to discuss about my academic status?" I ask her. But as she begins to stammer an answer, I hear my mother fiddling with the lock. "Thank you very much." I hang up before the woman can explain, and I put the phone into the cradle just as my mother bursts through the door with an armload of grocery bags and a smile on her face that says she's gotten past her gloomy mood.

My mother says I should stay in bed; she'll take care of the food and everything. I put a smile on my face and sink back under the covers again, trying not to think about my academic status. Just another item on the long list of things I avoid telling my mother.

∽∞∾

Paul Anka's soft crooning and the whirl of the heating system in Uncle Fergie's Toyota Camry are the only constant sounds during our ride to Jersey City. My mom sways back and forth to the music, commenting from time to time on the joys of heated car seats. Uncle chuckles proudly each time. I'm sitting in the back lamenting that my mother and I can't just stay in my apartment while she's in New York, but it's a given that we have to stay with the Fergies; it'd be impolite of us to refuse an invitation from family.

It turned out Mom went grocery shopping for nothing, since Uncle Fergie didn't bring Auntie to pick us up from my apartment and he didn't even come inside. Instead, he called my mom's cell phone and told her he was outside waiting. He arrived at 2:30 p.m. sharp, rousing me from the tail end of an uneventful sleep.

As usual, he's quiet, though he and Mom spoke in rapid Twi for the first few minutes of the car ride before falling silent. I don't understand anything in Twi except salutations and insults, and Uncle surprises me by cursing occasionally, calling bad drivers lunatics and idiots. He's over sixty, though he doesn't exactly look it—a full head of hair graying at the temples, only a slight potbelly protruding from his sweater vest and white button-down shirt, the sweater vest and too-large bifocals aging him more than anything else. He's a strange mix of dignified and frumpy, and his potty mouth doesn't add much clarity to my understanding of him.

"So, we are very excited to see your new apartment," my mom starts to say.

A car swerves in front of us, though, and Uncle Fergie says, "*Kwasia. Eh! Stupid obroni fool can't drive properly.*"

I can't help it, I laugh, even though it's wrong, since he's just called the man an idiot and a white fool. My mother turns and gives me an admonishing look from where I sit in the backseat like a kid.

The moment's made even better when my mother gently scolds my uncle in return, saying, "I don't believe poor driving has anything to do with being *obroni*, since you are Ghanaian and you have just switched lanes without a signal."

And then she chuckles, a forced, polite laugh, and I know it's meant to make light of the fact that she chastised a man who's not her husband and who is at least a decade older than she is.

He grunts and shifts uncomfortably in his seat, but the next time someone crosses him on the road, he doesn't curse.

Soon he pulls the car into the front drive of a luxury high rise. Auntie Fergie runs to the car from the lobby, flapping her arms wildly, her long curly hair flying about as she jumps up and down. Her excitement is contagious and my mom starts hopping, too, as soon as she gets out of the car. I sort of want to jump along with them, but my head begins to pound as if to remind me that I have little to be excited about. Uncle Fergie drives off to park the car in the garage, and Auntie leads us inside the building and into the elevator to their place on the sixteenth floor.

I'm in ecstasy because of the transcendent food Auntie Fergie has cooked us for an early dinner. I pour all my attention into devouring the meal. I am the food and the food is me. Conversation flitters around me, but I have no idea what my elders are saying. Quite the typical situation when I'm stuck with my mom and any aunties or uncles who refuse to acknowledge the fact that the American girl doesn't know Ewe or Twi, that the American girl is not a girl anymore and there's no need to exclude her from adult conversations by speaking in words she doesn't understand.

Since I'm not expected to say anything, I can focus all my attention on the delicacies that I don't get to eat often now that I don't live with my mom. Today it's a dish called red red, black-eyed peas in a meaty tomato sauce with a heap of fried plantains on the side and filets of fried tilapia for good measure. Over the black-eyed peas, I sprinkle dried cassava, my favorite part of the meal aside from the plantains, which my childhood self thought of as parentally sanctioned candy with dinner.

Aside from asking how I'm doing and hugging me and patting my head and hugging me more and asking me how the hospital was and if the doctor had prescribed any painkillers, Auntie Fergie says very little to me. But, unlike her ornery husband, she's not quiet and has a lot of stories to tell my mother. They haven't seen each other since my college graduation two years ago, because when my mom visited last spring, there hadn't been time to make the trip to New Jersey to visit them in the faculty housing where they used to live.

"Fergie and I are getting older, Enyo, we deserve the finer things!" Auntie bursts out in English at one point during dinner, and they both laugh and chatter away while Uncle shovels food into his mouth almost as quickly as I do.

As I mash a slice of plantain against the roof of my mouth and savor the sweetness, I take in the features of their new apartment. The Fergies' decor aesthetic, similar to that of my mother, revolved around the familiar: family photos on the wall, wooden statuettes, kente cloth hanging from the edges of bookcases. Auntie and Uncle have always boasted an admirable collection of Nigerian videos, while my mother and I only have a handful of the classic Nollywood witchcraft comedies and romance sagas; the Fergies keep all their DVDs and videos in a glass display case next to the entertainment center because the latter overflows with tapes and CDs and photo albums. The clutter that felt cozy and inviting in their old home feels out of place here in their expansive new living room, the modern design of the kitchen clashing with the mortar and pestle Auntie must have used to grind up spices for the black-eyed peas. From the dining room where we sit, I can see the large plush white couches and the huge flat screen TV. The kente cloth and the wooden statuette of a woman holding a basket on her head and a baby on her back seem tiny and misplaced on the marble mantle.

After dishing more food from the pots in the kitchen into ceramic serving bowls for the dining table, Auntie Fergie excuses herself and returns with a disposable camera.

"Take a photo of us, Fergie, a photo of us girls."

Uncle obliges, snapping a quick picture without giving us much warning, though he takes another when Auntie protests that none of us were ready. Then he puts the camera on an empty chair at the table and plunks down in front of his meal again.

In the meantime, Auntie has leaned her head away from the table, letting her long curls fall straight down toward the floor. Her head disappears for a moment, and when she straightens up again, her curly hair sits in a pile in her lap. She grins.

"I don't need the wig anymore today, do I, Akosua?"

Her short Afro looks far more flattering than the wig she's so abruptly removed. I've never seen her without the wig; I didn't even know she wore one.

"You don't ever need the wig, Auntie. Short hair fits you so nicely."

"Oh, you really think so?"

"Mmm-hmm."

"Thank you, my girl. What a good girl. So nice to say to an old woman."

"Oh, you're not an old woman."

On and on this could go. Most of our conversations proceed in this manner. I say something nice in a little girl's voice because that's the respectful way to speak, and she congratulates me on what a good girl I am or my mother on what a good girl she's raised. Now Auntie chooses to congratulate my mother, in Twi, and the conversation progresses without me.

If only I were Wisdom. These words pop into my head as I'm forking a bite-sized sliver of fried fish. Because Wisdom has only been in the States since his sophomore year of college and grew up all over Ghana, he knows both Twi and Ewe fluently and a few sayings in a handful of the other scores of dialects spoken in Ghana. He would be able to carry a conversation with Auntie Fergie and my mom; the women wouldn't have the freedom of being able to say whatever they wanted. The first time Wisdom cooked for me, he fried me some tilapia almost as good as the fish on my fork right now. He never burned his fish or made it too oily, either. He had a mental timer for cooking certain foods, he would always declare, wriggling his thick eyebrows, looking goofy yet competent. "It's a good thing I do," he joked, "since you don't know how to cook Ghanaian food."

"So, ahem." Uncle Fergie actually articulates "ahem," as if it's a word and not just an approximation of a sound people make when they're clearing their throats. And he doesn't do it in the exaggerated, pointed way that people do when they say the word. It's a natural sound that comes from him. The sound is enough to get his wife to stop talking mid-sentence. "Akosua. I would like to hear more about how school is going for you."

I feel my heart speed up in an instant. If the Fergies are my emergency contact for school, explaining how they found out I'd been to the hospital, perhaps my dean had also contacted them first to inquire about my weak schedule this semester? Maybe even my mother knows...

"School is fine," I say. "You know, in grad school nowadays, everything goes in ebbs and flows, sometimes you've got a big course load, sometimes you feel like you're practically not in school at all."

"Hmm." He wipes his mouth with a napkin, continues to eat. "Well, I suppose it will not be easy, keeping abreast of studies while you are nursing your head and becoming reacquainted with your father."

My fork clatters to my plate, a chunk of plantain falling off the end and plopping onto the white lace tablecloth.

"Oh," my mother says. "She doesn't need to talk about that right now, please, it's okay. What she does with him is her own decision."

"What?" I want to say more, but my voice catches in my throat. How do they know about Daniel's offer? "What?"

Uncle takes a long drink from his glass of water, then resumes the important work of stuffing his face. "Listen, my girl, these things should not be so taboo and hush hush. My brother, he has a child, too, that he lost contact with for, what, six, seven years. Back in Ghana, you know? It is okay to miss your father. He has moved back to the States for your sake, he is near his child, finally willing to make up for time that is lost. Let it be, Enyo, let them talk."

I raise my hand upward, pressing it against my head. I wonder if I'm still in the hospital and dreaming, if somehow my uncle and aunt and mother were able to get into my head, extract my thoughts, and voice all the reasons I should or shouldn't contact my father. I wonder anew at the strange mix of meddling and secret-keeping that seems to govern my family.

"*Tso!*" My mother's eyes gleam, black and earnest. "I wouldn't dare stop her. Do you think that is what I have done, Fergie? I haven't said a word to her about it. I don't care if she talks to that man. What I'm upset about is why she hasn't said a word to me about it herself. I don't understand why the girl didn't just tell me. Why wouldn't you tell me?"

I look at Auntie. She has no answers. She's looking at me, too, expectantly. I turn to Uncle, who is still eating, every few seconds or so glancing up at me with only his eyes because he can't be bothered with the effort of lifting his head too far from his plate. I cannot look at my mother. Finally, I say to Uncle's bowed head, "How did you and Auntie find out?"

"My dear. How do you think we knew about your head accident? Your father told us." He pierces a slice of plantain with his fork, pops it into his mouth.

"What? How did *he* find out?"

"Oh! Mercy Akosua." My mother never says my whole name like that. "Please, eh? We know you have begun to speak with your father. You don't have to continue to lie."

"But I haven't spoken to him," I say, my voice too loud for this table of elders. It's like I have no control over its volume. "I absolutely have not. Where would you get that crazy idea from?"

My head begins to throb as if their words are beating against it. Suddenly the dinner table's a barrage of confusion, back and forth, Uncle accusing Auntie of getting her signals crossed, my mother accusing me of lying and disrespecting Uncle and Auntie with my loud voice, and Auntie pleading that they should leave the poor girl alone, that she is embarrassed to discover that she loves and misses and needs her father.

"I'm not embarrassed—and I don't miss or need him—I just, please, let's straighten this out," I plead, clutching my forehead with both hands.

In less than a minute, the confusion is cleared up. Yesterday Auntie Fergie received a phone call from my father, who the Fergies hadn't spoken to or visited since his return to the States three months ago. He'd frantically asked if they had visited his daughter Akosua in the hospital. He had heard I had an accident of some kind, he said to Auntie, that I had hit my head. Auntie assumed then that my father and I must have been in contact with one another, so she called my mother to console her on the state of her hospitalized daughter, assuming that my mother knew everything about my head and my father.

I am so mad that tears are burning in my eyes. I blink them away, refusing to let my relatives see me cry. They are not looking at me, though. My mother's looking down at her plate, and Auntie and Uncle are exchanging glances. I feel violated, like before I even had a chance to decide about my father on my own, they have taken sides, for and against, and my mother, who matters the most, is clearly against.

I will brain Daniel Cobblah.

"This guy at school, Daniel Cobblah, he says his cousin works with Daddy—with my father." The tears drop warm against my hand, not bothering to touch my face before they fall. "He keeps meddling."

"Oh, Cobblah," Auntie says. "Is he related to Kwesi—"

"Yes, yes, so Daniel told his cousin who told my father who told you and on and on and on . . ." I can't get out the words I want. I can't say what I mean. "Nobody even said anything, but all anybody had to do was say something . . ."

My mother releases a tiny nervous laugh, one whose wings flutter quickly and then disappear. "*Tso.* My daughter. It's okay. It's only a misunderstanding, it's fine."

"No, it is not fine, it is crazy, and I totally understand why you run away from it all, why you're in Windsor, *Canada*, and far away from the memories of him, and the judging voices, and all the feelings . . ."

As soon as I say "voices," my mother is on her feet, by my side, pressing one palm against my forehead and one behind my head as if she can hold it all together. She thinks I'm losing it, I can tell. She's saying I need to lie down, that I hit my head and that the doctor gave so many possible symptoms and mood swings is one of them. She wants to put me to bed immediately. I will obey. I am not sure whether this sudden pounding in my head, this thing that she will later laugh at and call a tantrum, is due to a concussion or me being plain pissed off. But I will let them think whatever they want. I will keep my mouth shut for the night if it will keep theirs shut, too. It's always like this. So many people talking to each other, everyone in the world talking to each other, except the people who should be.

5

Our stay with the Fergies feels like a vacation. Aside from that first dinner, the days press forward like a boat in calm waters. Uncle spends most of the time in his office or in class, and my mother and aunt lounge in their pajamas half the day, chattering away in Twi, trading recipes for spinach stew, akple, akla. While buried in bed, I enjoy the scents of constant cooking. The Fergies have two extra bedrooms, and Mom and Auntie force me to take the one with a queen-size bed while Mom takes the full bed. I sink into the white comforters and pillows every glorious night and even some afternoons, whether I have a headache or not. Each time I try to help with dishes or cooking, I'm admonished to go to bed, to listen to some music, to read a book or something, so I do. Ella calls to check on me, Alan and my coworkers send me a get well soon e-card, but, other than that, I don't contact the outside world and it doesn't contact me. I wonder why Wisdom hasn't called. I am waiting for something that I don't realize I'm waiting for.

It feels good to have no worries, no business to take care of, though I'm not sure what I've been doing lately anyway. Haven't I spent all semester flipping through the course catalog, trying to figure out what to add to my schedule to make it whole again? Even after the registration period passed, I continued to read descriptions of classes, ones that I wish I took last semester, ones I want to take next semester. At the library I manned the desk, fielding questions from students and professors and alumni about library policies and took pictures for ID cards and doled out privileges to people who, unlike me, actually seemed invested enough in their studies to visit a library. But when I wasn't working, I was laughing with Alan, with the undergrad work-studies, or in quiet moments, sifting through the same course descriptions. I have them memorized. But it all felt like an empty distraction. Nothing sparked anything in me.

Perhaps it's lack of discipline that's getting in my way; perhaps I need a process. Process is one of the first things I learned since I spent the earliest years of my life around my father as he methodically read textbooks and wrote his papers and graded student work. My first memory is of my father studying, of me studying my father studying.

The memory suspends itself in time: I recall no moments preceding it, and the ones that follow come years later. I know I must have been three because I know my parents replaced the shag carpet before I turned four; three is also the year I got my favorite stuffed elephant that still sleeps on my bed at my mom's place in Windsor.

My mother thinks I must have fabricated much of this memory, plucked bits from more recent recollections or from stories I've been told, but what does it matter if the moment feels true? I'm clutching Ellie the Elephant because I must entertain myself, because even though my father sits a few toddles away, I know to be good and quiet. I run my fingers through the shag carpet of our living room; my earliest memories involve my fingers and toes in the brown, yarn-like strands. I see my father in fragments: his white-socked feet. Black sweatpants. An arm in a white T-shirt. His thick hair. And most of all, glasses perched on his forehead. He's reading a fat red textbook—I like red and I like the books my parents read to me at night.

Although I know I shouldn't, in time I walk over to my father, lay my hand on his knee. I don't know if he speaks to me, I think he laughs—but I do remember his arms around me as he sets me on a chair beside him and places a coloring book and a box of crayons into my lap.

But I don't color. I watch my father read.

He taps his pen against his lips.

He bites the end of his pen.

He puts down the pen, turns a page, tilts his head, clears his throat.

After a few moments, he repeats the process.

My mother says this isn't possible, that a three-year-old cannot understand such things, but I feel that I did understand; what more matters than that feeling? Three-year-old Mercy Akosua Agbe understands her father's actions as a process, as something she needs to repeat.

With crayons and coloring book, little girl me undertakes the process.

Taps crayons against lips.

Bites end of crayon (and this, I know, is the beginning of my dirty childhood crayon-eating habit).

Puts the crayon down, turns the page, tilts the head, clears the throat.

Repeat, repeat, repeat this until you do it without realizing what you're doing, repeat this even if he doesn't notice that you are repeating this because of him. Even if he doesn't notice that you are watching him all the time.

Even after he left, I watched him. On our living room wall in Detroit hung a photograph of my father in full regalia, his doctoral cap perched on a head held high. My mother left it on the wall until I left for college. "Let it stay there," she would say with a laugh whenever I asked why she didn't remove the photo. "The least the man can do is encourage you to focus on your schooling."

Now that I'm at the Fergies', concussed with nothing but time to assess my stagnancy, I try to summon that discipline I once observed in him.

One afternoon, I go into my guest bedroom and sit on my bed with *History of the Asante Before the British*.

I tap my pen against my lips—I read an entire paragraph on the great woman warrior Yaa Asantewaa, all the while trying to channel him, my father—I bite the end of my pen, I put it down, turn the page, read on, tilt my head, clear my throat. I can see his glasses but there's no face behind them. I can see the words on the page but there's no meaning behind them.

Lately I find that as I think these thoughts, I cry, not even realizing I've been crying until I feel my damp pillow. I blame the mood swings associated with my head injury, and that helps me to give in and cry until I can sleep.

Thursday night I am at the tail end of such a weep-fest when my mother knocks on my door, slipping into the guest bedroom before I give her the okay. The lights are off, though, so she doesn't see my wet face.

"How are you feeling?" she asks, sitting on the edge of my bed. She reaches for my hand and I let her take it. Everything is back to normal now; she's been almost herself again since that dinner when everything blew up in our faces.

"I'm okay. My head's okay. I think it's not a big deal at all and I should be able to go back to work on Monday like I told my boss. And school. God knows I'll have a lot to catch up on there."

"I wanted to ask you something," she starts, and I think she's going to mention my father. Maybe she'll scold me for not mentioning Daniel's offer to put me in touch with my father. Maybe she'll apologize for not simply asking me if I was talking to my father instead of taking Auntie's word.

"Yes?"

"Thanksgiving is so soon, and you were supposed to come home, but maybe you should try and reschedule your ticket. Maybe they will let you use it at Christmas time instead. Why come home in two weeks when I have just seen you here, now?"

"But I'll need the break."

"What you will need is to study. As you just said, you have a lot to catch up on, missing this entire week while you recover."

"But my head . . . like, the doctor said I should be slow about my recovery. Maybe coming to Windsor would help."

"I think that getting back on the right track with school and work will help."

Maybe she knows about the trouble I'm in with the dean? Perhaps the dean has contacted her, or maybe Daniel Cobblah hacked into my student records and blabbed about my academic problems to everyone he knows, too.

Or maybe she knows about my academic trouble because she knows me. She shouldn't be surprised. Junior year of high school, the year whose importance teachers and counselors and parents hammer home, something similar happened to me. Top student at a top school slips from a higher-than-4.0 average to a 2.5. She quits the swim team, of which she'd been co-captain, and misses enough student council meetings to get fired. She sleeps through chores on the weekend, she nods off in class. Her doctor has no answer, but the school counselor has a suggestion, which she calls to share with the girl's mom.

"Therapy?" the mom laughs, rolls her eyes. "This is what I get, sending my daughter to this school full of rich people. Therapy. Depression. Anxiety. Only the wealthy have time for this nonsense."

The mother didn't say this to the school counselor, of course, as that would be uncouth. But she did say it to her lost daughter, followed by a bit of advice: "You are not depressed, my dear. Don't let people label you. Be strong, keep studying, and in time you will shake this thing off."

Now my mother says something similar, smoothing my hair into place as she insists that I shouldn't leave New York for Thanksgiving, that I should stay nearby so I don't fall behind in grad school. "You are a tough girl. You'll be fine."

She laughs and reveals those white straight teeth, the barely perceptible gap between the front two that is a mark of beauty in Ghana. Her skin stretches smoothly across her still-young face, and when she leaves me, I find myself wondering, if I had tilted my head into the dim light, would she have seen that I was crying?

Friday morning, I tell my auntie and mother a white lie. Instead of saying that I need to go back to school in the afternoon because the dean has summoned me, I say that I need to get some assignments and check in with professors and my boss. Part of it is true; I will go to the library and say hi to Alan and make sure I'm penciled in for work on Monday. But I also will take care of a certain self-assigned task, one that involves letting Daniel Cobblah know that I am not his business and never will be again. I will sass all the politeness off his face.

My mother and Auntie Fergie do not allow me to ride the PATH train into the city and then take the subway up to campus. Not all alone, not in my condition, despite the fact that I feel fine today. Auntie Fergie knows a West African food store in Harlem that sells goat meat, so we will all drive into the city together in the afternoon and they'll drop me off at school on their way to shop.

Uncle Fergie gladly agrees to go to his office early in the morning and return before two o'clock so that we can use the car. I'm not sure if he's more excited about the prospect of goat stew or of a womanless afternoon in his apartment.

Walking on the campus feels surreal. Though I haven't even been gone for a week, it feels like I've just returned from summer vacation. Except that it is cold. On the way to the dean's office, I pass the bench where I passed out on Tuesday. Some undergrads are lying on it side by side, making out.

"Ew, stop, do that in *private*, this is *public*," I blurt before I can stop myself.

But they don't stop or seem to hear me. And I guess I did collapse here in public, airing my private sickness for all to see, so who am I to complain?

I don't have to wait at all in the dean's office. Her assistant sends me right in, to my dismay; I wish I could sit and clear my mind before whatever will happen happens. Luckily, Dean Jervis gets a phone call as soon as I sit in the chair across from her massive mahogany desk, and she speaks in the type of coded, vague language that seems to be the stuff of true adulthood, of academic professionalism, of the state in life I'm supposed to be striving toward.

"Yes, well, that is a matter that we intend to attend to . . ." She flashes me an apologetic smile as she speaks into the receiver.

Dean Jervis is tan and long-legged with wavy brown hair. She's wearing a clingy wrap dress under a blazer. She looks like she belongs in this office; she also looks like she belongs on a runway somewhere. My armpits prickle; let the nervous sweating begin. Why isn't she an old white man? I know exactly what to fear with them; I am familiar with their brand of condescension. I have learned not to feel inferior to them, or at least how to hide under a mask of confidence. But a woman is another thing altogether. Dean Jervis, with her picture-perfect looks and her picture-perfect office, might as well be my mother or an auntie, prepared to call me out on my failures.

The longer I sit in the dean's office, the more I notice it's not perfect: the faux wood panels, the pleather chair, the way the dark blue carpet tufts up and darkens in a few coffee-stained splotches. Still, the dean has two framed diplomas nailed to her wall—one from Cornell, the other from Harvard—and a couple of plaques on her bookshelves. It's clear that she belongs, and once again I'm wondering how I got here, to this place, fighting to stay in graduate school to study a subject I'm not sure of at all.

My senior year of college, I applied to many jobs; as an American studies major, I'd taken a lot of history and literature courses and I thought I could teach those subjects to middle or high school students. I interviewed at some private and charter schools, including the one where I'd interned as a teaching assistant during the school year. But the idea of teaching kids made me antsy. Who was I to think I could mold young minds? What had prepared me for the world, my liberal arts degree in basket weaving? A couple of my uncles in Ghana had said that to my mother once, encouraging her to force me to study nursing or law or medicine, not something as impractical as history.

So I looked for graduate programs to apply to, rushing my applications, rushing the GREs, deciding upon history and African studies as my focus, since I'd done pretty well in those classes. In my admissions essays for the history programs, I wrote about my father's work as a civil engineer and how his passion for exploring the history of engineering inspired my passion for studying the history of emerging societies.

Really, I didn't know anything about my father's work as a historian, and I still don't. I don't know anything about engineering or civility or societies in bloom. I decided to study history on an impulse, without any real sense of direction, without any true sense of how my own history had shaped my decision. And now I'm about to get kicked out of a place in which I have no purpose anyway.

When the dean gets off the phone, she turns to me and apologizes, once, efficiently, and then proceeds with the matter at hand.

With me she is much more direct than she was with whomever she was speaking to on the phone.

"You are not enrolled in enough courses for your registration to be valid. You are registered as a full-time student, enabling you to receive federal aid and your current position at the library and even student housing. Because you have failed to maintain the proper course load, you have voided your status as a full-time student."

Her light brown eyes pierce into me as she speaks, but her voice is soft, an attempt at being comforting, I guess. It is not working. As she sorts through something on her computer screen, silent now, I hear my own heart pounding, or perhaps it's something in my head. Whatever it is, it is loud and it is painful and I am worried I have done something irreparable in letting my academics slide so far. I am supposed to graduate in May. What will my mom say when she finds out I've been kicked out instead?

Dean Jervis clears her throat. "All right, Miss Agbe. I've spoken to your dissertation advisor, and Dr. Hollingsworth sings your praises, assuring me that you'll be able to focus and get back on track. I've now entered you as a part-time student. Unless you have something to say to explain your academic hardship, you'll be put on probation at least through this semester, and next semester you must register at least half-time—which means no more semesters of low-credit language courses—or lose your graduate housing and your job. Do you have any extenuating circumstances to explain your current situation?"

What can I possibly say? I have no direction? I broke up with my boyfriend? My father moved back to the country and is actually living in New York and the fact that he's nearby is eating away at my skull?

I shake my head.

"You will meet with your faculty advisor to discuss your plans for graduation." She smiles at me broadly, stands up, reaches for my hand, and shakes it. "For now, just make sure you ace Spanish conversation."

As I walk across campus to the library to say hi to my coworkers, my legs feel like rubber but my heart soars. I've gotten a reprieve. I haven't been kicked out of my program; I've just been demoted to part-time. Dr. Hollingsworth, my undergraduate thesis advisor who's now my dissertation advisor, saved me from getting kicked out. He's been relatively hands-off with me, probably because he still sees me as the focused student I personified as an undergrad. I haven't done much lately to legitimize his faith in me, but I appreciate it nonetheless. His faith buys me time.

Now the only thing I need to worry about is money. The dean can't change federal rules. I'm only a part-time student; I've lost my loans for this semester. The balance for my Spanish class and the campus housing will sit on my student account until next semester, harmless, but before I can officially register next semester—which is only a few weeks away—I will have to pay off the balance.

"Akosua. You are well again."

I stop in my tracks, turn around.

I am face to face with Daniel Cobblah, who's been walking behind me with Pete at his side.

"I could tell it was you by your walk. You take heavy footsteps," Daniel says. He's bundled in a knee-length down coat; he wears mittens that make his hands look like paws when he waves them at me. Friendly paws.

"No, I am not well. Do I look well to you?"

"You are looking very nice to me."

"You meddled. Do you know what a mess you caused, telling your stupid cousin to tell my dad that I was in the hospital?"

"Please, Akosua, calm down—"

"A girl should not be forced to think of her deadbeat father when she's trying to ask a guy on a date!"

Pete ducks away, waving at us, at the whole mess, as he bounds toward the dorm where the Housing Department desk is located.

"You said you were going to leave me alone and that you would call off your stupid cousin so that he wouldn't talk to my dad about me."

"Eh, please watch your mouth." He puts an open palm a handful of inches away from my face. "Don't curse my cousin, *kpor nkume neda. Tso!* He is my elder cousin. He has helped to support me as I moved to this country." Daniel Cobblah's voice is rising to heights I've never heard, loud, sharp like a knife, or like an arrow shooting straight into my heart. "Watch your manners, o."

I stop my ranting, amazed. Daniel Cobblah has just yelled at me. The chocolatey-smooth serenity of his face has contorted with anger. Of course, he is upset that I haven't been respectful and polite, which I realize now must be the only thing that can get him to stop being so damn respectful and polite himself. I am pleased that I've gotten him riled up without having to resort to flashing him.

I force myself to breathe. "I'm sorry. I mean no disrespect to your cousin."

"Right. Good. Thank you." The lines on his forehead relax again. "It is not your fault, in any case. I, too, am apologetic. I should not have involved myself in your family affairs. I was only trying to help, but I see now that it was not right."

"Oh. You do?"

"Yes. I don't know, Akosua." He puts his mittened hands in his pocket and shrugs his massive shoulders. "Things that are helpful back home, in this country they are seen as interference. You are both an American and a Ghanaian. You are more complex than I considered."

Somehow this sounds like a compliment. My lips agree, as they raise into a smile. My body stops pumping adrenaline, and I no longer want to fight or flee.

"I guess I am. But I wasn't very fair either. I didn't see things from your perspective."

He takes a step closer to me, and though we're the distance that my high school established for safe dancing at prom, we are still closer than we've ever stood while facing each other.

"It is good we understand each other," he says, and I notice the power in his jaw as he sets it against the cold.

"Yeah."

"I called your apartment Wednesday and Thursday, but you did not answer. You worried me."

I tell him about Auntie Fergie and my mother and the Jersey City apartment that is my temporary home. "They're buying goat meat now. I should actually hurry. I'm supposed to meet them on Amsterdam in a few minutes."

"Mmm, goat." He chuckles. "One thing I have been missing lately, not having a good Ghanaian woman to cook for me."

"There are plenty of Ghanaian girls around who could teach you." Like Aku Aggrey, that sophomore I saw him with the other day.

"I don't want Ghanaian girls. I'm looking for something a little more sophisticated than a girl."

"I can't cook, but maybe—" I yelp mid-sentence; my phone is vibrating deep in my coat pocket. "Oh, that must be my family." I take it out to check, but it finishes vibrating before I have the presence of mind to answer.

Daniel takes the phone from me, pulls off one of his mittens, and begins to press some numbers into the phone. Then he presses the call button. In his pocket perhaps, or maybe in his book bag, his own cell phone begins to ring. He smiles pleasantly, takes a couple of steps backward, watching me watch him, and then turns on heel and trots toward the housing desk.

I find the nearest bench. I slowly ease myself onto it and continue to watch him until he disappears into the building where he works. My heart struggles to find its normal steady rhythm.

You are both an American and a Ghanaian, he said, accepting it as a matter of fact, accusing me of nothing but being myself.

It is refreshing, not feeling guilty to be me.

In the car, on the way back to Jersey City, I am grinning. I am celebrating a victory. I can feel it in my skin, beneath my skin, in all of my muscles and synapses, which have slowed their constant twitching, the twitching that hasn't quite died down since I fell. I can feel the difference inside but, I guess you can see it on the outside, too; that must be why my mother and Auntie Fergie have noticed and won't stop badgering me.

"You look like you heard some good news. Come on, you have to share it with your mommy. Your one and only mommy who came all the way to New York and has seen nothing but a sick, sour face since I arrived."

"I didn't mean to," I start, the guilt rising.

"I don't blame you; you were sick. I can't fault you for being clumsy and falling." She breaks into laughter, and Auntie joins. They seem pretty thrilled with our trip to the city themselves, and I know from the musky scent emanating from the grocery bags seated next to me on the backseat that they've gotten enough goat meat to make a feast.

"You must be feeling better," Auntie Fergie says, "tell us why."

"Is everything okay at work?" Mom asks.

"Are your professors okay with your absence?" Auntie chimes in.

I don't mention that I didn't check on either of these things during my visit to campus.

"Or have you heard a bit of good campus gossip?" my mother asks.

Gossip. There it is, that word, that thing that thrives on an itch in the brain, a twitch of the tongue, an empty space in the ear canal that longs to be filled with scandalous news and rumors. Even though my mother has been the subject of gossip in her day, has seen how it can hurt and how false it can be, she still sometimes wants in on some of it herself, like every other human being. She doesn't like to focus on rumors about people she knows, though. Generally, she likes to hear about celebrities and, occasionally, the lives of the young and the restless, i.e. my peers.

"Okay, ready for this one, guys?" I say, leaning so far forward that the seat belt presses against my bladder.

I take a deep breath. I am about to rewrite history. "This is actually about this Ghanaian girl on campus. I mean, she's like me—born here, hardly goes back, but she's Ghanaian. Born in Brooklyn," I add. "Anyway, she's a—she's a med student, right? Really on the right track, wins fellowships, scholarships, makes her parents proud. And she was dating this Ghanaian boy, also a med student—"

"Like your friend Wisdom?" my mother asks.

"Well. Yeah. Something like him. So this girl, Naa—"

"She's Akan, then?"

"Yes."

"Where from?" My mother pesters.

"Brooklyn." I know that's not what my mother meant, but I forge ahead. "So Naa was dating this guy who was born in Accra and came here for undergrad and now med school. She was totally thrilled to have landed him: cute, funny, stylish, smart, really kind—*and* Ghanaian?"

"Sounds like what *you* would want," my mom says, and she and Auntie giggle.

"Who wouldn't? Thing is, he turns out to be a real jerk. He acts like he's cool with her being American—"

"But she's Ghanaian," Auntie Fergie jumps in.

"And American," I say. "She's both. Anyway, he's only really comfortable with who she is when they're alone, or with Americans, but when they're actually with other Ghanaians it's like he's ashamed of her."

As I tell them about the time that imaginary Naa went to dinner with mystery medical school jerk, I remember the time that I went to dinner with Wisdom and his friends, the incident that occurred the week before our breakup on the street. I know I have to hold back as I story-tell. I don't reveal too many details or else it will seem too real. I leave out the lavender perfume that I wore that late August night, the silver bangle wristwatch with a tiny heart pendant attached, given to me for no reason other than because-I-love-you-and-why-not. I don't mention his dark blue dress shirt and blazer, his perfect line-up. *Dapper,* I think as he takes my arm after picking me up at my apartment, *what a handsome package for this man of mine, sweetness wrapped in sweetness.* My linen eyelet dress, white, tight-bodied, loose-skirted and brushing against the backs of my knees, feels clean against my skin. I feel clean. There's no sweat. We're the most beautiful people alive, and finally, without my even having to beg, he's going to show me off to his Ghanaian friends from high school, the ones who, like him, have been transplanted for some reason or another—usually education and/or career—to the States and New York specifically.

"It's not that I'm embarrassed by you, silly," he says as we ride the subway from Harlem to midtown where we're meeting them. "It's that I thought you'd be bored, you know, we all know each other from school, we all will be speaking pidgin or Ewe or Twi—"

"Well, I understand pidgin, I just can't speak it well. Besides, I'm your girlfriend. Your friends are gonna have to hang out with me at some point, right?"

"I guess. But I still think you'll be bored." He kisses my cheek. "Not that I'm too worried about that, you know, considering how you look in that dress. I'm going to have to start inviting you to awkward outings with my friends more often, 'cause it really gets you fancied up, doesn't it?"

Everyone's already in the lounge where we'll be eating, drinking, and possibly dancing. The truth is, it took me quite a long time to get dressed; I tried on six other outfits before deciding that this one feels most like me. All I wanted to be was me, even if that meant we'd have to be late.

"What up, what up, man?" Wisdom greets two of his friends, Kwame and Michael.

"What de go on?" Michael replies in pidgin, grinning, shaking Wisdom's hand vigorously, giving me a one-armed hug. I understand pidgin well enough because my cousins in Ghana speak it all the time, and also because my grandmother, before she died, spoke her own version of it on the phone with me, the only way she could communicate with her American granddaughter. A mix of English and Portuguese and Ghanaian words and constructions, pidgin is my kind of language because it's a blend.

"Chale, I dey fine," Wisdom replies, and then gestures to me, his hands splayed game show hostess style as if to say, here she is, my girl Akosua, but he doesn't actually say these words or anything more on the subject of my introduction.

Kwame and Michael I've met before, briefly, but it's the girls Wisdom is always reluctant to introduce me to. Rebecca and Sedi, Kwame and Michael's girlfriends, respectively, flutter their hands at me in greeting, blow air-kisses at Wisdom to say hello to him, and I both love and hate the restrained, cool nod and smile he flashes at them in return: the Wisdom I know from day to day is rarely this cool.

The candles make the room seem smudgy, dreamlike; after a half an hour has passed, the wine kicks in and heightens the effect.

Mostly we talk about people and things and places I don't know, though Rebecca and Sedi—and on occasion, Wisdom—kindly fill me in on the missing pieces I can't know about since I'm not part of this circle of friends.

"Look at that girl dancing. It's like she literally has a stick up her ass," Sedi says at one point, giggling.

The woman dancing near the bar is white, or as Wisdom and his friends say, *obroni*. The woman dressed incorrectly for this trendy Manhattan establishment. Her turtleneck, jeans, and hiking boots make her stand out in this club full of women in dresses and stilettos. Earlier I heard her loudly declare her disdain for the high drink prices to her gaggle of girlfriends, speaking in an accent not unlike my own, vowels elongated beyond all reason, a tinge of nasalness, and I know she's probably from Ohio or Michigan or someplace else in the Midwest.

"Stick up her ass. I'd never quite visualized what that expression meant until now," Sedi says, and everyone at our table laughs.

My insider knowledge allows me to make the not-even-that-witty crack, "Well, stick-up-the-ass is a disorder quite prevalent in the suburban Midwest."

Wisdom laughs, as does Michael. Both went to undergrad in Ohio before moving out here for graduate school.

"You say?" Sedi asks, wanting to be filled in on the joke, and Wisdom tells my joke all over again, except in Twi this time, and my already mediocre joke about the stereotypical polite-but-stiff Midwesterner gets lost in cultural and linguistic translation. He translates it for them with such earnestness and laughs heartily at the end, his eyes saying, "Isn't my American girlfriend funny?"

Rebecca and Sedi hear a song they like and get up to dance, holding hands and twirling circles around each other, their hair and bare shoulders shining. The guys sit and drink and hype up the girls and their dance moves. I smile, my second glass of red wine really getting to me now, and it's great because they're happy and pretty and gyrating, and everyone's having fun, and here's my boyfriend by my side, this beautiful man running his hand across my forearm and leaning toward me to whisper in my ear.

Before he can say anything, I turn my head and kiss his lips that were poised, I'm sure, to say something sweet to me.

He smiles.

"Hi," I say, grinning.

"Hi."

"What were you going to tell me?"

"Oh." He nods toward Rebecca shaking her ample behind on the dance floor. "Just that that's the kind of skirt I thought would look good on you."

Rebecca has on a skintight Lycra skirt that shows off her perfectly smooth, dark legs from ankle to mid-thigh; her tank top is shiny and red and flatters her perky boobs and petite figure.

"What's wrong with what I'm wearing?"

"Nothing." He flashes his white teeth at me. "I told you. You look beautiful. But in that skirt, you'd look hot."

"I think I look hot in this dress." I *thought* I looked hot in this dress.

The girls come crashing back to the table, laughing. Apparently, the Midwestern woman whose dancing we teased earlier heard Sedi and Rebecca talking in pidgin and asked, "Are you Africans?"

"I mean, Africa is not a country," Sedi says to us now.

"*Aaaa*frican," Rebecca drawls, exaggerating the woman's accent. "Are you, like *Aaaa*frican jungle people, because that's totally awesome!"

I sit through their teasing, stung, as if they're making fun of me instead of a stranger. I talk like her; I am an American; I am foreign to my own people; I am strange, too.

"You know," I say, alcohol buzz infusing me with bravery, "technically you *are* Africans. Think about it, if you meet someone from

Guatemala or Honduras or something, are you sure you would know? Would you just say Hispanic or Latino or something else generic and inaccurate, or worse yet, think of the person as Mexican or something more familiar to you?"

"Hmm." Sedi shrugs. "I guess that's true. Who knows, maybe sometimes it's better to generalize than to guess—"

"Don't get me wrong, it *sucks* when people act like all of Africa is just one country," I say. "Obviously it's not, and there are so many differences—"

"Even within the same country," Michael chimes in.

"Exactly," I say. "But let's face it: Americans are ignorant of other countries, especially developing ones. They're not going to be able to catch those subtle differences. I mean, even I can't always. You know, people hear my name's Akosua Agbe and they just think 'African.' They don't think Ghanaian, they don't think Ewe, and they definitely don't think American."

"But you are Ghanaian," Rebecca says, reaching her hand across the table to pat mine. "One thing I don't understand is why Ghanaians born here or in England or someplace are afraid to admit that they are Ghanaian when they—"

"It's not a matter of being afraid," I try to explain, and I feel Wisdom's foot press against mine. "Hey, what are you doing, Wisdom honey, I'm talking," I laugh, and it's all good-natured, and I'm happy to be sharing this moment with these lovely people who I will finally convince to understand me, and the wine really isn't bad, and I take another big sip, perhaps more accurately called a gulp. I turn back to face my audience. "Okay, can I tell you what often happens to me?"

"Tell us, Akosua," Kwame says, grinning at me.

"So I'm from Detroit, right? Born there, went to school in the suburbs. When I'm outside of Michigan, like here in New York, if people ask where I'm from and I claim Detroit, they say I'm trying to be cooler than I am, that I can't claim Detroit because I'm from the 'burbs. But if ever I say I'm from 'outside Detroit' or a suburb, then I get accused of not repping Detroit, as if I'm ashamed of the place. If I say I'm Ghanaian, people ask how I can be Ghanaian but not know any of the languages or how to cook the food properly or how to get around in Accra. But if I say *I'm* not Ghanaian, that my parents are Ghanaian or something like that, then I'm accused of being ashamed of my heritage."

Sedi and Rebecca are nodding their heads, but I am too tipsy to discern whether they empathize with my plight or think I'm weird. Michael, though, breaks the awkward silence, laughing and winking at me. "Wisdom, your girl is wise, o."

And everyone laughs and drops the subject.

Throughout the night the girls treat me like their new best girl-friend; they pull me up to dance when the DJ plays another song they like, and I do a good job of pretending that I'm not awkward and self-conscious on the dance floor. Michael and Kwame take turns dancing with all of the girls, including me, and Michael and I exchange tales of snowy winters back West.

Wisdom, my boyfriend, has moved away from me. He dances with Sedi and Rebecca and the *obroni* woman and anyone who will have him, which seems like everyone. He is handsome. He has some unnamed charm even though he's not particularly muscular or model-like or anything like that; he possesses an appeal that attracts people. And he can move on the dance floor. But not with me, not tonight. He drinks far past his limit and enjoys himself with everyone except me.

During the subway ride to his apartment, he sleeps, but he doesn't rest his head on my shoulder as he normally would. Wordlessly, we pass the stop where I'd get off to go to my apartment, and I get off at his stop and he lets me walk into his apartment with him. We walk side by side. We undress and then redress for bed, side by side. Side by side, we lay in the bed and eventually fall asleep, without speaking to each other, without touching.

When I can't stay asleep, I shake him awake.

"Mmm?"

"Wisdom. Are you up?"

"Mmm."

"What's wrong with you tonight? I don't think your friends were annoyed, so why are you?"

"You're too much sometimes. You don't know when to talk and when to be quiet."

He dissolves into snores, and I resolve to pretend the night did not end with this tension.

But of course, now, I know the ending of this story, though knowing the ending does not stop me from playing it on repeat in my head, where it seems the incident will forever live in present tense. It happens again and again every day in different ways and causes a pain more substantial than any concussion, because Wisdom's supposed to love me for who I am and he didn't, he doesn't, and the rejection squeezes my heart until I feel it in my chest. There's moisture dripping down my nose as I tell my story to my mom and Auntie Fergie from the backseat of the Fergies' Toyota Camry on the way back to Jersey City.

Today the story isn't mine; it's Naa's bad luck, and even as I'm crying, I laugh and add the good part, the part that started my telling of this story in the first place.

I say to them, "And now she's finally got it, a good guy, a good Ghanaian guy who likes her for who she is. And the medical student is on his knees begging for mercy, saying, 'Okay, Naa, I should have loved you for who you are.'"

Mom and Auntie Fergie laugh at the medical student's misfortune but also at the story itself.

"It's simply unnecessary drama," my mother concludes, waving her hand dismissively. "What does that girl expect? He's a boy, not even a man yet, so it means he's even worse."

"What do you mean?" I ask.

"He's still a baby. If grown men don't know how to act, how can a young man like him know? Naa was too hasty to throw the doctor out. Besides, this new man, he will cause problems too."

"Isn't that what men do?" Auntie Fergie quips.

"Not your Fergie, he has been whipped into submission over the years!" My mother hoots.

Back and forth they joke, but I tune out. How could things have gone so wrong for Naa and her man? Is my mom right to say that Naa jumped the gun, that she was too quick to judge him? But it doesn't matter because it is over between the couple. It's not as if he's done much to get her back; he hasn't even called since I left the hospital. And besides, it's liberating, she is lifted by this new guy, this Daniel character, because he seems to understand who she is, whoever she is. Best of all, there's no overwhelming passion; he's methodical and polite and good-looking and relatively simple to understand, compared to Wisdom.

I pull out my phone and look at Daniel's number, and I tell myself that this is going to be good. I'm still crying, but the tears must be a quirk of my post-concussion syndrome, something I don't quite understand. I can't be crying from sadness; that wouldn't make sense because I am happy.

6

We don't cook the goat meat stew until the following day, Saturday, because Auntie thinks the feast will be a nice going away dinner for my mother, who will leave on Sunday.

"Going away feast? This feast is going away with me," my mother jokes, but not really, because she is serious: she will freeze some of the stew, along with a few slabs of the uncooked meat, and take it on the plane with her to Detroit, the city she still considers her true American home, where she will pick up her car from the airport and drive across the border to Windsor and her lonely condominium community.

I help to prepare the food. I've been feeling better since my campus visit yesterday. Mom, as usual, thinks it's a state-of-mind thing. She thinks that since I went back to campus and spoke to my professors and employer, I have espoused a mindset of productivity.

I believe it is a Daniel thing. Since I didn't actually speak to any professors or my boss, since all I did on campus is speak to Dean Jervis and Daniel, I know it is Daniel who has put me in healthy spirits. I conjure an image of his face as he took my cell phone from me and entered his phone number. Daniel always wears a calm confidence that is his skin; he is assured without being cocky, the way that Wisdom was. Wisdom always tried too hard to fit some sort of cool persona. Right? I'm not sure. But when I probe my brain further, trying to ascertain what the difference is between Daniel's brand of confidence and Wisdom's, I'm still not sure.

The only thing I am sure of is that, while Wisdom has not contacted me since picking my mom up from the airport, Daniel has sent me two text messages since I saw him yesterday on campus. The first one

I received last night at ten o'clock: *Thinking of you before I go to sleep. Sweet dreams and hope to talk soon.* Nothing particularly thrilling, but at least it stilled the thoughts in my mind so that I could fall asleep quickly. I only spent ten minutes reminiscing on the texts that Wisdom used to send me before bedtime, stuff like, *You up? Come over?* or, the only slightly more classy, *I miss your bosom as my pillow.* But then there were the ones that would unravel me. *Thank you for being you so that I can know what it's like to love so thoroughly.* How could he expect me to sleep, writing me something so sweet? In fact, sometimes the messages we sent each other would leave us so restless at night that one or both of us felt compelled to climb out of our beds and make our way across town just to see each other.

Daniel's messages put me at a greater peace. That is how he is different; he is not agitation in my veins, but tranquility. He told me to have sweet dreams, and I did sleep well (though I dreamt of nothing, but that can be a blessing, too). In the morning, I woke up to a chime from my phone and another message from Daniel. *Morning, pretty girl. Enjoy that goat for me.*

And so I laughed, sprung out of bed, and volunteered to help cook the feast. I will help in any and all ways.

Thus, I am pounding strips of goat meat to a second death.

"This place where we got the goat meat is not very good at preserving the flesh so that it is tender, but, luckily, we are used to that," Auntie says as she grinds together a colorful assortment of peppers in her lopsided clay mortar and pestle.

"Why is that?" I ask, hitting the meat with my fists.

My mother snorts; she's standing on a chair fishing through a cabinet for the Fergies' good dishware.

"Because, my dear, when we were growing up," Auntie says, "we didn't have things like a freezer to keep the meat, or meat tenderizer—"

"Unless you were rich," comes my mother's muffled voice, but I can still hear the derision in her tone.

"Right. No freezer. No bottles of meat tenderizer. Actually, hardly any meat. At least for my family and me. Goat was not something you would have every day, not even beef. Sometimes chicken. Mostly we ate fish—easier to find. Goat was a delicacy, but what we really loved was the unhealthy stuff."

"Like what?" I ask.

"Chicken butt! They used to sell us chicken butt from trucks going down the road." Auntie shakes with laughter. "The British must have dumped it on us in truckloads. Africans will eat anything, they figure."

"Chicken butt?"

"The butt of the chicken. The fattiest part, so delicious but not very good for you." Auntie Fergie has to stop chopping in order to wipe the amused tears from her eyes. "My mother thought it was good for us because it was meat. Maybe for this reason I am a fat old lady now and your mommy is not. Enyo, didn't you eat chicken butt as a girl?"

"Of course, and it shows. Not all of us can be as skinny as Akosua."

My mom is thinner than I am; I used to be able to squeeze into her pants, but that was back in high school and, since then, I've grown, while she hasn't. Still, she always speaks as if I'm the same shapeless, skin-and-bones girl I was until late in high school when everything started blooming.

"Except for all those hormones and preservatives in American food," my mother adds, her nutritionist voice kicking in. "Maybe that's why you have the tatas that no one in my family has. Or maybe it's your father's side of the family."

"Does his side of the family look like me?"

"Yes, of course, my darling. Those Agbe women, long, tall women like you, slender, but then, pow! Out of nowhere, big chest, big bottom." She lets her laughter loose. "I tell you, that's probably why the man had to stray. None of that on this body here."

She and Auntie chortle away as my mother slaps her own bony body; I have no clue why this is amusing, and, though my mother winks at me as if to give me permission to acknowledge the joke, I refuse to humor her with even a tiny smile. Is it really funny to contemplate my father's rejection of my mother?

Auntie Fergie wipes the sweat from her brow and puts the pepper mixture aside to be added to the stew later. "Enyo," she says to my mom, "leave the dishes; I will get them out and wash them later. Please do me a favor and finish the onions and tomatoes for the stew so that I can make some fufu."

"Don't we have enough food with the stew, jollof rice, *and* white rice?" Mom asks as she emerges from the cupboard, red clay plates in hand.

"Fergie always likes fufu on Saturdays," Auntie explains of her husband, who is supposedly grading papers, though I can hear the TV blasting soccer from the den.

"If only," my mom scoffs. "My husband would be eating the same thing everyone else is eating."

Auntie simply laughs and pulls out a box of fufu powder to which she will add water to create the heavy Ghanaian staple. "It's no trouble—just comfort food from home that I like to give my husband. As you know, it's not even the real thing, just the second-rate American way of making it, but he doesn't even complain. He's grateful."

"Oh, *grateful*." My mother begins to chop onions. Growing up, Sundays, when my mom prepared all the food for the week, was the only time I ever saw her cry. I've never seen anyone more sensitive to chopping onions. Rivers pour down her smiling cheeks as she and Auntie begin to discuss the distinction between traditional fufu and the way it's made here due to time and material constraints.

As I try to pick up little bits of their Ewe, my stomach churns at the idea of eating fufu. As with oatmeal or creamed spinach, the consistency of fufu, which is like a mushy ball of dough, does not appeal to me. Sticky, warm, made of roots like cassava, not unlike dumplings—that's how my mother describes fufu to curious non-

Ghanaians. She never cooks it but enjoys when family or friends make it for dinners or parties. I remember how Wisdom would visit the Long Island apartment that Sedi and Rebecca shared with another girl, Rena. They'd make fufu and stew for him and whoever else went to visit, usually their boyfriends, and then Wisdom would return to me, droopy-eyed, stuffed, and sated until the next time the girls decided to treat the men.

It occurs to me that maybe I'd like real Ghanaian fufu; every time I've seen it here, it's made by mixing some white powder with water, like magic.

"What's the difference between Ghanaian fufu and the way people have to make it here?" I ask, cutting into my mother and auntie's conversation.

"Uh-oh. She's trying to be sneaky and pick up our Ewe," my aunt says, nudging me playfully with her shoulder. "Poor thing."

"The first and most obvious difference is that back home it's made of real, fresh cassava and plantain and they're pounded for a long time until the consistency changes," my mother says, arching her eyebrow at me. "Most people don't have the time and means to be pounding roots all day. And fufu is supposed to be room temperature, but here we usually have to heat it on the stove to get the texture right. Didn't you pay attention when we went to Ghana last time and your auntie made it for you? Don't you remember the difference?"

I drop the slab of meat I'm holding onto the cutting board. "Don't you remember that you've never made fufu for me or taught me how to make it or told me anything about what it's like to make or do anything in Ghana? Don't you remember that you've never taught me any of these things?"

I give the meat one final slam with my fist, wash my hands, and storm out of the kitchen. On my way to the guest room that has been mine since we arrived, I pass Uncle Fergie in the den, who is perched on the couch in sweatpants and a white undershirt, his eyes glazed over as he watches Arsenal play Chelsea, his bare feet twitching as he mimics the plays he'd make if he were a British football star instead of a Ghanaian professor living in New Jersey, USA.

"Men." I can't help but snap at him, but he's too engrossed to notice.

In the guest room, I throw my clothes into my duffel bag. I stack up the books I brought here to fool my mom into believing I have classes to study for. I accidentally drop one on my foot. I don't feel a thing.

I want to be ready to leave as soon as my mother is out of here and back in her Canadian hideout.

There is not much to pack, so after a few moments I flop on the bed and its sanctuary of fluffy pillows and lilac-smelling sheets and comforters. None of it is a comfort to me. My body feels as though my cells are itching. I'm still waiting, wanting something. I know now, my mother and the Fergies confirmed it, that my father knows about my head injury and asked about me. But he hasn't asked *me*. Three months in the States, a head injury bad enough to send me to the hospital, and yet he won't call. I reach for the bedside table, for the phone, press a button, and I've reached him.

"Hey! Didn't expect to hear from you, Akosua. Was just thinking about you."

That light and springy voice, melodious the way it is when he's happy. A tenor maybe? Definitely not a baritone like Daniel's.

"Wisdom. Hey."

In the background I hear a lot of noise, maybe a radio, a TV. Or perhaps people. Perhaps today is one of those days on which he's eating fufu in Long Island with his Ghanaian friends.

"Hey, gal. I thought you'd still be hanging out with your mom. How's your head? Guess what I'm doing?"

"Oh, it's very clear to me what you're doing."

"What's that?"

"You definitely seem to be having a great time despite the fact that your shoddy medical attention almost got me killed," I snap.

Wisdom laughs, but only after a moment has passed, as if he's not sure whether I'm just being funny Akosua or if I'm really pissed.

I'm really pissed.

"You never even called to check up on me. Daniel has sent me text messages. I saw him on campus and he asked about my health. Ella, too—she's called and emailed and texted. But you, you couldn't do anything at all, and then when I call, you have the audacity to act all cool as if everything's fine."

"Actually, Akosua," he says slowly, in that infuriating way he speaks when I'm angry, the tone of voice that lets me know he's trying to highlight my irrationality by sounding composed, "I'm quite aware that everything's not fine. You hit your head. Moreover, you broke up with me months ago. You are still angry at me. I can understand why. We had some misunderstandings."

"You do not understand why, or else you would not call our issues *misunderstandings*."

"The last time I saw you, that night in the hospital, you made it pretty clear that I was annoying you. That it was more stress for me to try to sort out our issues than for me to just give you space. So I was trying to give you the space to enjoy your mother, relax, get better, and—"

"Oh, please, don't bullshit me." My head vibrates. The ache that had receded creeps its way into my skull, curls up and makes itself at home again. "I can hear people in the background. You're not giving me space, you're out with your precious friends."

"I am not out—"

"Wisdom, which one of them are you cheating on me with? Huh?" I cannot believe these words, but once they are out, they are out, so I must run with them. "I mean, which one's the one you were interested in while you and I were dating?"

"No one!" He sputters as he says these two words, and I can picture him pushing his glasses up the bridge of his nose as he often does when frustrated. "What are you talking about? Those girls, they're my friends. They're all dating my guy friends, for another thing."

"That wouldn't necessarily stop someone like you."

"I am not your father," he replies in a level voice.

"Shut up. My issues with you are not my issues with my father. They're with you. And how I wasn't good enough."

"Of course you're good enough," he said. "In fact, too good. Don't you think I know that? I wasn't embarrassed by you, not ever. Don't you see it's me who's the one with the problem? I get awkward and stupid around my friends, and—"

"Nobody needs your excuses now. Nobody needs you. In fact, when we broke up, I said we could be friends, right? I take it back. I take back that suggestion and in its place, I extend a big 'fuck you.'"

"What is this?" Now his voice rises; now he's ticked off. "Are you mad? You, my friend, you better be saying this shit because of hitting your head."

"No. I'm not. I'm saying this shit because I don't want to be your friend anymore."

But at this very moment, a wave is rising in my throat to accompany the orchestra of pain playing my every sense: my ears ring, my head pounds to a steady rhythm, my stomach churns. The light of the sun glares through my window, and I glare right back at it: *vex me if you dare.* It dares. The sun is a knife, silver blade flashing. My pain is a howl, all vowels and no teeth.

I am lying in darkness, a heavy blanket over me. I've never known pain like this; it's probably worse than the initial concussion, and much more embarrassing because I fear I have brought it on myself. Did I really throw a fit? My mother, my Wisdom. The people I love. I blame them for this migraine. Or do I blame this migraine for my fit? *Migraines, sensitivity to light, ringing in the ears, fatigue, insomnia, inability to concentrate, mood swings, depression.* Mood swings?

Where does my head begin and where does my head injury end?

Perhaps it ends here: me sprawled out in a similar darkness, a heavy blanket, this one not figurative, over me, because I am seven and curled in my bed in shame because I have failed, and I am similarly embarrassed and the only person there to make it all better is my daddy.

Second grade, my first and last D, my first history quiz. My mother praised me for having the courage to show her the grade instead of hiding it, but she sent me to my room nonetheless and said she and Daddy would be in to talk to me in a few minutes.

Yet after fifteen minutes of crying under my hot blankets, worried about what they would possibly say or do to me, their A-and-B student who had sunk so low that I was basically nothing, I hear my parents by the door, whispering to each other.

"Let me talk to her first," comes my father's deep voice, and I shudder. I have heard him yell before, though on rare occasions: at my mother when they fight, over the phone if relatives in Ghana upset him; once, at a strange woman who came to the door when my mother was at work, and he'd shouted at her, "Never show your face here again. This is where my wife and daughter live." He's never really yelled at me, though he's used a stern voice if I fail to drink my milk at dinner.

I fear that now I'll be subject to that sharp and rare shout of his, the one that chastised the stranger at the door, the one that chastised my mother.

The door creeps open. I hear his footsteps pad on the carpet. I feel his presence standing over me, and then the pressure of him sitting on the bed next to my feet.

"My dear." I refuse to move or make a sound. "Akosua." He says my name just once, and I know now to pull my head from beneath the blanket.

"Did you study?"

I shake my head.

"How many times did your mommy and I ask if you had studied for your quiz?"

My parents check all my homework assignments, and I happily tell them about school because I love it and my teachers and all the stickers and stars I earn for my good marks.

"I know, but—"

"How many times?" His voice is low, measured, his face serene and controlled.

"Lots of times," I answer, running my fingers across the red truck, blue truck pattern on my bedspread.

"So why didn't you study?"

"Because it was easy. Because it was boring," I finally sputter. When I was supposed to be studying for that quiz, I was instead looking through my parents' old albums, at my baby pictures, at the aunties and uncles dancing and laughing, at my mother with an Afro and bell bottoms, my father tall and smiling with a hand firmly planted on my mother's back. "The stuff we were supposed to learn is boring. Michigan history, the history of Wayne County. Our school history. It's not fun and it's not even real."

Now my father takes my hands in his, looks into my eyes. "Mercy Akosua. My daughter. History is always very important. All kinds of history. If your mother and I have not taught you that, have we taught you anything?"

Even at seven, I know the meaning of "rhetorical question;" elders ask a lot of questions of me and I know that only their answers are the correct ones. I keep my mouth shut and listen.

"Do you know, Akosua, that there is no reason to *know* unless you attempt to know fully? That is what our lives are about. Your mother, myself. We came to this country to learn. So that I would be a better engineer. So that your mother could be a doctor."

"But she isn't a doctor," I say, something strange rising in the pit of me, because I've never heard anyone speak of my mother as a doctor. *She works in hospitals. She helps people stay healthy. But she's not a doctor.* Somehow, suddenly, the fact that she isn't seems all my fault.

"Your mother had a family to raise, us to care for, and her goals changed," he replies, his eyebrows now stern, warning me not to pursue the subject any further. "We stayed in the US for you, for any future children of ours, so that you may have the best education. So that you may understand. Do you know that although I am an engineer, I am also a historian?"

I shake my head.

"Yes. I study the history of engineering, of building things, so that I may better understand my place as an engineer. Right now, you are in Michigan. You live in Wayne County. These are places where you dwell. You must understand the history of these places."

I feel small in my bed, snuggled in comforters. Already I'm afraid about living up to his speech. But if he can tell, he says nothing. He looks at me as if I'm a fully sapient being instead of seven and confused.

"Do you know how these white people will judge you if you don't know the history of their country? If you don't learn about their presidents and their constitution, if you don't learn about their European philosophers and all the wars they fought and in whose name?"

My father lifts his forefinger, gently taps my forehead with it. "But you will have outwitted them because you will learn that knowledge well *and* more. You will know that history and your Ghanaian history, black American history, history of Asian peoples, of the ones native to this land, and of the ones who took this land over from the natives. All of it. In here, in your head. And no one can question your knowledge because you will know what they think you should know, in addition to everything else they do not know."

As he speaks, I drink in his words, not fully understanding, but they feel soothing nonetheless. He speaks with a rhythm, an urgency that somehow lulls me, and at any rate, a lecture is better than a spanking or a punishment (bedtime without snacks, no TV, no coloring books and modeling clay).

"Do you think that any of my colleagues can challenge my opinions on a project when I'm helping to plan the building of a hospital? Or a school? Or when I'm in the classroom teaching new engineers about what is right to do? No. Because I know the history of what I am doing. I know the foundation of building foundations. I know—"

A knock sounds at the door. My mother enters the room, wringing a dish towel in her hands.

"Dinner is ready. Akosua, are you listening to what your father is saying to you?"

"Yes, Mommy," I reply automatically.

She turns and leaves the room, not touching my daddy.

My father, I expect, will go on with his lecture. You can't interrupt him once he gets going on something like this. But his face is creased now, his back arched as he sits at my feet, like my mother's sudden entrance into the room has unraveled his whole speech.

He stands up, brushes my disheveled hair back into place. "Go and wash your hands for dinner. Okay?"

My father hesitates before he leaves the room, picks me up and sets me on my feet. "There we go. You are a good girl."

And then he leaves, and I'm standing with my head whirling with the desire to please him, to go back in time and study for my failed quiz, or better yet, to go back in time and witness everything that has ever happened in the world so that I may know its history.

He is around to witness the B+ I get on my next history quiz, but not to see the A I earn in the subject at the end of the school year.

"Don't worry." My mother keeps lying, a lie to save me. "I am sending him all of your report cards. I am sure he is very proud."

∽o∾

Awake. The pressure lifts, but only enough to know that I am me now, that I am not seven and hiding in my bed. I climb out of that memory, feeling rusty as I climb back into who I am now. This one I did not suspect, this story creeping up; its narrative, I did not realize, has been playing in my head on repeat but with the volume turned down low. I had forgotten about this day, my failure at age seven, my daddy's reaction. What would he think of my current failures, my stagnant stint as a master's student? Would he sit here at my bedside, pat my hair into place, and call me a good girl?

When I open my eyes, it's not him but her sitting in the space of the curve of my body in the bed: my mother. She presses a cool washcloth to my forehead.

"I knew it had to be the headaches, not you, that would cause you to talk to me so disrespectfully," she says quietly.

"When?" For an instant, I don't know which me I am, which time this is, why she is sitting on my bed.

"In the kitchen." There's an edge of panic to her voice. "In the kitchen, an hour ago. You were upset, the fufu—"

"Oh. No. Yes. I remember."

She accepts this answer, or refuses to probe any further. "You know I didn't mean to tease." She chuckles a little. "Or rather, I did, as usual. I was only playing with you. Don't be upset."

"It's just my head injury," I say, and as my eyes adjust to the light filtering through the shuttered blinds, tears sliding down my mother's cheeks.

She notices me noticing her. "It's the onions," she says and holds up a dish towel as proof that she'd been in the kitchen recently. "You were yelling into the phone."

"Because of my headache. It came on really suddenly, actually."

"Who were you talking to?"

"Wisdom."

"Oh, Wisdom. The nice young man in medical school who picked me up from the airport."

"Mm-hmm."

"Your good friend?"

"A friend," I say, and blurt, "I think Daniel Cobblah and I will probably start dating."

"Oh." She raises an eyebrow. "I see."

"Mm-hmm." I refuse to tell her any more. Any stories I'm going to tell her I've already told in some form or another. More than anything, I am so tired right now of the way we speak or unspeak to each other.

"Well. Auntie Fergie says her sister used to suffer from migraines and the best thing to do is rest and keep still."

"Yeah, rest," I echo, unbelieving of the notion that my mind ever rests, but almost immediately I am engulfed by the kind of deep sleep that the body can only achieve to escape an unbearable hurt.

In the morning, I feel better, a shadow of headache remaining, nothing like the initial onset of the migraine. When I wake up, I discover I've draped my hand over my eyes while sleeping; when I remove my hand, I immediately want to replace it: I don't want to see anything in this room or in this apartment. I want out of this space. My mother's impending departure makes me feel like a cranky child with separation anxiety and an adult who is finally free.

All four of us—the Fergies, my mother, and me—climb into the back of their family car for the drive, first to LaGuardia Airport and then on their way back to Jersey; my aunt and uncle will drop me off at campus. I have my duffel bag, but also something extra: Tupperware filled with the dinner I missed last night while holed up with my migraine. Usually, a ride to the airport means that I'm leaving home for school and my mom is imparting final words of wisdom before I take off. Study hard but loosen up a bit; loose girlfriends make bad company because they reflect poorly on you; you are not a girl, you are a woman, conduct yourself as such, on and on. Today, though, because my mother and I aren't in the car alone, she refrains from saying much unless it has to do with my head.

"If anything feels strange," she says from the front seat as Uncle Fergie inches us into the Holland Tunnel, "do not hesitate to call a doctor. Better yet, go to the emergency room."

"And call us," Auntie chimes in. She is seated next to me in the back, and every so often she reaches over and pats my knee and says, "Ohh, Akosua, you and your mommy are leaving me." Now she says, "You can always stay with us anytime you need to."

"Just call somebody," my mother says. "Better to check yourself into the hospital than to have to be dragged there."

"Yes, Mommy." I slip into my little girl voice without meaning to.

The silence is an odd one for my mother and me, perhaps because we know we would be speaking to each other if it were only the two of us. Maybe the Fergies don't feel the strangeness in the air, maybe they do. Nonetheless, it is my mother who presses play on the car's sound system, starting up whatever disc is in the CD changer.

At full volume blasts the familiar opening guitar notes to the Prince Nico Mbarga classic sung in pidgin, a Nigerian song called "Sweet Mother" that every West African must know.

"All right!" My mother begins moving her arms and shoulders to the highlife beat.

Auntie Fergie sings along as well, her voice much higher pitched than I'd expected.

"Somehow this seems rigged," I say, my knees bouncing to the music of their own volition. Even Uncle Fergie in the driver's seat has unleashed his deep baritone and sings out a couple of bars every so often. "Mom, you planned this didn't you? You want to make me miss you and cry before you leave, huh?"

My mother only laughs from deep in her chest and continues to sing. When she gets to the part about how mothers suffer when their kids feel sick, my mother cranes her neck and gives me a knowing glance.

We pull up to arrivals at the end of the lengthy song, and the finale is playing like a soundtrack as my mother utters her parting words to the Fergies, as she promises to call them and me when she lands, as she kisses my forehead, smoothes down my unruly hair, and slips into my hand what I know from routine must be two twenty-dollar bills.

As I watch her walk into the airport, Prince Nico's voice, which sounds like sand and silk at the same time, sings about how you can get another wife or husband, but you can't get another mother.

And as I mouth the final lyrics, a knot of regret forms in my throat, and I wish I'd said more when my mother was here. I worry that perhaps this song playing as she leaves is foreboding, that maybe this is the last time I will see my mother's tiny, graceful form making its way across this earth.

But like every other time we part, this feeling subsides when she calls in a handful of hours and announces, "Back home, safe and sound, miss you, my dear."

She cleaned my whole apartment. She disinfected and re-scented and humanized the place. It's not my place now; it's hers and mine, because she touched it. I can smell her perfume but too faintly.

Will I ever stop feeling lost when my mother leaves?

The migraine I had yesterday during the goat feast has faded but has also faded me. I am exhausted. I crawl into bed. I pick up my cell phone, scroll down to "Home." But I shouldn't call. Maybe my mother is sleeping, recovering from her flight. *Sleep it off, Akosua, sleep it off.*

Instead, I push the up arrow until "Daniel" is highlighted.

After four rings, his low rumble of a voice comes on and speaks to me kindly. "Hello. This is Daniel Kweku Cobblah, currently unavailable to take your call. Leave me a message. Have a blessed day."

"Hi. It's me, Akosua. About that goat you wanted me to enjoy for you. Why don't you come enjoy it yourself? I know it's Sunday and your shift ends late . . . but it's never too late to come by my place." I am ruffled by these last words I've spoken; they didn't come out the way I intended. Determined to salvage the message without seeming too flustered, I take a moment to think, then forge ahead. "It *is* Sunday night, after all, and our ritual is to walk home together after work. Why stop our tradition just because I'm temporarily out of commission? Hope to see you soon."

I am sleeping when the phone rings to announce his arrival. It's after eleven. I buzz him in. In the time it takes him to ride the elevator up to my floor, I hope to make my bed, wash my face, brush my teeth, and warm up the goat stew or the rice or at least *something*, so that I look like a person who has her shit together.

Instead, when he arrives, I have a toothbrush hanging out of my mouth, foam dripping down my chin. I mumble greetings, and he walks into my apartment holding a large brown paper bag.

After I run to the bathroom to rinse my mouth and glance in the mirror too quickly to see myself, I return to the living room, and suddenly I find myself rushing forward to embrace him—it is nice to have him in my apartment after months of our Sunday night ritual. I know at the very least this is true: though I poke fun at him with my mother, Daniel Cobblah is my friend.

"You brought some food?" I ask him, peeking into the paper bag in his arms.

"No. It was outside your door. I only picked it up."

I nearly rip the bag while opening it, which would have prevented me from seeing the note written in blue ink on the side of the bag in the half-elegant, half-scribbled handwriting that I know so well.

> *I made these for you yesterday. That's what I was doing when you called. Giving you space to get well, but do call if you need me. Enjoy, and rest your head. Love, Wisdom.*

"Fried fish?" Daniel peeks into the glass container filled with a batch of perfectly fried tilapia.

I hurry to the kitchen to hide the fish in the fridge and warm up the stew in the microwave. "Yeah. Tilapia. My favorite. My aunt must have dropped it off. She sent me home with a lot of stew and also this fish, and I guess I forgot it in the car. So she brought it to the door."

"I see. How nice of her to return."

"Ready to eat? How are you? Why'd you get off work so late tonight?"

"Oh. You know how it is over there. The work never ends," he says, smiling. He takes off his coat, holds onto it awkwardly; awkwardly, we stand together in my apartment that seems too small for the both of us. "I feel very honored to be here, Akosua. Thank you for the invitation."

I take his coat, hang it on the back of my desk chair. I like his cable-knit sweater; it is light gray and looks warm and safe and like something a grandfather might wear. But he is not my grandfather, he is Daniel Cobblah, and besides, my mother might joke, my grandfathers were way more suave at Daniel's age than Daniel, both my father's father and my mother's father being city men, being dapper, being quite a hit with the ladies, and then my mother might laugh and shake her head and mutter something about Daniel's pocket protector.

Now is not the time to think of my mother.

Plus, Daniel is standing in my muggy, overheated apartment, pulling off his grandfatherly sweater to reveal a white button-down dress shirt, one with no pocket protector in the chest pocket. With his shirt untucked, he looks a little disheveled, a little less formal, so I invite him to sit on my bed, the most comfortable seat in my room, while I perch on the desk chair. We begin to talk like we do at the housing desk, except this time, there's a room and furniture and no Pete or undergraduates milling around; there's the rich scent of tomato and peppers as the stew warms in the microwave; there's the promise of the kind of intimacy I like best: a shared meal and conversation between two people making an honest attempt at understanding each other.

7

Friday at the library is label-making day, and I am the queen of making labels.

Alan sits at the front desk, assisting the patrons who come into our office to pay fines or ask questions about library policies and borrowing rights. Sheena, the undergrad work-study who comes in on Friday afternoons, sits in the chair next to Alan, studying for her Classics exam in between helping Alan with the patrons. I sit in the back, hidden from the view of others, because I am responsible for the all-consuming task of creating new library cards for groups of visitors who have requested or paid for library privileges of some sort. It's a big list because there's an oral history conference taking place at the school next week before the Thanksgiving holiday, and all of the visitors will need access to the stacks and the computer labs, and some of them have prepaid for borrowing privileges. Our boss requested that I let Alan and Sheena handle the library patrons so that I could focus on the new ID cards.

And then our boss left for a day of meetings.

Alan turns up the volume of the radio that we're supposed to keep on low and on classical or easy listening stations. "Too loud, Sheena?"

"Nope. I've studied this stuff a million times, so no big deal."

"How 'bout you, Mistress of Labels?"

"I like that one, Mistress of Labels. Put on some holiday music, Alan, I feel festive." I stick the label on an adjunct professor's card, a big red A. "Being an adjunct professor is just as shameful as being Hester Prynne?"

"That's your future, Professor Agbe," Sheena says. She's a double major in history and poli sci. She wants to be a poet but also wants to justify her expensive college degree, so she's come up with a plan: in two years, when she finishes undergrad, she'll go to law school, practice corporate law for a few decades, and retire early, living off her amassed fortune and writing poetry. Sounds like a terrible plan to me, but I don't have a plan, so who am I to judge?

"Please don't remind me of my future." I hide the adjunct card at the bottom of the pile; out of sight, out of mind, right?

"Why not?" Sheena stretches, shaking her strawberry blonde hair down her back. "As if you have anything to worry about. Professor Hollingsworth *still* uses your research papers as a model for all of his undergrad history courses. And that international research award you won your senior year? They don't give those out to just anyone ..."

I need her to stop talking about my so-called bright future. *The past doesn't guarantee the future,* I want to scream at her. Instead, I reach toward the pile of library cards too fast and knock them off the table. Plastic clatters to the floor, and conversation stops while Sheena and Alan help me clean up my mess.

"You ladies need to stop talking about academics all the time," Alan says, switching to the R&B/hip-hop/rock station. "You gotta enjoy youth while you still can."

"Hey, I had a good time last weekend," Sheena says indignantly, putting her flashcards down. "My boyfriend came to visit from Cornell. And I mean, he goes *crazy* when he gets to the city because there's, like, stuff to do here. We went to this party at the basketball frat."

Alan scoffs and rolls his eyes.

"And we went to a club. This one in Chelsea, downtown? We have fake IDs. What, you don't believe me? Check online, I posted pictures."

As Alan and Sheena fool around, looking at pictures of Sheena and her preppy boyfriend drunk and frightened at the club, I laugh along but concentrate on putting my library passes into nice, neat categories. Visiting scholars. Transfer students. Undergraduate students. Non-degree students. Professors Emeritus. One week borrowing, three months, a year. I love this job because of my coworkers, but also because it's the only place right now where everything is relatively easy to figure out. I know all the rules. Each situation and person fits into the boxes with relative ease.

"What have you done for fun recently, Sue?" Alan asks me.

"She's got a concussion, leave her alone," Sheena says. "Besides, she's a grad student. She's busy."

"She seems all healed to me."

"I am all healed." I am sticking barcodes onto the visiting scholar cards. "I've been kinda low-key, but still having fun. Cooking a lot, having dinner with my friends." I pause. "Been hanging out with this guy for the past week."

It's okay to tell Alan about Daniel Cobblah, even though we're all employees of the university, because Alan doesn't really know anyone who'd be interested in gossip about me, I figure. I tell him and Sheena about how every night since I returned from Jersey City, Daniel has been coming over for a late dinner of goat stew and rice. I tell him about how Daniel and I have begun to laugh real laughs now, about how we watch TV shows and movies and how he's always reluctant to leave my apartment when he has to go.

I don't tell Alan about the fried tilapia that's going bad in the back of the fridge because I can't bring myself to eat Wisdom's food with Daniel.

"You only see this dude at night?" Alan says. "What's his deal?"

"Oh, he has classes during the day and he works late. You know. So he comes over after his shift . . ."

"Mm-hmm. Sure."

"What?" I put my cards down, walk around so that I'm standing face to face with Alan and can clearly see his expression.

But he wears a poker face. "Sounds a little . . ."

"Oh, Alan!" I laugh. "It's not like that. I'm a take-it-slow kinda girl, plus I'm concussed. There's no kinky stuff right now."

Sheena leans toward me, speaks in a hushed voice even though no one is around but the three of us. "This guy in my dorm, he only visits girls really late if he wants to, you know, lay the groundwork for, like, that kind of relationship."

"What do you mean?" I ask, hating that I am essentially asking her for dating advice.

"A booty call kind of relationship," she says matter-of-factly. "So he comes over late all the time, everything's cool, friendly, platonic. Then one day—wham—something happens. You hook up or whatever. Then the next time he wants to come over, he calls late at night and asks if he can visit. You think nothing of it because he's always over late at night. You don't realize he's calling because he wants to hook up again. Since you've done it before, why not again? You've essentially set the precedent for the booty call."

Alan can't contain his laughter, but he quickly grows serious again. "You gotta admit, Sue, it *is* kinda shady. Do you ever go *out* anywhere with him, or just stay in?"

"He works late. Come on, guys."

"Always?"

"Well, when he's not working late, he's in class or he's got study groups. He's an engineering grad student. He's busy. Plus, this weekend we're gonna go out."

"Okay, well, that part sounds good. Let us know how it works out. And avoid that booty call trap," Alan says, and the three of us laugh, though mine feels forced.

An elderly couple walks into the office, and Alan and Sheena direct their attention toward them. I return to my own work, shrugging off their comments about Daniel. They don't understand that Daniel is one of the good ones. Too polite for his own good, really. He's not a New Yorker, not a Detroiter. He's not smooth, at least not consciously so: he's a country boy, and one from Ghana where propriety reigns. His voicemail message urges callers to have a blessed day. He hasn't even tried to kiss me. He does not know what booty call means.

Besides, today's Friday, and half the reason I am singing inside is that Daniel and I both have Friday nights and Saturdays off from our jobs. He can't need to study tonight, lord knows I have nothing much to study for, so there's no reason why we can't have a date tonight, and maybe hang out tomorrow, too. And tomorrow night, Ella and I have plans for a girl's night. We haven't seen each other since I returned from New Jersey, and I have to fill her in on my blooming relationship with Daniel.

I call Daniel's cell phone on my way home from work.

"Oh, no, no, no, Akosua, you have gotten my schedule wrong. One more hour of work left for me today."

"No, I know. I just wanted to say hi." I am whispering to him, as though I am the one talking on the phone at work instead of him.

He, on the other hand, chuckles loudly. "Good, good. You cannot get enough of me. I'm happy to discover this news."

"Ha. Yeah. Well, I'm also calling so we can make some plans for tonight. I want to . . . *go* somewhere with you, you know, *do* something. We don't have to spend all evening cooped up in my apartment."

"Okay. We can go to my place instead."

"*No*, silly. I meant let's go someplace that's not where we live. Outside. Where do you go for fun?"

"I don't know, I'm more the type to stay in . . ."

"We could go out to dinner and a movie." I'm realizing maybe he doesn't go out much at all. Maybe all of his experience in this city has involved working and studying. Maybe I can show him the city. "Tomorrow during the day we could walk around, look at all the Christmas displays that are being put up in stores. Nothing too complicated or expensive."

I regret that I added that last part about money; my mother always tells me I shouldn't present myself to men as a cheap date, because then they won't treat me as the queen I am. I almost laugh just thinking about the gulf between who I am and who my mom wants me to be.

"Hmm . . . please, dear Akosua, I am not sure I have the time for both dinner and a movie tonight. I have plans with some people I know, some international students. We have a meeting tonight for international engineers."

"On a Friday?"

"Yes. You see, Friday evenings are when we are all free."

"Okay . . ."

"But you and I could meet later on, a little after eleven o'clock."

"Eleven o'clock! That's so late. I wanted us to have a fun evening out, you know, like the full evening. By eleven, we'd both be so tired."

"I could come over and we can spend time together. Or you can come to my place. I would walk you home if it got too late, or you could spend the night if that would be easier."

"I love that you're so serious about school, but do you have to go to the engineering meeting every weekend?" I say, hating the sound of my voice, the wheedling neediness.

"Yes. I have a responsibility to this group." Responsibility, the word vital to who he is. A man compelled to follow through on his commitments. Why would I want him to change? "It seems we are destined to meet tomorrow night then."

"But tomorrow night I'm meeting up with my friend Ella. I was gonna go over to her place to relax and catch up." And gush about how romantic you are, if only you could be romantic.

"Can you cancel?" he asks without hesitation.

"Um, I don't think I want to. I think I want to see my friend as I planned, and I think you need to be a little bit more accommodating. Can you cancel your club meeting?"

"Eh! American girl!" His voice tells me he is amused, but I'm far from finding humor in this situation. I begin to wonder if any of this is a great idea.

But then we settle on a compromise that satisfies us both, though it requires me to negotiate with Ella.

Ella has a twenty-minute window before she heads to a work event in Harlem, and she agrees to meet me in Morningside Park. I try to make it worth her while by bringing coffee and Hungarian pastries.

Of course my detour to buy treats makes me late, and Ella's already waiting for me, radiant in a long black coat and drapey black pant-suit and, of course, her self-made red scarf. She stands next to the statue of Carl Schurz, one of our favorite meeting spots from our college days. She smiles and hugs me in greeting, though I do catch her glancing at her watch as I explain why I want to make a slight change to our plans.

The smile has slid off her face by the time I'm done talking. She crosses her arms. "No way. Roger and I are not going on a double date with you and Daniel. Are you kidding me? Besides, Roger's got other plans, that's why tomorrow's the perfect night for you and me to have our get-together. If I'd known you were still thinking about this Daniel boy . . ."

"What's wrong with Daniel?"

"First of all, he's dull as bricks, according to everything you've told me about him."

"Oh, come on—"

"Second, the rumor is, he's dating that little girl," Ella says. "That Aku Aggrey girl."

"No, he's not. He told me he's not looking to fool around with young girls."

"Oh, he said that, so of course we have to believe him," she sighs. She twirls the end of one of her millions of tiny long braids around her finger, looking half-bored, half-amused. "You really banged your head hard, huh? Is that what changed your mind about him?"

I haven't told Ella about Daniel's text messages, about the phone conversations we've had and our late night dinners this week, but when I do, she seems unmoved. "That boy is eatin' you out of house and home, controlling when and where you spend time together. Your boy Wisdom looks like a saint in comparison—"

"Wisdom?"

"Yes. That boy calls me every night to check on you and your mixed-up head. I don't even feel good leaving you here for Thanksgiving. By the time I come back you'll be off in a commune or something, living with both boys as your concubines."

I laugh, though the thought of Wisdom and Daniel in the same room makes me shudder. "You don't have to worry. While you're off in Atlanta with Roger's parents enjoying the holiday, I'll be in Jersey with my Aunt and Uncle Fergie getting fat and happy."

I don't tell her that I want to invite Daniel to Jersey City for Thanksgiving dinner; she won't understand that it's just as friends, that it's only so he can eat a good, authentic Ghanaian meal since I certainly can't make him one. I have already asked the Fergies for permission, and they are excited to meet this young Ghanaian engineering student and figure out how they might know him or someone else who knows him.

"You're changing plans for him, cooking, and who knows what else. This boy is running your life and you barely know him or vice versa," she says. "At least Wisdom never tried to do that."

"Are you serious? Wisdom started this thing where he'd comment on my clothes and stuff, like he was my self-improvement guru. That night we went out with his friends—"

"Girl, that was the first time you went out with his friends, he was nervous and stupid, cut him some slack."

"You've certainly changed your tune from hating Wisdom to now advocating for him."

"Listen. I never hated the boy. I just hate the way you get around him sometimes. All that boy did was act a little childish, but instead of really setting him straight, you dumped him outright. He's got image issues. You'd think someone like you who has them yourself would see that in him. He messed up. Go ahead and be pissed at him for things he said that made you feel like he was questioning who you are as a person, but honestly, you two are still so hung up on each other that this Daniel distraction makes no sense."

"He's not a distraction. He's a friend. Maybe soon more," I say.

"Akosua, if you *have* to be with someone—which you don't—it's better that the guy is Wisdom. A little misguided, but at least he's not skeezy like Daniel who I swear is messing with that little Aku girl."

A laugh escapes before I know it. "Just come out with us. Just meet him. You don't even know him. You only know what the rumor mill says about him."

Finally, she agrees to meet Daniel and me for drinks after our date tomorrow night, since her boyfriend Roger won't be available for a double date.

I finish off the rest of my pastry, and Ella pulls her knitting project out of her bag, getting ready for her subway ride to work. She always needs to read or knit when taking public transportation.

"Akosua, I've known you for, what, like six years now, right? And even when you were good, you were never all that good at taking care of yourself."

We both turn away from the street and toward the park, looking down at the concrete path unwinding, the tree branches reaching up to the blue-gray sky. "Ella, who's taking care of me if not me?" I laugh, feeling like my mother, or what I imagine my mother must feel like, laughing for no reason.

"Chance. Circumstance. Occasional diligence on your part, but mostly the help of good friends like me."

"Mm-hmm, of course."

"Don't laugh, girl, I'm not joking. Not to be like a mom, but I worry about you." She wags her unfinished green scarf toward me. "Maybe you should come to my knitting circle some time. It's so relaxing. It will get your mind off things."

"I don't think I have the dexterity for something like that." I accidentally drop my last bit of cheese danish on the ground, underscoring my point.

"Or, okay, you could come to group therapy with me. It'll help you get things off your mind."

"You must be joking," I hear myself say, but I don't need to look at her face to know that she's serious. She has told me about this group before, some sort of counseling session for first-generation Americans. I always figured it was more of a social thing than a therapy thing, and when I tell her this, she sucks her teeth.

"Not sure why you think that when I keep telling you it's real therapy."

"I don't have enough real problems for real therapy," I say, and instantly regret it.

"Thanks a lot, I guess that means I do?"

"No, no, I don't mean it like that. You don't have enough real problems for it, either. Your life is nearly perfect."

"Right. Nearly perfect." Ella rolls her eyes so hard I can feel it in my bones. "See you tomorrow, girl." She air-kisses both of my cheeks and walks away.

∽∘∾

In the morning, I feel restless, my muscles ready to jerk me into action before my brain's fully awake. I push the blankets aside, automatically reach up to close the blinds on the window to block the sun's assault. I feel funny waking up without Daniel here, not that I've ever woken up with Daniel physically here, not that I'm even close to ready for that juncture in our relationship. But for the past few days, I've been waking up to the now-familiar feeling of Daniel's presence lingering from the night before. Anyone could see that I adore him now, and that I regret that I didn't get to see him last night. I have to wait until the evening to see him. Can I wait until the evening to see him? My Spanish books await. Maybe Daniel will come over for lunch. Maybe we can study together. I'm out of bed and pacing the room, wondering what I'm going to do all day until our date.

Until my breakup, I never had to wake up to a lonely Saturday ahead of me. Wisdom and I always spent the night at the other's apartment Friday night—even if it meant that he'd come over late after studying or I'd come over at three in the morning after hanging out with Ella and her friends—so that we could always wake up together on Saturday.

One rare weekend a few months back, we missed a Friday night. I arrived at his place at nine the next morning because I'd accidentally fallen asleep at Ella's place after going to a birthday party with her.

"I called you all night," he said when I finally let myself into his apartment, bleary-eyed and guilty. "I got worried."

He lay on the couch, a baby blue blanket covering him, and I can see him even now, a fresh image before my eyes, cozy, arms open. I smiled at him. "You look like all you got is sleepy."

"No," he said, sitting up, blinking against the light of the lamp I turned on when I walked in the door. "I couldn't sleep. I've been staring at the ceiling. I can't sleep without you here," he said, and he lifted up the blanket to welcome me onto the couch with him, kissed my lips, and promptly fell asleep. I pressed my head against his bare chest, warm, and marveled at how well we fit, how immediately his arms wrapped around me, how he clung to me like a lucky charm. How useful I felt, loved but most of all loving.

I shouldn't think of any of this right now, not him, unless the *him* is Daniel Cobblah, who is the man I am missing right now.

I stop pacing the room, stride to the bathroom, brush my teeth, and, avoiding my face in the mirror, wash it nonetheless. On autopilot, I leave the bathroom and head straight to my room phone, ready to dial Daniel's number and see if he's not interested in starting our Saturday together with an early lunch.

Thankfully, my phone rings, waking me from my stupor, saving me from calling Daniel and committing the sin of appearing too eager. "Thank you, Mom," I say, assuming she's the one calling me. I scramble to locate my phone amidst a jumble of sheets and comforters on my bed, but when I find it, I'm surprised to see FERGIES across the screen.

"Hello, girl. Eh, this is your Uncle."

"Oh, hello, Uncle Fergie. How are you?" My voice raises octaves until I sound twelve again. I wonder if my voice will always do this around older Ghanaian aunties and uncles, if I'll be forty-five years old and still in genuflect.

"Fine, fine. I am just grading some papers to prepare for Monday." But in the background, I can hear the fuzzy noise of fans cheering on TV, and I can picture Uncle Fergie sitting on the couch pretending to work while watching soccer.

"Oh, okay. That sounds nice." I sit at my desk, pull a random textbook into my lap. "I was actually about to study, myself."

"Nice, nice. What a good girl. Listen, eh, Akosua. Your auntie has gone to visit a sick friend in Princeton and she will be gone all weekend. But she wanted me to call and check on you in her absence. We haven't heard from you."

"Oh! Oh, me? What about the sick friend? Is the person okay?"

"Yes, yes. I'm sure of it. Gifty, the wife of Dr. Akrofi Edwards. You may know them. They live in Grosse Pointe, Michigan, but are here visiting their daughter and son-in-law. The son-in-law is earning his PhD in electrical engineering at Princeton and she will graduate from Columbia Law in the spring."

"Oh, yes, I do, of course . . ." My throat dries instantly; how could I not remember him, my father's old school buddy, the uncle I adored simply because my father seemed to adore him.

"Yes, he was friends with your Daddy. Speaking of your daddy, my girl, time is not on your side—"

"I'm actually doing well. My head feels fine," I hear myself blurting. "I mean, yes, I'm fine, and it's so nice of you and auntie to think of me, especially given that Auntie Gifty also isn't feeling well. Is it serious?"

Uncle Fergie begins to grumble under his breath, and I cringe, wondering if I'm going to receive some sort of admonition for interrupting him and changing the subject. But then he speaks loudly enough for me to make out the words, "Lady issues," and I realize he's just answering my question about what's wrong with Auntie Gifty.

I smile to myself; my mother and I would have a laugh about an old man like Uncle Fergie regarding menopause or menstruation or whatever "lady issue" as if it's an illness. The disease of womanhood.

An awkward pause ensues and I consider ending the conversation until he clears his throat. "Ahem. Well, I just wanted to check on your health and let you know that you can call your auntie and me if you need anything. Your mother is like a younger sister to us. We Ghanaians in this country must help each other wherever we are, you know? The foot does not go on a mission and leave the thigh alone."

"Yes, Uncle. Thank you very—"

"You know, I knew your daddy, too, but not as well as Akrofi did. I don't excuse your daddy's careless treatment of you and your mother . . . How valuable our fathers are . . . Do you know that I have no children of my own?"

"Oh. Yes, Uncle." Talking to Uncle Fergie for any length of time is new to me. In fact, I feel as if I've rarely heard him speak, since his wife always talks enough for the two of them. I don't know if the subject matter is tough for him, or if he's distracted by the soccer game, or perhaps eating the serving of sardines and dried cassava that I'm sure Auntie Fergie left behind for his breakfast. Whatever the cause, he's sputtering his words out, leaving large gaps of space between sentences that don't exactly follow each other anyway.

"There is no excuse, but your father has struggled in this country. I have not spoken to him since his return but have heard about him . . . It is all a shame, eh? It is often on the young generation's shoulders to act. Do you understand me, girl?"

"Um. Yes, Uncle. Thank you." I try my best to sound grateful for his . . . wisdom? Though I don't fully understand what he's getting at, I know at least that it must have something to do with my being a good respectful girl and doing what's expected of me. Whatever that is.

"Hey ..."

"Yes, Uncle?"

"Hey ... hey ..." His voice raises in volume, the words more staccato, or should I say *word*, because all he keeps repeating is "hey."

"Are you okay, Uncle?"

And then at the top of his lungs he booms, "Hey! *Kwasia!* Get off your ass and do something! You fool, o ... you useless fool!"

His words startle me so much that I jump, knocking some books off my desk, upsetting my chair so that it falls backward and I nearly fall with it. I stick out my arm and catch myself but instead of standing up again or righting my chair, I sit on the floor. I can't move because I am shaking. I am shocked. I picture him in his argyle sweater and button-down dress shirt, his big glasses, his fuzzy graying hair, and the image is incongruous with what he has shouted at me. Instantly, my arms goosebump and tears spring to my eyes.

"Oh. Dear Akosua. I'm sorry, o. These footballers, they get paid too much. It makes them lazy."

And Uncle Fergie shouts once more at the TV screen, quickly wraps up our conversation with a kind, "Take care," and then hangs up and returns to watching his soccer game in solitude.

I lie down on the floor in a heap, my cell phone still in my palm, dazed. I resign myself to a day of staring at the wall and daydreaming. I could pick up the history books I knocked off my desk when Uncle Fergie scared me; I could read the history books, too—bite the end of my pen, put the crayon down, turn the page, read on, tilt my head, clear my throat, and repeat the process, internalizing the words all the while. But what difference will it make?

Maybe Uncle really did mean those words for me. Maybe he can sense that I lie every time I mention that I'm studying, every time I mention anything that has to do with having a purpose.

I pull out my laptop, clicking on the page I've bookmarked for easy access: the graduate history course catalog. But instead of diving into it for the millionth time, I open a new email draft. I put Dean Jarvis's address in the recipient field and Professor Hollingsworth's address in the CC field.

> *Thank you both for allowing me to continue in the program as a part-time student. I feel honored that you have enough belief in my academic capabilities to give me a second chance. However, in light of certain personal struggles, I have decided*

But I can hear my mother's voice in my ear, saying, "You don't have to tell everybody everything. 'Personal struggles' sounds like there is something wrong with you."

> *However, upon further introspection, I have decided that, after this semester, I will*

I will what? My fingertips and lips begin to tingle, and I realize I'm barely breathing. I inhale, exhale, and shut my laptop.

My uncle's words rattle in my skull. *My girl, time is not on your side.* Surely there is nothing wrong with my father; Uncle would have told me that. Of course, the more probable explanation is that my father doesn't plan to stick around in the States. He will leave again. But this time, he won't be leaving my mother and me, because we aren't his anymore. Suddenly, but not for the first time, I want to ask my mother how she feels about all of this, if she ever thinks of calling him up just to see if he sounds the same, if she ever thinks she can forgive him—and forgive me if I want to talk to him again. I wonder if she ever thinks about what it was like to be his and misses it, and if she ever wants to be someone else's. To feel loved and loving, not just by her daughter, but by a person who would sweep her off her feet.

And I laugh out loud because if my mother could hear my thoughts, she'd do the same, only wilder.

8

Daniel does not know where he wants to go. All he knows is that he's probably going to eat a little bit with some guys from his engineering study group, so I tell him to go all out and eat a full dinner before we meet.

I eat Wisdom's fried fish, a little soggy by now, but still buttery in my mouth.

Since Daniel does not know where he wants to go, I decide, thinking, so much for Ella's theory that Daniel is a control freak, he is a docile creature lost in the city and he doesn't know what movies he likes to see. I want us to go to a lounge before the movie, have appetizers and drinks or something, but I nix the idea when he doesn't seem that excited about it.

"Never mind. I shouldn't be drinking anyway," I say. "Had a bit of a headache earlier, not sure drinking helps that."

"In that case, maybe we should stay in and rest."

I ignore what he says and we go to a theater in the Village that shows indie films. I pick a Japanese movie based on a Murakami short story I like. As the theater darkens and the movie begins, Daniel whispers in my ear,

"Subtitles."

"Yeah?"

"I didn't bring my glasses."

I look at him, smile. "Hey, I didn't even know you wear glasses. I've never seen you in them. I want to see."

"Well, I did not bring them. I didn't know I would need to be reading in a movie theater."

"Um, didn't you say you were studying earlier? Wouldn't you have needed them for that?"

We get shushed by the people sitting behind us, and my face grows hot as I sink into my chair and worry about whether Daniel will even enjoy the movie at all.

Daniel is good. He is quiet. He seems to be watching, though I am appalled by his good manners during the movie. Not that I am rowdy while watching movies, not that I enjoy talking back to the screen, but I do like sharing the occasional whispered commentary with my viewing partner. Whenever I say something to Daniel now ("Oh my God, can you imagine dying like that, because of a clothing addiction?"), he just smiles and nods as if I've thanked him for unlocking my dorm room door.

I don't mean to, but I imagine Wisdom watching this movie. He introduced me to this theater; he said that because he was always busy with school, he liked to come here whenever he was free because they play movies about a month behind the bigger theaters. So anytime he thinks he's missed a movie's release, he remembers that he hasn't and comes here.

"Plus, I like the big bang blockbuster stuff, but sometimes I need a break from being a man," he said on our first date here, which was our fifth date or so.

I rolled my eyes at his arrogance, at his blatant stereotype, but he laughed, *just a joke, a joke, I'm not sexist*, said his hands raised up in surrender.

But it can't be a joke, can it, that, as we're watching some Spanish romance, Wisdom's removing his black-framed glasses and sliding them back on, removing them, replacing them, pinching at the corners of his eyes, and when the heroine almost dies, he pulls out a handkerchief—

"Are you really—" I start to ask, but then he drops his handkerchief and takes hold of my shoulders and pulls me close for a kiss that is our first kiss, which might as well be the only kiss in the history of kisses. We end the kiss and he tucks his handkerchief away.

We watch the movie with heightened awareness. The words and music seem louder, the colors brighter, the subtitles on the screen larger. It is the most excellent movie I have ever seen. We stay through the end of the credits, holding hands. When the lights come on and I turn to him, I notice that in fact his long eyelashes are a little matted with wetness, but I don't mention a thing. I know that I am starting to love him.

"I don't understand what is happening," he says in my ear, but he is not Wisdom. It is Daniel, my date, Daniel Cobblah, Housing Department Staff Level II. "The subtitles go too fast."

I don't know what he's talking about. There's hardly even any dialogue in this movie. I am mildly annoyed because this boy, Daniel, is not enjoying our perfect evening out, because he doesn't like to read subtitles, because he does not notice the pathos in this storyline, because he leans over and kisses me during the most depressing part in the movie, and this isn't even romantic sadness, it's just bleak bleak bleak, the most starkly sad movie in the world, and his lips are like pillows and I'd always admired them from a distance, but now that they are on mine they feel wrong because they aren't *his*.

"Ah, shit," I mutter, but when he asks what I've said, I just smile and pretend that utterance came from someone else's bewildered mouth.

Daniel has set a fast pace as we walk from the movie theater to the bar where Ella said she would meet us.

I feel like I'm running to keep up, because my mood has dragged me down. "Wasn't that the most depressing movie you've ever seen?"

He laughs, reaches for my hand, pulls me up so that I'm walking at his side. "Lots of movies are depressing."

"Yeah, but this one was a special kind of depressing. There wasn't any yelling or crying, no violence or blood or desperate pleas for help. Just a barren, limitless landscape of death."

"What a thing to overhear. Hey, hon."

Out of the corner of my eye I see a flash of red: Ella has on boots that match her red scarf. She puts her arm around me from behind; she has crept up on us as we're entering the bar. She sticks out a gloved hand to shake Daniel's. "I'm Ella, not sure if you remember me from undergrad . . ."

"Yes, yes, I do." He grins. "Very nice to meet you. You look lovely," but as he says this, he puts his arm around my shoulder, so I assume that he's just being kind to her. Though she does look lovely. It's no sin to point this out, is it?

I was a little worried that Ella might be mad at me, since the last time I saw her, I possibly insulted her and her knitting circle and her therapy group, but she flashes me her usual warm smile and seems more excited to be here than I expected.

Still, I am self-conscious. I feel a slight headache coming on so I don't drink, since I'm not really supposed to drink anything so soon after my concussion anyway. But I *want* to drink, just a little something to help mellow me out. I can hear myself talking on and on like someone's paying me by the word.

"Ella, the whole movie," I say, "it's this guy who was sad as a boy, then is sad as a man, then is happy for a split second with his wife who's perfect except for her clothing addiction that kills her, and then he spends all this time obsessed with her clothes . . ."

"What did you think of it, Daniel?" Ella asks.

A sheepish grin spreads across his face. He takes a swig of his drink. "Hmm. I thought it was . . . interesting."

"Please see this movie so that I have someone to talk about it with," I say to Ella.

"Not if it's going to depress me like it has you," she replies, winking at me.

We drink. I sip at my Sprite. Ella, who can drink anyone under the table, has three martinis. Daniel slowly works on one black and tan. We hardly have anything to say, and, because drawing Daniel into the conversation has proven difficult, we maintain a strange pattern. He talks to me about something at length (an engineering class, an odd occurrence at the Housing Department, what he's buying to take to his family in Ghana for Christmas), and Ella observes the conversation. Then Ella talks to me about funny things that have happened at work, or about her and Roger's date last night, and Daniel will nod and smile and not speak. It is tiring to me. I suddenly don't care if Ella likes Daniel or not. Nothing is meshing; I want to return to my apartment and the goat stew and the novelty of talking to him in a place other than the housing desk. Perhaps we've taken too big a step, going out to the movies, a bar, meeting with my friend. I need to relieve my bladder.

"I have to pee," I announce and gulp down the rest of my Sprite.

What am I doing here? I sit on the toilet without pulling down my pants. I rest my head on my knees and look at the floor and wait for an answer.

For a moment I feel too exhausted to actually pull down my pants and do what I came here to do. I have never had penis envy before, but now I do.

It would be so much easier. To pee, I mean.

I finally finish what I came in here to do, flush, go out to wash my hands. The bathroom is all dark wood, dingy, not well lit. I splash cold, cold water on my face because I feel a headache coming on. My face in the mirror is covered with droplets of water. I imagine the drops of freezing water as tiny mirrors all over my face, reflecting my image back at me, infinitely. But I can't see any of these images, not even the one that I'm meant to see, my face in the mirror on the wall, because water is dripping into my eyes and stinging.

When I return to the table, Ella is laughing, but not in her eyes. "Your friend was just telling me about how you cussed him out last week. I find it hilarious that a week ago you were cussing him out for meddling in your life and now, here we are." She giggles and signals the bartender for another.

I notice that while I was gone, my empty glass was replaced with a full one. I take a sip of what I assume is a refill of my soda.

"It's shandy," Daniel says as I cough and put the drink down. "This one is Sprite mixed with—"

"Sprite mixed with beer, I know, I know. I am Ghanaian after all," I hear myself grumbling. Daniel seems unfazed by my snarky response.

"She's not supposed to be drinking, I thought." Ella's eyebrows are raised, her lips pursed.

"It's light. I told the bartender not to make it strong." Daniel smiles as he says this. He pushes the drink toward me.

I take a sip. "I reacted like that because I had been expecting pop—soda—and I got something else on my palate instead. It's really not that bad."

"Have you given any second thought to talking to your father, by the way?" Daniel says.

"You must have had more to drink than I thought if you're asking her that again," Ella snorts.

"I won't pressure her," he says. He makes his patented polite smile. "I only want to let her know that I am here for her, that I can help her talk to him if she wishes." Then Daniel looks at me and reaches for my hand across the table. "I want to be supportive of you. I care."

"Aw. Thanks." I clutch my drink like it's the steering wheel of the car that is taking us on this long and crazy ride.

Silence returns, though this time it is thoroughly disheartening to me since I am already feeling the effects of the beer. I can't handle beer well. I can't handle anything well. Alcohol-wise.

No one tries to speak anymore. Only drink. Ella gets drunk enough that she needs to eat something; she orders a tray of shrimp quesadillas that the two of us devour, and I barely blink when Daniel orders me another shandy, and then a third that is the end of me. It is the end of me because I feel the start of a migraine coming on, or at least a dull ache in my head that could be a migraine caused by my head injury or could just be my body pissed at me for drinking or for being in a bar or for being in a bar with these people on this night when I need to be home resting.

The last coherent part of the evening comes when Ella puts down her last empty glass with a flourish of her hands and declares, "Well, Akosua, I got a promotion at work, and Roger and I are going to move in together. That's part of what our girls' night was to celebrate. That's the big news, and I'm happy to share it with your wonderful housing engineering friend in our company."

"Oh my gosh!" I reach my arms out to hug her and spill the rest of Daniel's drink in his lap. I squeeze Ella tight nonetheless. "How wonderful, oh my gosh. I mean, you're happy, right?"

"Well, I consider it good news, yes, and I'm excited. A little nervous too, but—"

"So congratulations!" I linger in the hug, I get lost in it, I let my weight go in her arms, because it is great, it is fantastic that she's happy, but also that she is warm and embracing me and I am safe in this moment.

The rest of the evening occurs in flashes of unconsciousness and pain-tinged memory.

I slump into the backseat of a yellow cab.

"Are you sure you'll be okay without me?" comes Ella's voice.

"We will be fine, please, do not worry." Daniel's deep chuckle.

The door slams shut and the sound reverberates in my skull. I turn my head to see her go but catch only a glimpse of her scarf trailing behind her in the wind like a hand saying goodbye, or like a red flag warning.

I lean my head on Daniel's shoulder, not of my own volition; the car turns down a street and gravity leads me to crash into him. He laughs gently. "We got you quite drunk tonight, didn't we?"

The car horn blares, wakes me for a moment during the long ride uptown. I hear my mother's voice from some other space and time:

"Agbes are not very good drinkers. Your father could never hold his liquor, my dear."

I put my hands over my ears to silence her, but his hands are already there, on my cold cheeks, waiting.

This blackness is different, it's not drunken blackness, it's migraine blackness, or it's drunken migraine blackness. Whatever it is, it is flirting with me like crazy as I stumble into the building. I'm falling to my knees, and he's strong enough to pick me up without very much effort at all. We are in my apartment. We stand near my bed. He tugs at my shirt.

"You need me. Let me help you change."

I lie in my bed, my head sinking into the pillow. My eyes are blurred but when I blink I clearly see his face, his teeth so white. I feel a draft from somewhere, I feel it run through my pajama top, which is open, which is confusing to me, almost as confusing as the glimpse I get from the corner of my eye of his khaki pants on my floor. The tips of his fingers rest on my collarbone, and until I close my eyes, everything under my skin shudders with an alarming violence.

9

Panic. I wake and my alarm clock reads 9:47 in digits whose bright red color underscores my panic. I sit up. I don't remember the night before, not where the narrative has broken. My head feels twice its weight, but I can't tell if it's from the alcohol or the receding migraine.

I lift my head from the pillow nonetheless. I lift myself and look around my room.

Daniel is nowhere to be found.

The last thing I recall is my body shaking from my headache, from the cold, from the heat of his fingertips resting on my skin, and I don't understand what he was doing. What was he doing here, undressing me?

The light from the sun pouring through my window is shining on my face, nearly blinding me. I shut the shades and notice the lamp light is on, too. I lean over to shut that off and stand in the middle of my apartment, my hands in my hair, on my head; I am confused and I am reeling. I am wearing the same charcoal dress pants I wore last night but I now have on the shirt from one of my cotton pajama sets. As I press my fingers to the buttons, I remember.

He pulled off my shirt over my head, my arms hanging in the air like a surrender. He said something about helping me change into pajamas. But when his hands found my bra clasp, I pushed them away.

What are you doing, Daniel?

I want to spend the night here.

I said something like thank you, thinking he wanted to sleep on the couch, to stay and make sure I would be okay. But then his hands ran up my bare arms, to my shoulders, to my back, to the bra clasp.

I want to spend the night with you, Akosua. His voice rumbled and he pressed close enough that I could feel the vibration in his chest as he spoke. *Isn't that why I'm here?*

I'm sick. No.

But the clasp came undone in his hands; he tried to pull the bra off.

I mean it, no. I pushed him away from me with a force greater than intended. He stumbled. I almost apologized out of habit, but I stopped myself. I shut my mouth, shut my eyes. My head pounded. And it kept pounding after he gathered his clothes and left, slamming the door.

I pick up my phone. Ella answers after three rings, emitting a sound more groan than voice. "Who's this?"

"Me. Akosua."

"Ooh, hon, I don't know about that bland boy Daniel. He drove me to drink beyond my limit. Good lord, is he boring . . ."

"Yeah, I'm really sorry. You're okay, right?"

"Yeah, are you? Did you find your way home okay?"

I bite my lip; I remember when she asked last night if we could make it home without her help. I remember Daniel saying yes. "Well, I am home."

"What? Did something happen?" Her voice is no longer sleepy.

"No. I mean. It's fuzzy . . ."

"But you only had three drinks. Is that really enough—"

"I shouldn't have been drinking with my headaches, you know? I knew that, I just, I couldn't be sober anymore on that terrible date, and I didn't know I'd have such a terrible migraine, but the pain and the alcohol, they both just knocked me out. And Daniel . . ." I don't know why I feel so embarrassed to say it outright. "Let's just say he had ulterior motives for helping me get home."

"Oh, Christ. I knew I shouldn't have left you. I should not have had so much to drink. I totally let my guard down."

"It's not your fault. How is it your fault I'm an idiot and he's skeezy?" I pull a sweater over my head, but it doesn't help; I continue to shiver. "I really didn't feel well, Ella. In the car, I must have passed out. In my room . . . everything's foggy. I felt myself slipping. If he had waited a little longer before he . . . tried, maybe I wouldn't have been able to say no and push him away."

"You had to push him away? The word 'no' wasn't enough for him to get the picture?"

"I know, I know. But after that, he left. Nothing happened. I'm fine." But I don't feel lucky or fine; I feel so violated knowing that he's seen any part of me undressed. That his hands were on my skin. That he hadn't cared that I wasn't sober enough to say yes; that he had stormed out when I said no. I feel naked no matter how many sweaters I put on.

"No one's ever seen me . . . no one but Wisdom . . . I just . . ." I exhale. *Slow down, Akosua, slow.*

"You should call the campus police."

"What? No. And say what, that I passed out and woke up to my date trying to make a move on me but he stopped when I told him to? That's not anything."

"Maybe it's not a crime, but it's still something. He was wrong. God, I can't believe I drank so much that I lost my head like that and left you alone."

"I can't believe I lost my head, either."

I try to sleep it off. Lying in bed, I can't help but run my fingers across its wrinkled surface, press my nose close to the cotton and breathe in. Smells like dryer sheets. Smells like my lavender perfume. The scent of my mother is long gone from this room, but the scent of Daniel has not replaced it. Nothing seems changed. No evidence of his presence, no evidence of his trespass. I wrap more blankets around myself and sweat myself to sleep.

So much for our Sunday daylight date, our walk down the streets of the city. Our glimpse at Christmas lights.

Just after noon I take a shower, a scalding hot one, one in which I continue to sweat. But I like the way the water stings my skin, the way the fog matches what's happening in my head, the way whiteness fills the bathroom and clouds the mirror so I can get dressed again without having to see myself.

Ella calls, but I don't answer. My mother calls, too, and I listen to her voicemail.

"Mercy Akosua. Shame on you, leaving your Mommy without a phone call for the last couple of days. Are you still mad that I suggested you stay in New York for Thanksgiving? I want you to focus on your studies and relax without having to travel. I will see you when you fly home for Christmas. I'll take lots of days off from work and we'll have a good time, okay? But first you have to call. Love from your Mommy. Bye-bye."

I can't tell her. I can't tell my mommy that her little girl is stupid and careless. That I'm so messed up in the head that I almost let some guy I barely know hurt me.

I wonder if she even knows I'm not a virgin anymore. I know, I know, I'm twenty-four, but that doesn't mean anything in my mother's world. Matt, my high school boyfriend (whom my mother acknowledged only as a "school friend," since I was not allowed to date until college) was half-Greek and half-Nigerian. We bonded over feeling like outsiders and started hanging out soon after I turned sixteen. I didn't ridicule him for his love of emo, and he didn't mock me for liking alternative rock. Depending on the crowd, people teased him for acting too white or too black, and people poked fun at me for not acting black enough. But everyone agreed that Matt and I, the misfits, fit together, except perhaps my mother, who was disturbed to see me attached at the hip to anyone other than her, especially to a boy.

What she didn't have to worry about—though I know she did worry—is that Matt and I would attach in that special, procreative way. Our nearly three-year relationship fizzled out halfway through freshman year of college, when I took a train to his campus to visit him. He'd set up candles in his dorm room, scattered rose petals on the bed, and burned us a mixed CD of love songs that he entitled *At Last!*—but we ended up chastely spending the evening creating elaborate dance routines for "My First, My Last, My Everything" and binging on anchovy pizza. "You worried about what your mom would say if she found out?" he asked, and I said yes, but that wasn't the whole truth. I could see our future unraveling in my mind: the post-consummation endorphins would drive me to fall in love with him, testosterone would drive him to cheat, and then where would I be? Heartbroken. It didn't matter that I had no evidence to substantiate those fears. I couldn't see any other outcome.

That's part of what makes Wisdom exceptional: unlike any other guy, I felt comfortable with him. I'd dated a few other people, but not for more than a couple of weeks, nothing that ever got anywhere too physical. It didn't seem worth the risk, and I couldn't be bothered with the painstaking process of getting comfortable in my skin. But Wisdom changed everything. What would my mother think when she found out that I finally *could* be bothered, hot and bothered, doing unladylike things with Wisdom, the boyfriend she didn't even know about? One door leads to another, she often said about dating. Maybe she would blame me for putting myself in a compromising position with Daniel.

I won't wait for him to call anymore. I've been waiting, trying to be fair, trying to give Daniel Cobblah Housing Department Staff Level II a chance to redeem himself by at least checking up on me.

I put on my clothes, layer by layer: underwear, top and bottom, corduroy pants, my favorite bluish-purplish button-down blouse, a black sweater. A purple hair clip shaped like an African Violet. My winter coat. I don't usually, but today I put on makeup, not too heavy as makeup goes, but heavy for me. A mask of foundation. Lipstick instead of lip gloss. Eye goop. Color on my cheeks. In the mirror, I look like another version of me.

Daniel's graduate dorm is only a few blocks from mine. He gets the best pick because of his affiliation with the Housing Department. Over the past three months, on our Sunday walks home, I have seen the outside of his building a few times but have never gone inside, just as he'd never gone inside of mine until some fool named Akosua had the horrible idea to invite him over for goat stew.

There's a white stone the size of a golf ball propping open the door of the apartment building. I pick it up, hold it in my hand. It feels cool and smooth and real. Somehow the feel of its irregular shape grounds me. I put the stone in my pocket, something I can hold.

There's a pair of computers in the lobby and I type his name into the university search engine. Daniel Kweku Cobblah, Housing Department Staff Level II, Graduate Student in the School of Engineering and Applied Sciences. The listing includes the name of his dorm and the phone number and the apartment number. 3C. I think of calling to warn him I'm here, but I don't want to hear his voice in my ear.

I plow up all three flights of stairs and I am pounding on his door.

He opens it wearing a white towel tucked around his waist.

So normally this would be a treat. I have never seen him shirtless but have suspected that something like this might lurk beneath all the pomp and circumstance of clothing. I have never been acquainted with someone with an actual six pack, clearly defined stomach muscles and pecs and veiny arms.

Except this is not a treat because looking at him makes me feel like my skin is growing a second skin.

"Oh. Akosua. What are you doing here? I thought that you were not well." He smiles but it's just for show. There's nothing accommodating about the way his lips turn up and the way he does not move his body from blocking the entrance to his apartment.

I barge past him.

"I definitely was not well. You made me drink even though I said I couldn't."

"I don't believe I forced you. You could have said no."

I hate that he has a point. He strides over to his closet and pulls out a short sleeve polo shirt, pulls it over his head. His apartment is set up a lot like mine except that everything's newer and there's more space. He also has a full kitchen; I see a pot of something red boiling on the stove. Instead of a full bathroom, there's only a sink and toilet. He must have just come from the communal showers down the hall.

"Excuse me, please, dear Akosua."

I look away while he finishes dressing.

"If you are okay," he says as I stare out the window at the sunny, cold world, "I am very glad. I am sorry that we got carried away last night. I suppose if you felt a headache coming on we should have stayed home as I suggested." He walks around so he's standing in front of me, reaches to clasp my hands in his. "Now, if you are feeling okay, perhaps you should go home and rest some more. Tonight I have some nice plans for us. In fact, I am cooking this stew for our dinner."

"I didn't know you could cook." I don't let him touch my hands, stuffing them into my coat pocket instead. "That's nice of you to offer." I hear my own heart pounding. It seems absurd, now, to accuse him of something nasty; he's the same old block-of-wood, overly formal Daniel Cobblah that I've known. Still, I linger.

"Is there something else? Or shall I walk you downstairs. I'm really very late for a meeting I have—"

"There is something else. I mean, it's very silly, really, but you know, I blacked out from the alcohol and probably my head injury, too."

"Yes?" He puts a hand on my shoulder, begins to walk me slowly toward the door, as if I won't notice he's moving me.

"So I only remember certain parts of the last part of the night—"

"Yes?"

"And I remember—"

"Akosua, I'm really in a hurry."

I notice that his eyes are trained on the open door. "Are you expecting someone?"

"No, I told you, I have a meeting."

"Well, excuse me for asking, but I just need to settle the little matter of how and why, number one, you were pantsless in my room, and number two, you basically, like, tried to take my clothes off, and—and—"

"*Tso*! Akosua, my darling." He laughs, I can't tell if he's nervous or amused. "Do you recall spilling a drink on me?"

I remember my hand swinging wildly as I hugged Ella to congratulate her on her promotion and—whoa, Ella's moving in with Roger, like a real adult woman—I remember the drink splashing on his lap. "Yes, I remember."

"Right. So I took my pants off to clean them up a bit." He shrugs, begins leading me out the door again, this time pulling me by my elbow.

"And my shirt? And trying to take off my bra?"

"I just wanted you to sleep comfortably."

"I mean, why did you have to do that? I barely know you."

"I didn't think you would mind. My whole aim the whole night was to make you feel comfortable. You were uptight, so I thought if you had a drink . . ."

"I think it's funny that you're calling me uptight, because you are the most uptight person I know."

By now we are doing a strange kind of dance, facing each other, my back to the open door. He steps forward, knowing I will step back and inch toward the door and out of his room. I step forward, my hand outstretched to push him back into his room because I am not yet finished sorting out what happened.

"I remember that I had to push you away. That you were saying you wanted to be with me. Would you have, like, kept going if I hadn't made you stop?"

"Akosua, you are misremembering things. You were confused. I would never do the things you are suggesting."

I could be imagining things, but I think—no, I know—that his eyes have made their way down to my chest, where they linger for a bit. I wrap my sweater tight around myself. "You got pissed off when I said no. You left me there drunk and sick. It's clear what you wanted. You're so slimy it's ridiculous, I mean, who takes off someone's shirt when they're passed out—"

"Maybe you shouldn't have passed out."

"Maybe you shouldn't be an asshole. Seriously, fuck you. Fuck you and go to hell. You know what you were trying to do with a half-unconscious person."

"Do not insult me in this manner, o. What kind of jungle boy do you think I am? Do you think that just because I am African—"

"I am African, too. It's nothing related to that. Stop trying to distract me from the truth. You did something really wrong last night and you're trying to pretend you didn't."

"Excuse me."

This voice does not belong to someone in this room. This voice belongs to someone behind me, someone in the doorway (I turn around to face it despite Daniel's desperate grip on my elbow), someone in a towel, a female someone who I think I remember is a sophomore in the college (she once came to the library to pay her fines; we exchanged shy smiles because each could tell the other was Ghanaian), someone who now smiles at me and extends her hand in greeting.

"Hello, I am Esther Essilfie. Sorry, o, I am not dressed properly. You look familiar. Are you in the African Students Association?"

I whirl back around. Daniel doesn't even wear a poker face; all of his features have distorted, his hands clasp his mouth, he is horrified.

I am screaming obscenities.

"Wow. You're shitting me. Are you *serious*? Are you absolutely serious?"

"Akosua, it's not as if you and I were a serious couple yet . . ."

"Yet? How was that going to happen given that it seems like you're a serious couple with this young lady here?"

Behind me Esther Essilfie is gathering all of her clothes from a pile on the floor in the corner, rushing to the door, screaming, "Lunch is off! Cook your own stew, Daniel Cobblah."

"Look at what you have done." Now his hands are gripping his head.

"What *I* have done? I haven't done anything! You did it! You are a cheater. You're cheating on this girl. What about Aku Aggrey? I saw you with her, too."

"Oh, she's just—"

"You shut up, I don't want to hear it. You were too busy for me until next semester. Now I know why. Ugh, you are a cheater *and* you need to learn a lesson about consent."

"Lower your voice."

"No," I scream as loudly as I can. "No, no, no! What are you gonna do about it?"

He grabs at my forearms, trying to get me to calm down, trying to lead me out of the apartment. He wants quiet. He wants me gone. He wants to deal with the girl in the bathroom, to placate her, to tell her I'm just crazy and jealous, which she will probably believe since I am acting so out of control, but how dare he, how dare this nothing person treat me like a nothing person? I will kill him, I will scratch his eyes out for leaving me like this, for treating us like this.

"Shame on you, Akosua. This temper tantrum is not becoming of you."

She hits him. She is me, I suppose, but I don't feel like it: I am somewhere else, standing by the stairs, horrified at this person who looks like me except that she's doing something I would never do: beating Daniel Cobblah about the head and neck with closed fists. She's hitting him hard and fast enough that he can't even find a way to take hold of her arms, to subdue her or force her to stop. All he can do is keep his hands over his head, over his eyes, because she throws her punches indiscriminately.

"You are gonna pay for what you did to us! How could you do this to us when we are innocent. We were innocent," Mercy Akosua Agbe screams without any mercy at all, and standing by the stairs watching her, watching me, I am crying because I realize that by *us* I don't mean myself and Esther Essilfie and Aku Aggrey and anyone else Daniel's messing with. "How could you do this to us?"

"Are you crazy? What are you on about? Get out of here."

Now he's being mean; we have finally seen Daniel Cobblah lose his religion. I have erred in simplifying him to nothing but a polite country boy who knows nothing of cheating, of rudeness, of perversion. Vile. I watch and listen to myself screaming and hitting without any concern for the neighbors, and one guy from across the hall comes out, asks what's going on, and Daniel says, "Get this crazy girl away from me before I lose it."

I am myself again. These words have awakened me. I take from my pocket the stone that was propping open the door, and as the guy from across the hall tries to pull me away from Daniel, I think about what I am about to do. I think, and then decide it's right. I hold the stone and aim for Daniel's head, I want to hit him right between the eyes and watch him fall backward in pain and in shock.

I miss him by a mile. Still, I pump my fists up in the air and congratulate myself for trying.

At home, my euphoria wears off. I hit him with my fists, yes, I swore at him, I really let him have it. But I still feel violated. He tried to play me for a fool, which is what I am.

In minutes all the makeup on my face has washed away as I cry without end. There is no end to my tears. For once, my brain is still. I am not thinking of anything; I am remembering nothing. History is not repeating itself again and again in my head. I am not thinking of my father. I am not thinking of Daniel and how I yelled at him the way I want to yell at my father. I am not thinking of Wisdom. I am only thinking of myself, finally, and how I have no idea what or who inhabits this skin.

My phone rings and rings. First my cell phone, whose messages I don't bother to check. Then my room phone, and I can hear the voices playing on the answering machine.

"This is Ella. You need to call me back and tell me what is going on. Are you okay?"

Then my mother, a short, dispirited message. "Akosua, please call me. You usually call every day. I am worried."

I don't move from my spot on my floor all day Saturday. I cry the kind of cry that racks your entire body, and because it hurts both my body and my head, I try to stop, but the trying makes it worse because the fact that I cannot stop alerts me to the reality that I am finally breaking for good. This won't end. I wonder when it'll stop, these trickles down my spine, if there's an end to all this sweat, all these headaches.

Through blurry eyes, I watch the sunset. The minutes, the hours stretch on as I shake. I stop crying, but only because my body is exhausted from it. I sleep the night away; on Monday I am disappointed to find myself awake, so I shut my body off again and sleep.

By Tuesday night I have disconnected my room phone and put my cell phone on silent.

I am binging on Wisdom's fried fish. By now I have learned to put the filets in the oven, not the microwave, for maximum crispiness. I eat two or three at once; it seems he made enough to last me a lifetime.

I have missed my make-up Spanish quiz on the *pluscuamperfecto*. I have missed three days' worth of work without calling in. Every moment in which my head is not leaking tears, I am either eating the fish or I am sleeping off the overeating and the crying. I am worried about how worried I am not about school and work. I can only use my two-week-old concussion as an excuse for so long.

Still, I reconnect my phone and call my school's health services to make an appointment; I was supposed to schedule a checkup, anyway, at least this way I can talk to someone about what's wrong with me.

But when I call the health center's appointment line, I hear a message that informs me that health services is closed and no longer taking appointments—I glance at my alarm clock, 8:00 p.m.—and that the health center is also closing for the Thanksgiving holiday but will reopen next Monday. For emergencies, I'm instructed to call 911 or press one to speak to a doctor or nurse practitioner on call. If I simply need to speak to someone who might offer "non-judgmental support and healthy, feasible options," I can press two and reach the college's peer counseling hotline.

Not wanting to burden a doctor or nurse with problems that I'm not sure are in my heart or my head—and feeling like the nebulous wording of the peer counseling hotline's services rather suits my nebulous state of being—I press two.

A sweet but somehow sober-sounding female voice answers, "Good evening; this is Helpline Peer Counseling. How may I help you?"

Inhale. "Um, this is not exactly a . . . I'm not sure if this is the kind of thing you deal with, and I am a graduate student, not an undergrad, but the health center is closed and the message says you can give advice about options . . . ?"

"We offer our services to members of the undergraduate and graduate communities, and, in fact, we even accept calls from the general public. So it's no problem," the girl says in a way that is not quite cheerful, but is definitely a little eager. "Go ahead and tell me anything you'd like to tell me."

I pause, bite my lip and consider for a moment whether what I'm doing is pointless and maybe even a little wrong. Pointless because how will this barely trained undergraduate student help me figure out what's going on in my head; wrong because I once was a barely-trained undergraduate student working the peer counseling hotline. As a freshman, I'd trained for the program, graduating from trainee to man the lines until my supervisor pointed out that I gave too much advice to callers, which is precisely what you're not supposed to do. You're only meant to support, to guide someone to vent, to prevent self-harm, of course. Mostly people called up to talk about academic pressures and issues with their boyfriends or girlfriends. Mostly you just repeated comforting phrases, got the person to lighten the burden of their thoughts, and then suggested they go to see a real counselor the next day. I felt guilty and useless whenever I hung up after a fruitless conversation with some sobbing student, and so I quit after only a couple of weeks. So maybe it's wrong that I'm going to ask this young girl for the answers to my life's current questions even though I know that she can't give me any answers, not only because she probably doesn't have them, but also because it's against the rules to say much of anything at all.

But this girl seems eager to hear me vent: "Go ahead, no one will judge you here. I'm listening. Tell me."

So even though I don't have to, I tell her my name. I tell her my age and my farce of a position as a graduate history student. I tell her about how I hit my head two weeks ago. I tell her the doctor's diagnosis, post-concussion syndrome, and that so far I've suffered from some of the symptoms the doctor warned me may or may not occur: headaches and migraines, difficulty concentrating, depression, trouble sleeping, too much sleeping, sometimes dizziness and disorientation and blackouts. Erratic behavior. As I speak, she continues to prod me gently, saying, "Mm-hmm . . . yes . . . that must have been very difficult for you . . . keep going," so I keep going. I tell her about Daniel, about what he did, what he tried to do to me, and what I'm pretty sure I did to him, yelling at him for treating me as poorly as my father treated my mother. I tell her about my father. How seventeen years ago he left my life; how three months ago he reentered it, but not of his own volition or mine. How I've only heard rumors of his return. How he never contacted me himself. Wisdom. Dear Wisdom. How our breakup was sort of like a tantrum: he threw one that questioned my authenticity, my identity, and I threw a bigger one, extricating him and our relationship from my life. Trying to. Trying really hard to but doing it stupidly, with Daniel, who doesn't care about me.

I pause to breathe, to wipe away these unwanted tears that continue to leak as I vent everything to this perfect stranger, this wonderful anonymous undergraduate girl, someone who probably had been dutifully perusing her biology text or chatting with co-peer counselors before receiving a phone call from me, a frantic lunatic. My tears turn into guilty ones, because I'm wasting her life in addition to my own.

"Ako . . . Akosua?" comes her voice, finally.

"Yes?"

"Akosua. Am I getting that right?"

"Yes."

"Excellent. Are you currently suffering any of the symptoms related to your head injury?"

"A dull ache behind my eyes. Incessant crying, which I guess is depression. Maybe."

"Are you alone right now?"

"Yes. I mean, no. I'm with you, so . . ."

"Are you going to need to head to the hospital? Maybe you could call a friend and have them come over and walk you to the emergency room. You sound pretty upset, which is definitely understandable. And I know you're probably not wanting to worry anyone, but it's okay to seek help. No one will be mad if you go to get checked out, which would be much better than if you got hurt or if you hurt yourself . . ."

"No, no, I'm not going to do that. I am seeking help. That's why I'm calling you. Given everything, given all I've said, what's—what's wrong with me?"

"Excuse me?"

I explain to her what I mean, and what I mean is that I want to know from an outsider who has never met me or seen a scan of my brain, a person who might offer an honest, unbiased opinion: where does the injury start and end? My headaches, are they because of my father, of Wisdom, of Daniel, these mystifying creatures called men; are they because of my mother, her sweetness, her bitterness, her wild and uneasy laughter, her perfection, her being my beginning and end? Or are my headaches caused by the way my head hit the edge of the tub sixteen days ago? Am I crying now, for instance, because of the depression and irritability associated with post-concussion syndrome, or because I am upset that some boy I barely even like has seen me vulnerable, has made me feel foolish, has reminded me of the ways that men can hurt women? When I throw a stone, throw a tantrum, throw myself on the bed and cry myself to sleep—who or what has taken that action?

I hear the girl, my dear peer counselor, draw in her breath. She does not know what to say.

"Sorry," I say. "Sorry. I rambled."

"No. Don't apologize. It's just . . ." I think she's going to say, *It's just that this is not in my job description*, but instead she says, "It's just that I can't answer these questions for you. No one can."

"Why not? I mean, can't you just tell me, does this sound like stuff that a head injury can make a person do? Or is it just me?"

"To that end, do you think you're who you are *because* your father left? Would you have been that person anyway? You're asking me to decipher the impossible puzzle of cause and effect and what makes people do what they do."

I don't like what she's saying. I don't understand what she's saying. I massage my forehead with fingertips I discover are drenched in sweat. "Are you suggesting that I need a shrink?"

"Well, health services does offer a total of six free, half-hour sessions to students with the school insurance, and many students find that a useful option—" She cuts herself off, sighs. "Look. I'm just gonna talk to you straight right now, person to person, you know, student to student or whatever. You must have taken a psych or philosophy class at some point, you know all this stuff."

I clasp my head in my hands, befuddled that she's speaking so frankly and with an air of such knowledge. "Yeah, I did take some psych stuff and took a pass/fail philosophy class that I didn't really get..."

"Well," she says, and already her voice has lost that guarded politeness of a peer counselor and taken on the confidence of a budding academic. "Your head injury, the migraines, the blackouts—there's no doubt they may have had an effect on your life. Other people. Circumstance. But you're *you*; you're, like, a person. Your actions count for something. You're not just a jumble of insults and injuries that have been heaped on you."

"But—"

"You don't have to be, like, a slave to your past."

"Slave?"

"Poor choice of words, I mean that you can move beyond your past. Maybe you need to look back at it and really understand it, and yeah, maybe a shrink can help with that. But either way, it's like, stuff happens to you. But not *everything* just happens. You're not some passenger in your life."

What she's telling me, what she's really saying to me, is that it's all myself: the pains in my head and neck and back, the ones in my heart and mind, the impulses I'm aware of, the ones I'm not, it's all me, unreconciled, but it's me.

I clear my throat. "So you don't think I need to call a doctor, you know, given my concussion and everything?"

Then there's a pause I can only describe as uncanny. At first I'm not sure whether it's a pause in my brain, like the synapses have stopped jumping and my brain has clicked off, or a pause because the peer counselor girl thinks I've asked something completely idiotic and doesn't know what to say. There's silence for a few heartbeats, for long enough that I say "hello?" and check to make sure the phone hasn't somehow disconnected from the wall.

In fact, the pause came from someone putting me on hold and someone new—a deeper female voice—picking up the phone.

"Good evening, this is Helpline Peer Counseling, how may I help you?"

"Oh. I was actually talking to someone already. I think maybe something happened with the phones?"

This new girl, who is not *my* peer counselor, makes an embarrassed little laugh. "I'm sorry, but you were speaking to someone in training. I'd stepped away from the phones because of an emergency, and left unsupervised, she spoke in a manner that is not in keeping with our policy and objectives here . . ."

I keep the receiver to my ear, but I don't listen to what she's saying because I get the basic idea after a few seconds. My peer counselor, the girl in whom I put all my trust (well, maybe only a negligible percentage of my trust), is a renegade peer counselor. Worse on the phone than I was years ago, this girl has not only broken protocol in talking to me straight, person to person, as she said, but she's also offered dangerous opinions about my health that could give me a false sense of security.

The supposedly better trained peer counselor with whom I'm speaking now offers to give me the phone number of one of the advice nurses so that I can talk to a trained health care professional about my head injury.

I do call and speak to a nurse practitioner, but only half-heartedly. I don't tell her about Daniel, Wisdom, or my father. I don't even make much mention of the cause of my headaches, the fall, passing out, the ambulance ride to the hospital, the talk of post-concussion syndrome. I am all talked out, so I focus on symptoms.

The nurse thinks that stress has exacerbated some neck and jaw muscle tightness, making my headaches worse. I should schedule an appointment for a checkup after the holiday to make sure my physical head injury has healed, but in the meantime, to alleviate the pain, I can take showers in which I alternate between hot and cold water, let the extremes pound upon my skull until the tension and pain run down the drain. I can scream into my pillow to relieve the jaw tension. I can rest my head, drink chamomile tea, and try to fall into a sleep that's not frenzied or depleted but gentle, tranquil rest.

10

It is Wednesday morning. Exactly two weeks ago, I left the hospital with my mother. For the first time since then, for the first time since before then, my head finally feels clear. Clear considering whose head it is.

My body is another thing. I don't quite feel it belongs to me. It belongs to Daniel, whom I haven't heard from and of course haven't seen; I haven't left my room again since I confronted him on Sunday. I don't want my skin and what's in it to belong to Daniel. It has never belonged to anyone but me; not even Wisdom could claim it because he never tried to force me, never made me feel powerless. But even though good sleep and hot and cold showers and screaming have eased some of my tension and hurt, I still feel Daniel's fingerprints and eyes on me: my body belongs to him at this moment.

What does not belong to him, what I will never allow to belong to anyone or anything again, is my mind. My will. I can do whatever I need to do on my own.

But I don't know what I need to do. Not in the big picture. I know I need to sleep better, eat better, rest better. I know I need to lay low until my head injury's completely healed. But the problems of my mind and heart, whatever those two intangible spaces are, anyway, stump me. I don't know what they need at all. Part of me wants to ask the renegade peer counselor—after all, she had confidence, and that must count for something, right?—but she's probably been fired, and after all, what does she truly know about my life?

So instead I stick to the simple solutions. Obviously, I need to go to work. I haven't called out sick, just failed to show up for the past couple of days, and the idea of calling Alan or our boss with some kind of excuse causes the bottoms of my feet to itch, my head to ache from the prospect of spinning lies. Instead, I rise from bed, shower, dress. I will walk to the library. I won't offer any excuses, I'll just apologize and be the best mistress of label-making I can be.

Outside, though, I feel like an alien. I'm worried that people on the street will notice that I'm drenched in sweat, that it's my fault I'm drenched in sweat. It's about forty-five degrees outside, yet I dressed myself in thermal underwear—top and bottoms—a turtleneck, a wool sweater, and my winter coat. Within minutes, drops of water trickle down and collect in what feels like a puddle between the underwire of my bra and the skin of my chest, and though no one can see any of this activity, I feel like a freak show on display, I feel like all of these layers have disintegrated and I'm down to nothing but sweat and flesh and bones, and I am losing it again, my calm, my sense of purpose, and now I feel myself veering off the path to the library and heading toward the housing desk, where Daniel Cobblah will see what a mess he's made of me and will have to pay for what he's done, he'll *want* to pay for what he's done when he sees my face.

Luckily, when I enter the dormitory where the housing desk is situated, Daniel is not there and Peter's preoccupied with an undergrad who is filing a complaint about her roommate's constant smoking. I sneak past without attracting his attention. I head for the vending machine alcove off to the right of the housing desk a few good yards away, close enough that if I peek my head around one of the pillars, I'll see Daniel's entrance but far enough that he shouldn't notice me. I'm protected by rows of snack and soda machines, so many that, at first, I worry if I'll be able to hear anything. I glance at my watch, at his name on the placard at the desk: Daniel Cobblah, Housing Department Staff Level II. He's clocked in today, I know that for sure. He's probably off in "the field."

I peel off one layer, my winter coat, and watch Pete watch the girl's mouth move. When she bends down to pick up a piece of paper she dropped on the floor, his eyes greedily devour her butt, and they peer down her shirt when she leans over to sign the complaint he's filing on her behalf. I'm smart, I know to steer clear of people like Pete, so how is it that I'd missed the signs with Daniel?

As the girl walks away from the housing desk and out of the building, Daniel strides in. I know he's coming because I hear him, his rumbling voice. He says, "Good day, miss," to someone, maybe the girl Pete just finished with, as he enters the building.

"Did you see that girl?" Pete greets Daniel as Daniel settles behind the desk.

Daniel chuckles from deep in his belly. "I'm no longer looking at girls. I got woman troubles, o, for real. Trying to get out of the doghouse."

"Which one's pissed off this time?" Pete asks.

"Which one isn't?"

And then the two of them busy themselves with a boy who approaches the desk to ask for guest passes so that his parents and sisters can see his dorm room.

As I watch Daniel accept ID cards from one of the sisters, who looks about sixteen, I wonder what I'm doing here. What I'm doing caring about any men, period. Maybe my mother's right about men being of no use to me. Daniel's hand lingers as he takes the girl's ID card, he brushes his fingers against hers, lets his eyes linger on her body, and I wonder if this is something all men do, or just ones like Pete and Daniel? Or, more precisely, if all men have the potential to behave as Daniel did on Sunday night. This is a stupid thought, though, useless. I'm not all women; why would Daniel be all men? Why can't I live in the gray area? I peel off my sweater. I am hot and feeling a little faint.

The family leaves. Pete and Daniel elbow each other, commenting on the jailbait that just slipped through their hands. They say that, jailbait. Who talks like this? And what a great lot of good it did throwing the rock at him. He looks perfectly fine now, unscathed. I wanted him to look contrite as if an auntie has scolded him for mistreating a nice young Ghanaian girl, but if I go flying at him, hurling accusations and fists in his direction, I won't be that nice young Ghanaian girl.

I crouch by the vending machines for what seems like ages, watching Daniel conduct his business, straining my ears to hear him speak. He's cordial, almost generous. When the patrons leave, he and Pete clown around like any guys would. I try to remember what I've heard Daniel talk about with Pete but cannot conjure anything specific except that on the day that I attempted to ask Daniel out, Pete had called Daniel a player. Why hadn't I listened?

"Akosua."

I know that voice is not Daniel's because it's higher pitched and more familiar to my ears. It's Wisdom, standing right next to me with his hand on my shoulder.

Somehow I manage not to cry out in surprise.

"What is going on?" His voice comes out as if he's stifling something; he sounds like he's choking on his words.

"What? What are you doing here? The med school campus is uptown," I whisper.

"I know where my campus is. I came down here to keep an eye on you."

"Keep an *eye* on me?"

"I went to your apartment but I saw you leaving. So I thought I'd come, too, and make sure no one was bothering you."

"You followed me? Are you crazy?"

"Are you? Coming here where this boy is, always looking for trouble, huh? When I saw that you were heading to where Daniel works, I knew I had to come. Besides, it's perfect, because I'd love to have a word with this boy."

I put my finger over my lips. Wisdom's blowing my cover.

"Oh, I don't care if that boy hears me. If he wants to hear, let him. He's a fool." Wisdom's hand clutches my forearm, and I see in his eyes an intensity I haven't seen from him in a while. "Ella didn't want to tell me, but I convinced her to, and I know now that this fool tried to take advantage of you."

"Well, he tried but he didn't." I reach for my winter coat, shrug it onto my shoulders. I don't want Wisdom knowing what happened. I don't like that anyone knows. "What did she tell you?"

"Enough to let me know I needed to come down here and set some things straight." Wisdom never gets this visibly mad. His guise of calm often enraged me when we fought, conveying what I perceived as indifference. But now his eyes bulge and every muscle in his face trembles as he struggles to suppress his anger.

"Wisdom, this doesn't really concern—"

"Either you tell me or Daniel Cobblah tells me. You can't just let people pick on people with brain injuries."

I grab hold of his forearm to prevent him from walking away from me. "I'm not *brain* injured, Wisdom—"

Wisdom shakes me off, and before I can stop him, he strides right toward the housing desk.

"May I help you?" Daniel asks, his meaningless smile plastered on his face.

"Daniel? Wisdom."

Daniel doesn't notice Wisdom's acerbic tone, or he pretends not to. He sticks out his right hand for a shake; Wisdom stares at the hand defiantly; I stand in the corner paralyzed. This is my worst nightmare, these two men meeting up. They must know each other minimally, I've always thought, by virtue of attending the same not-so-large graduate institution, by virtue of being Ghanaian men at said institution. But apparently the network isn't as large as I'd assumed; Daniel has no idea who Wisdom is or why he would arrive at the housing desk, pissed.

"What's good, *chale*?" Daniel asks genially once his and Wisdom's eyes connect and Daniel recognizes the Ghanaianness of Wisdom.

"You tell me what's good. Could you do that?"

Daniel, for the first time, truly diverts his attention from the paperwork. "What do you mean?"

"You know Akosua Agbe, don't you?"

Daniel laughs that belly laugh again, the one I've grown to hate. "Oh. What is this, eh? What has she sent you to do?"

"Nobody sends me anywhere. I'm doing this on my own. I want to make sure nobody's bothering her." Wisdom has balled his hands into two ineffectual-looking fists at his sides. He looks so wiry and small in comparison to Daniel, even though Daniel's seated and slouching a little behind the desk. Nothing can hide Daniel's hulking muscles.

"Nobody's bothering her that I know of." Daniel leans back in his chair yet still manages to look menacing behind the smile. "Here I am thinking somebody has come to make friends and instead you come and accuse me."

"I'm not accusing you of anything. I'm asking you to leave her alone."

"What? You want to chop that crazy girl? Well, go ahead. I'm sure you will be joining a long list of others."

"For your own sake," Wisdom says, and I notice his fists re-clench at his sides, "I ask you not to say such things because I don't know what I'll do."

"Little boy. Go home. This is my place of work. Your big speeches mean nothing. I barely know that girl."

"You know her enough to get her drunk or whatever you did Saturday night. Don't fucking pretend."

Pete holds his palms up in the air. "'Scuse me, young man, I'm gonna have to ask you to leave. This really isn't the place . . .'"

But already Daniel has risen to his feet, his hands in his pockets. "Listen here, little boy. One thing you need to know? This your Akosua Agbe? She's a tease, o. The whole time that I know her, she acts as if she wants it, *ashawo*, always around, always inviting me over, but then? She drinks, what, two drinks and is useless to me."

"She has a *head injury*. She shouldn't have been drinking," Wisdom snapped.

But Daniel continues as if Wisdom hasn't spoken. "God knows that if she weren't such a sloppy drinker, we would have had a better end to our evening."

"Shut your mouth, o, I'm warning you." Wisdom's voice sounds like a high-pitched bark, he is another person right now, and as I stand back and watch, hiding in the alcove, I don't feel like myself at all because I have never encountered a Wisdom like this.

"Do you realize you came here to embarrass yourself and scold me for nothing? All I did," Daniel says as he steps from behind the housing desk, right into Wisdom's face, "was take a drunk girl home and leave her there. I'm sure other men have done much worse with her. That's probably why you want to chop her, too, right? Because you think New York girls are easy, too—"

In one motion, Wisdom steps back and takes a wild swing at Daniel's face with his right fist. Daniel ducks out of the way so easily, as if he expected Wisdom to try to hit him. Wisdom grips his own right arm with his other hand, puffing air in and out of his mouth, muttering Ewe curse words under his breath. Chuckling to himself, standing with crossed arms, untouched, Daniel seems like a goliath, what with the stone I threw at him and now this punch, but Wisdom and I are two peas in a pod: we both failed in our attempts to knock him down.

Abruptly I am no longer crouching near the vending machine like a coward; I'm sprinting toward the housing desk to do anything I can to stop Wisdom from getting his ass kicked. Though Wisdom's still holding his right arm at the shoulder, he's spewing insults and threats right in Daniel's amused face, and I run to his side and grab his left elbow, pulling him toward me.

"Stop," I say. "Please, Wisdom, let's go."

"I will choke you," Wisdom says to Daniel in a softly menacing way, and I believe him, but Daniel just laughs.

"Okay, okay, you gotta get this guy outta here, Sue," Pete says to me, shaking his head.

As we walk away from the housing desk and out of the dormitory, my hands wrapped around Wisdom's left elbow, I glance behind me and catch a look on Daniel's face that I know I'll never forget. The corners of his mouth have turned up slightly like little hooks—his polite smile, same as always.

Wisdom stands beside my bed, shivering without his shirt on. Goosebumps cover his skin, the muscles in his chest and stomach tense from the cold and the pain of his injured shoulder as he attempts to lift his right arm above his head.

"Fuck," he hisses, dropping his arm to his side before he's able to raise it much more than a few inches from his waist. He hasn't looked me in the eye once; during the walk to my apartment, he refused to speak or look anywhere but the pavement. In fact, this "fuck" is the first thing he's said to me since he threatened to confront Daniel, tried, and failed.

"You think you need to see a doctor?" I'm sitting on the bed in front of him, looking up at him, but not exactly *at* him. I can tell he doesn't want to be seen right now: he lost his cool, he caused a scene, he not only lost a fight but he managed to hurt himself without even making physical contact with his supposed opponent.

"No, I don't need to see a doctor. I'm a med student," he grumbles, attempting again to raise his arm, this time raising it slowly in front of him, perpendicular to his body.

"Well, yes. You are. But what if you dislocated it?"

"It's not dislocated. This is the shoulder I injured playing football in high school. I just strained it a little. I probably just need a hot shower."

I rise from my bed and walk to my drawer, pull out a spare towel, and hand it to him. "Okay, shower here. And if you're not okay afterward, we're going to the hospital."

"I think I'd know whether I need to go to the hospital," he mutters, but he takes the towel and in no time his pants and boxers lie in a puddle at his feet.

Regarding Wisdom in a towel, I'm amazed at how the sight of him nearly nude feels almost clinical now. Or does it, really? Wouldn't it be nice to take off my clothes and jump in the shower with him, not in any sexy way, really, but to be close to him, better yet, to get clean together? He can make me feel like myself again; once upon a time, wasn't he the only person with whom I felt most at home in my skin?

"What's the problem?" Wisdom snaps at me, startling me out of my gaze.

Finally our eyes meet, and his look hurt, guarded. He adjusts the towel at his waist, his eyes darting away from mine.

"What are you looking at, Akosua? The wimpy boy who can't fight that Daniel fool? Well, let me tell you, I was fucking pissed, if I'd been calmer I could have knocked him out . . ."

"Shush. Are you kidding?" I stand up, and now I'm face to face with him. I could step closer, lay my hand over his chest, but I don't. I hold my right hand in my left, tight, willing myself to stay in control. "Do you think that's how I see you? You care enough to defend me. That's kind. But it's also kind of silly. I kicked him out of my room. He didn't do anything to me. I took care of myself."

"I guess I did that thing you're not supposed to do," he muttered. "What do you call it? White knighting?"

I bite my lip; I don't want him to think I'm laughing at him, even though I do find humor in his use of the phrase. "It was nice of you to talk to Ella to see how I was doing."

"Of course I'd do that," he says, and he's the one to make the move now. He steps forward, wraps his left arm around me in a tight hug that catches me off guard so that my nose smashes against his bare chest. Into my neck he mumbles, "You're so dense sometimes. I clearly love you. How many times do I have to say it?"

"Well." I feel my body stiffen. "I feel bad that your shoulder's hurt. It's my fault. You really shouldn't have gotten involved."

Wisdom moves away from me, turns toward the bathroom. I said the wrong thing, I know. As I hear the shower water turn on, I throw myself on my bed and feel an unsettling mix of satisfaction and disappointment. I cover my eyes with my hands to block the late morning sunshine that's streaming through the blinds. There really isn't anything left to do but sleep.

I doze off, awaking when I hear the bathroom door open followed by Wisdom's heavy footsteps and a rush of steam from his long hot shower.

"You don't have to hide your eyes. You've seen me in all my scrawny glory before."

"Oh, quit being a baby. You're not scrawny. And like you said, you could've kicked Daniel's ass if you weren't so angry and out of sorts." Still, I don't uncover my eyes. I don't want him to see them when I ask him this question that's been on my mind since we left Daniel behind. I know what it means to "chop" a girl—in pidgin, it translates to "eat," but it can also mean to have sex. But the other thing . . . "What did he call me—*ashawo*? That's not Ewe, is it?"

"No. It's just slang."

"And it means . . ."

"It's not nice."

"None of this was nice. He insulted me and said gross things about me in front of you and Pete and whoever else happened by the housing desk, all the while showing no remorse for trying to strip me down while I was practically passed out—"

"Please, let's not put the picture in my head."

"Um, it's about more than the picture in your head, Wisdom. It's about the feeling in my skin. I mean, this is an actual thing that happened to me. It's more than some macho argument about staking your claim on a girl."

Wisdom sighs and I feel the weight of his body as he sits on the bed. I open my eyes and take him in: he's dressed again, the towel draped over his shoulder. The collar of his Oxford button-down dress shirt looks a darker blue than the rest of his shirt; he's always rushing out of the shower, too impatient to dry off properly.

"I didn't mean to make it seem like it's all about something macho. I have to admit I don't like picturing some other guy's hands all over you, but obviously that's nothing compared to the knowledge that that asshole hurt you. Why are you even hanging out with that guy?"

I sit up, clear my throat. "How's your shoulder?"

"Don't change the subject. I'm trying to understand what's going on with you. It's like you're so restless—"

"If you can't lift your arm over your head, we're going to the emergency room right now," I blurt out, "and please don't say anything about how you're a med student so you know what you're doing, because you definitely said the same thing when I hit my head and look how that turned out."

Wisdom's forehead creases down the center in the way that lets me know I've worried him. He takes my hand in his, begins to massage my fingers like he does, like he always used to do. "I know. I'm sorry. I don't know what I was thinking that night, not taking you to the doctor right away. I'm really sorry." He pauses, tilts his head to the side. "You must admit, though, that it's sometimes difficult to tell with you. You tend to be dramatic."

"Dramatic?"

"Yes. Sometimes. The way that whenever you get a cold you say you have the flu." A smile plays on his lips, his thick eyebrows wag up and down, he nudges me with his shoulder. "That time you screamed your head off because you thought you saw a rat in your apartment, but it was just your fuzzy cat slippers?"

"Well. That's a different kind of drama from hitting my head against the edge of the tub and getting a concussion."

"I didn't actually *see* you hit your head, so I couldn't have known how bad it was. Not that I didn't believe you. I just didn't know it was as bad as it was."

"Oh, of course. Thank you very much for the faith you have in me." I let go of his hand. "Of course you never believe me, and you never understand. Akosua *claims* she hits her head? Whatever, just come over and humor her and pretend you're concerned. Akosua *claims* you really screwed her over when you called her an embarrassment and treated her like some shameful piece of nothing in front of your friends? No problem, just offer a perfunctory apology and expect everything to go back to normal."

"No. I didn't expect everything to go back to normal after an apology. I thought maybe it might after ten apologies, and a million gestures to show you I care, and twice as many explanations." There, he's back, the Wisdom I know, calm, matter-of-fact, maddeningly practical. "But still, over three months have passed, and nothing's back to normal. I'd like to ask you to tell me what you want from me, but that seems too simple."

My face feels hot, but my hands and feet have grown numb and heavy. "Oh, you're so cool and calm and collected. Good for you. Just as cold as you were when you left me on the sidewalk on my ass. Cold-hearted."

He exhales, clasps his hands together, asks for mercy. "Look. I'm very sorry I left you on the sidewalk that night. When you tripped, I should've helped you up," he says quietly, his eyes large behind his glasses.

I find myself shaking my head. "It's more than that. I didn't trip."

"Yes, you did. Coming after me, you tripped on a bump in the sidewalk or something."

"Oh! Glad to know that this is how your memory warps these things."

"Exactly how do you remember things that night?"

"I didn't trip!"

"And you ended up on your ass how?"

"The force of your horrible words knocked me over!"

Wisdom shakes his head, stalks toward the door. "Because that makes a lot of sense, Akosua. Face the facts: everything isn't always all someone else's fault. You're always tripping over something."

When he slams the door behind him, he uses his right arm, the injured one, and I can't tell if it's the pain or his anger at me that causes him to cry out, "Damn it!" before he hurries down the stairs and away from me.

So, a short-lived recovery. I failed at going back to work, I pushed away my would-be hero, my would-be Wisdom, if only I'd let him be mine. So much for my agency, my starring role in my own narrative. I duck under my blankets again, I embed myself in the suffocating warmth of my bed, I erase myself from the rest of the day and the hope I thought I could feel.

∽○∾

Lately, I find myself sleeping. I dream of being awake, of things I've done in the past when awake, of things I continue to do over and over again when awake, of things over which I have no control. I have no control; I am out of it.

In my sleep, I dream of the phone calls that have plagued me while I'm awake. Auntie Fergie wondering if I'll make it to Jersey for Thanksgiving tomorrow, my mother calling to ask the same question and demanding to know why I've been out of touch. The dean's assistant, no doubt wanting to track my progress or let me know outright that I'm going to get kicked out because she's already heard that I skipped my Spanish quiz and will fail, fail, fail, as I am wont to do. Wisdom, calling for no good reason. There's no good reason why he should try to contact someone as fickle as myself, but he does, he doesn't give up. Ella, leaving messages, asking if she can see me before she leaves to spend the holiday with Roger's family. I dream of these phone calls, of these voices reaching out to me, of how I reject them but still crave them at the same time. And then I dream of Thanksgiving dinner.

I envision the dinner I expect to have. I'm in the Fergies' expansive apartment with its clean white walls and pristine furniture that all but swallow up the touches that would make their home familiar: family pictures, kente cloth, wooden statues, the smell of fried fish and plantain somewhat masked by the scents of lavender air freshener and Italian leather. Uncle's in the den shouting obscenities at the television screen. Auntie Fergie's in the kitchen, pounding at peppers in her Ghana-style mortar and pestle, singing church hymns in her high-pitched voice. I'm feeling small and lost in this confused space, uncomfortable because my mother's not with me, instead at home in Windsor by herself, picking at candied yams from a can because she hasn't bothered to prepare herself a proper Thanksgiving meal. I don't know how to behave at the Fergies—or at any auntie and uncle's house—without my mother present to do the work of being Ghanaian enough to get by.

"Do you want me to help you make stuffing for the turkey?" my dream-self asks Auntie Fergie. "Or should I peel some plantains?"

Someone has dressed me in a Ghanaian print dress that's too tight, the pencil skirt clinging to my legs so that my inaction makes sense: I'm only standing in the kitchen asking what I should do, but I make no moves toward acting. Blame it on whoever dressed me, right?

"Should I set the table now or do you usually do it later? Are we going to have some pie? Should I stay out of the kitchen? Am I in the way? Am I being good by staying out of it?"

As the last words leave my mouth, Auntie Fergie finally looks up from her incessant pepper grinding, confused. "Out of it?"

"Out of the way, that is."

But Auntie Fergie doesn't have a chance to answer the question of how good I am because the sound of Uncle Fergie's celebratory whoop overpowers the sound of us two women talking in the kitchen.

"All right!" he shouts. "That's my good man!"

And Auntie Fergie laughs, tittering about her silly husband, about how funny men can be with the games they love to watch and play, and asks me, "Why don't you be a good girl and bring your uncle some groundnuts and beer?"

She hands me a glass bowl full of peanuts, pats me on the shoulder, and begins to speak to me in Twi, a language I don't understand. She tries Ewe, the language my mother speaks, but all I can do is stand still and mute, tongue-tied.

Auntie laughs and finally says in English, "Just go and serve your uncle, silly girl."

I try to walk but can't because the skirt's too restrictive, and besides, the Akosua of my dream world has become conscious of the Akosua who's dreaming. Me, Mercy Akosua Agbe, I have imagined myself into a box, into a Ghanaian skirt that doesn't fit, into a Ghanaian family that isn't mine, into a conundrum. I laugh in my sleep. Or we laugh in my sleep. Myself in bed with a headache, and the version of myself standing in the Fergies' kitchen holding a bowl of nuts, we laugh until we snort and tears run down our cheeks.

"You have a headache," Auntie Fergie says, taking the nuts back from me, pressing the palm of her hand to my forehead. "Are you sick? You're really getting out of control."

But I actually am the one in control, aren't I? I'm asleep right now, I truly am, but if I'm thinking these thoughts at this moment, if Akosua in the pencil skirt is looking up at the ceiling and laughing along with Akosua lying in bed sleeping, then can't something be done? After all, no one chooses to paint themselves into a corner, do they?

Perhaps I really need to use my imagination.

I decide to invite a guest to this Thanksgiving dinner so that it's not only me, Auntie Fergie, Uncle Fergie, the kitchen with its rich smells, the den with its alluring soccer games. Yes, let's populate this dream world. Let's not bring my mother; that's too obvious, of course I want my mother there. And not Ella, no, she'd hate being here, she'd scold me and tell me to wake up, she'd say, "Are you really wasting time deciding who to invite to your little make-believe world when you could be calling me back in real life?" The Fergies expect me to bring Daniel Cobblah to their apartment for Thanksgiving, but, if I go, I won't bring him anymore, so why have him show up in my fantasy, and isn't it cruel, and again, much too obvious to bring Wisdom, oh Wisdom, how easy it is to conjure you up and dream of you: your high cheekbones, the way your glasses rest crookedly against your crooked nose, the creases on your forehead, the tightening of your facial muscles as you set your jaw against me and all of my crazy ways (how resilient you are in the face of my crazy ways), your deep brown eyes just as myopic as mine.

Who, in my dreams, would I invite to this Thanksgiving dinner to pull up a chair beside me so that we can share an awkward, indulgent, all-American meal?

Of course it's him. The one person whose face I can't ever fully visualize. The one who is only eyes, glasses, hands, maybe a mouth but it's mute; he's just fragments, pieces of him forever lost in the mess inside my head. My father: he taps his pen against his lips, he bites the end of his pen, he puts down the pen, turns a page, tilts his head, clears his throat, he repeats the process. But I can't, even in my dreams, begin to imagine him sitting down to have a meal with me. No matter how hard I try to force him in, he doesn't have a place in my dreams, not as anything but a broken image.

But maybe, I think, *maybe that's better than nothing.* And I lull myself into deeper sleep with the memory of my three-year-old self watching in awe as my father studies books filled with history.

∽⚬∽

I wake up to simultaneous pounding at my door and the ringing of my dorm room phone. I glance at my alarm clock: only a couple of hours have passed since my encounter with Daniel, with Wisdom, with the pieces of my father in my dream.

"Girl, open up! It's Ella, honey, it's me."

I smash my pillows against my ears. What will I say to her? She is moving in with her boyfriend; she's getting a promotion. I am getting muscle atrophy from lying in bed all day. My brain will melt from lack of use.

"What happened, did you talk to Daniel? Akosua, I'm not leaving until you tell me what happened. It's been a week. I'm going to call the police and file a missing persons report."

The thought of my mother's alarmed shout when the police call her in Canada and tell her that her only daughter is missing forces me to lift my head from the pillow. "It hasn't been a week, Ella," I shout through the door. "It's been ..." I count on my fingers, Sunday, Monday, Tuesday, Wednesday. "It's been four days."

"There you are. Now open up."

"No. I'm ... I'm naked. It's okay; thank you for coming; everything is fine. Happy Thanksgiving, Ella, really, aren't you going to miss your flight?"

"I can tell from your voice that you are not naked."

I am wearing about eighty-five layers of clothes. I am buried in a cave of sheets and blankets. "How can you tell from my voice?"

"Akosua. Do we need to report that boy?" It is not a question, it is a demand for an answer, and I shake my head even though she can't see me.

"No. No. I don't think so. I took care of it." By throwing a rock in his face that missed him? By beating his giant muscular self with my small fists and watching Wisdom try and fail to do the very same thing?

"Are you sure? Akosua, please, open the door. I won't be able to have Thanksgiving unless I can see your face and know that you're okay. You know I'm going away for almost two weeks, right? Open the door and let me have a look at your mug."

I don't want to. I don't want to open the door and let her see me like this. I'm sure she's in her traveling clothes, sleek and clean and like a woman.

"Okay." Her voice sounds final, disappointed. "I'm leaving. Roger's out waiting for the bus to LaGuardia and I'll miss it if I stay. Happy Thanksgiving. But don't think I'm not sending somebody over to take care of you."

It's not the guilt that gets to me, it's the way she said the word "care," and I fling the blankets back and climb out of bed and run to the door, swing it wide open, and see her departing back. She spins around. I hug her and say, "I'll take care of myself. Thank you so much. For everything. Always. See you when you get back."

And I only let myself see her smile for an instant before I hurry back inside and shut the door.

I linger by the doorway as I hear her booted feet go clomping down the stairs. When I think she's gone, I open the door again, considering going down to check my mailbox, which I haven't done in a while. But the air outside of my room smells putrid; the guys down the hall must have had another party, or else they've been storing a dead body in their apartment. I decide to try again later. But as I'm about to close the door again, I see a flash of red on the stairway: Ella's scarf.

"Ella, are you there?" I call down the staircase, but she does not answer. And because I don't want her to fly without it, because I feel it is imperative for her to carry this with her always, I trip over myself to get back into my room, throw on my winter coat, wipe the sleep from my eyes. Grab my purse, my MetroCard, and run down the stairs and to the street.

It is cold. It's almost winter. I keep forgetting, all holed up in my room, hibernating. I'm not thinking of anything at all, just running to catch the bus I see on the corner, the bus to the airport, the bus on which Ella is without her scarf, but the bus is not waiting no matter how hard I shout and wave my hands because I am too far away.

To wait for the next airport-bound bus will take forever, but, if I take the subway, I can meet the bus on one of its last stops before it crosses into Queens and heads to the airport. I jam myself into a crosstown bus first, then get on the five train to take it up a few stops to where I might be able to meet Ella's bus, hop on, and give her back her scarf.

I take in the sights of the city, the life on the train. People sit and stand and hang onto the safety bars: kids with backpacks, clutching their grown-ups' hands; men and women in loafers and heels and business suits; teens holding skateboards and bags of fast food and the hands of their crushes; a hipster with a handlebar mustache. Everybody sways as the train brakes and speeds up, and I'm reminded that I love this city. My first subway ride was with Ella. We didn't even go anywhere, just rode to Seventy-Second Street and walked back to campus, just because she said it was time for me to get to know the world outside my dorm room.

I clutch her scarf. I feel good. I am doing something good for someone who is always doing something good for me.

But when I get off the train at 125th and Madison Avenue, I realize how brainless my plan is. There are about three M60 buses lining this street: one that is cruising away from me, one that's accepting its last rider before it leaves, one that's easing up to the bus stop. Which one do I get on? And I don't have my cell phone. I can't call her to let her know that I'm standing on the street holding her scarf, and, even if I could call her, she would probably laugh and say, "You crazy girl. If I'd known this was all I had to do to get you out of your apartment..."

I wrap her scarf around my neck. I'll take care of it until she returns.

I turn around, go back underground, ride the train back downtown, then take the crosstown bus to my neighborhood, trudge down the street, sweating, to my own front door, which is open.

My heart gallops. Has someone broken in? Maybe Daniel has reported me to the Housing Department for my physical attack on him. Or maybe someone has actually reported me missing, like my mother herself.

"Hello?" I call out into my apartment. My voice sounds tiny. I pull the scarf tighter around my neck and try again with a bigger voice. "Who is there?" I demand. I might sound tough now, but I'm poised and ready to run down the stairs should an assailant pop out of my apartment.

I hear footsteps running to the door; my front door bangs open and Wisdom greets me, throws his arms around me.

"Oh my God," I say as he embraces me, his hand in my hair, smoothing it down. "You scared me! You used your key? It's fine, but you scared me—"

"No. You left the door open." His breath is warm on my cold face. "I had to come back. I ran out on you again, like leaving you on the sidewalk, like not taking care of you when you hit your head, and I had to come back, but you left the door open and I thought I'd finally been negligent enough to really screw things up."

"Huh?"

"I thought someone had hurt you or that you hit your head again. Or that you had run away. Don't ever disappear like that again."

Now he won't let me go; now I find myself unwilling to push him away. I choose to hold onto him, and we stand by my open door, tangled in each other, our heads at rest against each other's shoulders, the sound and the sensation of blood pounding in my ears because of the shock of his return, because of the nice surprise of his always being here.

"Mercy Akosua," he says in a voice that's more intense than loud, but even still, it's like someone turned the volume of everything all the way up.

"Yes, Wisdom?"

He says nothing for a moment, continuing to hold me so tight it almost hurts. One of his hands burrows beneath the collar of my coat and past Ella's red scarf to find the skin on the back of my neck.

His fingertips linger there, soft at first, but then not really, it's like he's trying to massage the tension away, or like he's not thinking about what he's doing at all. The other hand moves frantically across my coat and the body beneath it—arms, hips, back, shoulders—and finally toward the zipper of my coat.

"Mercy Akosua," he repeats, and this time he's nearly breathless. He pulls his head off my shoulder and looks me in the face for the first time since we started this embrace. Behind the lenses of his glasses, his eyes have grown large, they say everything, there's no need for him to speak at all, but when he does, he drops his eyes in the direction of my coat zipper and asks: "Can I?"

I nod. I let him unzip my coat and throw it at my feet. He embraces me again, like it's all he can do. I'm thinking that perhaps he doesn't remember how to do what I think it is he wants to do right now, that he's forgotten, but as I'm thinking this, he cups my chin and pulls my face close to his and there it is, there, those lips, and yes, it's happening again, the first kiss in history, the only kiss in history, and yes, we're moving, and yes, there's the bed, yes, let's stretch ourselves across it and across each other until I disappear into you and you disappear into me—

"Wisdom?" I hear myself say when we're lying close to each other, his hands reaching for either the bottom of my sweater or the buckle of my belt.

"Hmm?"

I slide my hands into his hands, squeezing, nestling my head against his chest where I hear his heart drumming as frantic as his hands' previous movement across my body, movement I have now stilled, because though almost every part of me feels warm enough to dissolve into him, there's a chill remaining in my bones. I don't want it to be like I'm erasing Daniel's trespass with Wisdom.

"Can we just rest a little? I'm so tired."

He wraps his arms around me tightly. "Of course. Of course." He kisses my temple. "I'm just so glad that you came back to me."

I like these words, the idea behind them, and I play them over and over in my head as we hold onto each other in the waning hours of this red-letter day. But when I reimagine the day's events, I wonder if I did come back to him or if he came back to me and I, as usual, reacted to someone else's movements rather than making my own.

11

In the morning, early, before the sun has fully arisen, Wisdom stretches and wakes me to tell me he is leaving. For Thanksgiving, he planned to drive to New Haven where some friends of his at Yale are cooking two turkeys and a boatload of Ghanaian food. He invites me, but I have to think about it: I promised the Fergies I'd come for Thanksgiving; in fact, I promised them that I would ride the train over yesterday. They must be worried. My mother must be worried. I have twenty-two missed calls and five messages that I haven't checked.

"Should I go?" I ask him.

Wisdom shrugs and says, as if it's no big deal at all, "I could also come with you. We could do Thanksgiving with my friends or with your family. Or we could each do our own thing. You decide. I'll go back to my apartment and get ready and rent the car and come back here. At least I'll give you a ride to Jersey City."

I agree, though I'm not feeling festive at all, not feeling like leaving this apartment, definitely not wanting him to leave just when I'm starting to feel comfortable with his most recent, much smoother reentry into my life. I stretch. I rise, planning to take a long hot shower while Wisdom is gone, but on my way to the bathroom, I pass my laptop and see that I have a new message from the financial aid office. The subject line reads, "Urgent: Your Impending Ineligibility for Federal Aid."

"Shit," I say, and begin to worry that if I go to the Fergies', if I call my mother back, if I do anything but hide under my blankets, all three of them will sense my impending ineligibility for federal aid, a.k.a. my impending failure to make something of myself, a.k.a. my impending expulsion from the club of worthy first-generation sons and daughters of Ghanaian immigrants. Uncle Fergie will ask how school is, and I won't know how to answer. Or better yet, Auntie Fergie will open the conversation by telling me that so-and-so's daughter heard from the auntie of her best friend's son—who's by chance from the same hometown as my mother and happens to work in my school's registrar office—that I'm flunking out of grad school. At the same time, if I don't go, I fear that the Fergies and my mother will begin to suspect that I'm hiding something from them.

"Maybe," I say aloud, "everything would be easier if I don't hide from them."

I sit down in front of my computer, but instead of opening the email about my financial aid status, I return to the draft I started a few days ago, the message to my dean and graduate advisor. I inhale, exhale, and inhale again.

> *Thank you both for allowing me to continue in the program as a part-time student. I feel honored that you have enough belief in my academic capabilities to give me a second chance. However, upon further introspection, I've realized*

I decide to freewrite, to type whatever words come to mind.

> *Thank you both for allowing me to continue in the program as a part-time student. I feel honored that you have enough belief in my academic capabilities to give me a second chance. However, upon further introspection, I've realized I need more self-reflection to solve the problem of my indirection. In the interest of self-protection, I've drowned myself in circumspection—*

I laugh at myself. Maybe I should tell them I'm dropping out to become a slam poet.

Maybe I should tell them I'm dropping out?

When Wisdom returns from retrieving the car and asks what I want to do, I tell him.

"I want you to come to the Fergies' place for Thanksgiving."

He readily agrees. We find the directions on the internet and Wisdom copies them down in handwriting that seems immaculate only if compared to mine.

"You get to navigate; I get to drive," he says with a grin, handing me the directions.

He's no doubt recalling our first and only road trip; four months into our relationship, we attempted to drive to Boston to visit one of my high school friends, but because I drove tentatively and he navigated shortsightedly, we got so lost that we ended up making a series of pointless loops that landed us back in New York City after two hours had passed. Laughing, we finally returned the rental car and paid for the train fare instead. "Is this really a good idea? I'm kind of surprised you want to do this. Should I feel nervous about meeting your auntie and uncle?" he asks as an afterthought, as we're heading out the door. "Am I dressed okay?"

Wisdom has showered and dressed himself in crisp blue jeans and a sweater with wide green and blue stripes running across it. I can see the damp collar of a blue T-shirt peeking out from his sweater's neckline. He smells like cornstarch baby powder, but also like aftershave.

"You shouldn't feel nervous about it, I should," I say. I've tried my best, dressed in gray pants but also a bright red African print blouse that Auntie Fergie had a seamstress sew for me a couple of years ago when she visited Ghana. The blouse came with a matching pencil skirt, but wouldn't it be tempting fate to dress myself up as I had in my dream? Besides, I don't want to look like I'm trying too hard to please them.

"Should we bring something?" he asks, knowing already that the answer is yes.

The dull ache in my head sharpens as he continues, "We really should have thought about this in advance. But I guess it was a spur of the moment thing. Us. Going to your family's place. Together." The way he's angled his head now, chin slightly down, makes him seem shy.

"It's not even a big deal like that at all. My aunt and uncle aren't even blood relatives. They wouldn't be judging you."

But won't they be? I think as Wisdom and I walk out to the car. He seems to stop worrying about meeting the Fergies, starts instead to converse about the friends he would have visited if we weren't going to Jersey, saying that I should really meet them sometime. High school mates, he calls them, and though I've always found those Britishisms that mark my Wisdom's speech endearing, I feel a pressure building in my head that makes it difficult for me to concentrate on his words. Because he's right, the Fergies *will* judge him and also me. Not that I can imagine many things they might find wrong with him: he's a budding doctor. He's well-dressed and holds a pleasant conversation, his eyes clear and alert; his dimples will charm Auntie and his penchant for discussing soccer—football—and African politics will impress Uncle. In fact, showing up with Wisdom can only help me, right, as I will seem special for knowing him. Well, I've always felt special for knowing him, even if not for the superficial reasons that the Fergies will notice first.

But there's also the fact of Wisdom's maleness. The fact that I'm bringing a boy, a man, means something, even if I don't know what it means (are he and I back together?) and even if they don't know what it means (regardless of whether we're long-lost lovers or lab partners, I'm going to walk into their home as a woman with a man on her arm). No matter how good Wisdom seems, or how well the two of us might seem together (do we seem good together, or do we seem like the mess that we usually are?), I'm still a girl with a man and that might strike them as an unsavory situation. *I'm twenty-four.* Still, I'm a girl with a man, what am I doing with a man, how close am I to this man, and what the heck, didn't I almost bring a different man? Sure, I asked the Fergies if I could bring a friend named Daniel Cobblah, and I'm going to introduce Wisdom to them as a friend, but to them, friend will sound like a euphemism for boyfriend. All of my aunties and uncles have forever inquired about my love life with the words, "Mercy Akosua, do you have a *friend*?"

I'm twenty-four. Still a girl trying to uphold her good girlness, and it occurs to me that everyone in the world will know that I'm bringing Wisdom to the Fergies' place for Thanksgiving. Maybe Auntie will tell a friend who'll tell a friend who'll tell my father. Somehow, he will hear. Maybe he's got spies scoping out my every move.

Maybe somehow my father will be there, I think, and from the eerie silence in the car—I'm only now noticing the eerie silence in the car—I know that I'm creeping Wisdom out. Is it possible that he and I are so connected that he's privy to the thoughts coursing through my gray matter?

Wisdom, I notice, has pulled over at the side of a road, in front of a diner.

"You're hungry?" I ask.

He's turned and staring at me gape-mouthed, his left arm draped across the steering wheel, his right arm gripping the parking brake. "You're talking to yourself."

"What?"

"I was inviting you to spend New Year's with my friends since I'm not going to hang out with them today, and you started mumbling something about being twenty-four, and now, what's this about your father? Is that what this is? He's going to be there?"

"No, no. I don't think so. I mean, he's not even . . . he's not even that close to my uncle or anything . . ." I squeeze my eyes shut. "Maybe we should eat at this diner, actually."

"You don't look like yourself." He shakes his head, jams his glasses further back on his nose with a forefinger. "This wasn't a good idea. You don't really want to go to your aunt and uncle's, do you? This is the kind of situation you're most uncomfortable in. Are we going because you think your father's going to be here?"

"*No*," I say, and scowl. "You can be such a know-it-all, are you aware of that?"

"Here we go."

"No, no. We're not 'here we going,' I'm not picking a fight." I want to lay my hand on his cheek, but instead I settle for his knee. "I don't mean to fight. Sorry. I guess I don't feel that great, though. I've been inside mostly for the past few days, you know. I guess I'm just feeling a little off-kilter out here. But yeah, you're right, we should have brought something. Maybe let's find a pie. I'm sure Auntie can't make pie."

"I thought you wanted to eat something at this diner." The evenness of his tone doesn't mask his exasperation; in fact, it's the mark of his exasperation.

"Let's keep driving and see if we can find a nice bakery on the way," I say and offer a smile, squeeze his hand. Sensing the need for generosity, I lean over and kiss his cheek. "Don't worry. I'm not trying to fight. I was just thinking too hard."

"Oh." Now he grins. "*Oh*, I see. This, my Akosua, is finally feeling affectionate? Did *you* really kiss *me*, shy girl?"

"Stop it, don't tease me . . ."

He lets go of the steering wheel and parking brake and now he's drawing my face to his and kissing me again, and suddenly I don't feel like we're the guy and girl who belong at an auntie and uncle's house, not right now, the places his hands seem to want to go, the fact that I don't seem to want to stop him, and as he casts aside Ella's red scarf and reaches for my coat zipper—again, the coat's in the way, though this time I feel quite hot beneath it—I feel a vibration on my lap that is unrelated to the situation and then from inside my purse, my phone begins to sing the special ring that indicates my mother's calling from her cell phone, which she only uses during an emergency.

He detaches himself from me and pulls my phone from the front compartment of my purse. "It says 'Mom Calling,'" he announces in a hoarse voice.

I realize that my headache almost disappears when he's touching me; so perhaps my pains are purely emotional and not at all medical, and I feel good that I'll have something positive to tell her, that I'm actually doing fine.

My mother. My mommy. I take the phone from his hands and answer it.

I breathe in. "Hello?"

"Akosua. *Tso, tso, tso,* shame on you."

"I know, Mommy, I'm sorry."

"Do you know how much I have called? Your auntie and uncle, too?" Her voice reaches a level of shrill I hadn't known she could achieve.

"I know, Mom."

"Well, did you have to go to the hospital? For your head?"

"No. No. I just . . . I got caught up in some things . . ." It occurs to me that maybe I shouldn't have been ignoring my mother's calls, how lonely she could be in her Canada condominium, alone for Thanksgiving.

"I'm sorry, Mom. Are you okay? Have you been okay?"

"Of course, except that I have been worried sick about you. I hope that getting caught up in some things means that you've been studying hard and are on the track to your—"

We say the letters together. "P . . . h . . . D."

I laugh. I manage to. A weak one. Next to me, Wisdom grins because he can hear our conversation. "I'm not sure, Mom. I'm trying to, like, figure out, you know . . ."

"Okay, okay. Later, *dzinam.* Listen, are you going to your Auntie and Uncle Fergie for Thanksgiving dinner or not? Are you bringing your friend Daniel? They told me you asked if you could, but then no one has heard from you in ages."

My throat is dry and I can't squeeze the words out. I fear that if I make a sound she'll hear in my voice everything that went wrong with "my friend Daniel," and how everything is my fault.

"Hello? Akosua. Tell me whether you're going. I have to be somewhere."

"To be somewhere?"

My mother sighs, exasperated. "Yes, *to be somewhere*. It's Thanksgiving, a day on which people share a meal with other people, unless they are like my mixed-up daughter Akosua."

"Where are you going?"

My mother does that same sigh again, informs me that she is going to drive across the border to Detroit and up to Bloomfield, Michigan, to have dinner with Auntie Irina and Uncle Ossei.

"Do you remember them?"

I do, but only from old pictures: the couple always dressed in their fanciest Ghanaian attire.

"They are having a get-together, like old times," she says. "Some new West African folks will be there, too. We want to welcome the families who have recently moved here and are celebrating their first Thanksgiving. You know that is normally Auntie Gifty and Uncle Akrofi's job." I can hear the smile in her voice when mentioning them, her best friends, my father's best friend. "But they are not in town. Do you remember their daughter, she's now—"

"Yes, Mom, she lives in Princeton with some PhD genius husband and she's gonna be a lawyer. Uncle Fergie already told me, so you don't have to say it."

"*Tso*! I don't hear from you for days and days and this is the attitude I have to hear?"

"Well, you don't have to rub it in that everyone's doing all this stuff I'm not doing."

"What are you talking about? You are in graduate school, aren't you? You will have your master's degree soon, and then you will continue and earn your PhD, so I am not—"

"You totally brought them up to rub it in my face."

"Rub what in your face?"

"Never mind, we need to look for a pie to take to Fergie's place."

"We?"

"Wisdom and I. We're in the car. I have to go."

My mother clicks her tongue. "I guess it was a blessing not to speak to you on the phone all these days. You are speaking to me so disrespectfully, and on Thanksgiving, a family holiday? I was waiting and waiting to talk to you, and when I finally do . . . ?" She sighs. "Say hello to your aunties and uncles. Goodbye."

She hangs up the phone.

Wisdom starts the engine without a word.

"*What?* Don't even say anything, she was totally about to start pressuring me about grad school, on Thanksgiving of all days."

"Come on, that's what parents do. That's especially what *Ghanaian* parents do."

"Oh. Yes. The expert speaks again. Why don't you share the rest of your knowledge of what it's like to be the child of a Ghanaian parent?"

"Ah!" He bangs a clenched fist against his knee. "You're always looking for a fight, Akosua. Please."

"I'm sorry. I'm on edge because I don't feel well."

"Oh, okay," he says, but in a voice that I can't read.

I can't tell if he's mocking me, his darling hypochondriac. I know that's what he's thinking, that I'm faking it, and part of me doesn't know whether I'm faking it, this hurt in my head, weakness in my limbs, nausea surging in my belly as if I'm floating out on a rolling sea alone in a leaky boat. But I'm not: I'm in the car with Wisdom and he's driving because (for better or worse?) he cares for me in the unfailing manner of many beloved people around me, in this unwarranted way that I don't understand.

I awaken when Wisdom pulls the car into the parking lot of the Fergies' apartment building.

He gently nudges my cheek with his knuckles. "Are you up, sleepyhead?"

"Yup."

"So much for navigator, you slept the whole way," he says, but he's smiling good-naturedly.

"I'm sorry."

"You missed the hordes of cranky Thanksgiving travelers clogging up the highway. And you missed this." With a flourish, Wisdom brings forth from the backseat a brown paper bag and shows me the gourmet lattice-crusted apple pie he must have bought from one of the fancy grocery stores he's embarrassed to admit he frequents. "It's organic, too." And then he rolls his eyes to hide his pride in the purchase.

I heap on the praise, telling him that Auntie and Uncle will love it.

We walk up to the apartment complex hand in hand, not letting go of each other until we're off the elevator and in front of the Fergies' door, where we know it'll do no good for them to see us touching.

Already, though it's barely one o'clock, I smell jollof rice and the pungent aroma of palm oil frying some meat, maybe beef, maybe goat or chicken for a stew. Rollicking highlife music wafts through the door.

"Oh, your auntie can cook, I can tell already." Wisdom licks his lips and presses his finger to the doorbell.

I barely have a moment to pat my hair down before the door swings open. Auntie Fergie greets us with her hands on her hips, face cracked open in a wide smile.

"Akosua, eh! We were waiting all week to hear from you, silly girl." She hugs me tightly, turns to Wisdom, hugs him, too. "You must be Daniel Cobblah. Welcome, welcome. Please, come inside."

Auntie bustles into the apartment ahead of us, going to the kitchen, I'm sure. Wisdom takes hold of my arm, holds me back for a moment.

"You didn't tell them we were coming? And you didn't tell them I'm not Daniel?"

"We only decided this morning that we were coming . . ."

"I thought you'd have called while I was out renting the car. I was gone for nearly two hours."

As we walk through the short hall that leads to the living room, Wisdom holds his head high and stiff, annoyed. I'm going to apologize to him, squeeze his elbow and vow to be more reliable on future road trips, but then I catch a glimpse of a figure sitting on the living room couch and realize that Wisdom and I are not the only guests.

I know it's not him, but it easily could be: the slow-moving smile, round face, glasses. The now receding hairline with its soft-looking graying hair. The slender frame impeccable in a professorial blue dress shirt and gray pants.

"My, my. Could it be?" He rises to his feet and booms in his rich, deep voice, "The daughter of Dr. and Mrs. Kofi Agbe, right here before my eyes? Akosua!"

"Uncle Akrofi."

I speak his name in a quiet voice and offer him a restrained smile, but when he moves to shake my hand I find myself embracing him, hard. I am sure in his arms, I feel righted. Probably more than I would feel if it had turned out to be my father and not his best friend sitting on the Fergies' couch. A flash of heat assails my face; I let go of him only to bring one hand to my cheek and ensure that my face is still dry.

His two firm pats on my back suggest I should consider the embrace completed. I let go of him but don't move too far from where he stands.

"I must have last seen you—when?"

"Ten years ago," I reply too quickly. "Or something like it, I guess."

I study his face and find hardly a crease, really no sign that he has aged except the silver hair. Perhaps my father looks the same, this unchanged, this handsome; perhaps Uncle Akrofi could tell me exactly how my father looks.

Auntie Fergie and Auntie Gifty emerge from the kitchen, holding glasses of water for Wisdom and me. Uncle Fergie follows them, a bottle of beer in hand.

"Hello, hello, hello, my baby." Auntie Gifty embraces me firmly but quickly, kisses my cheek. "Akosua, it is so nice to see you. Last week or so, I saw your mommy at Bible Study, and she just bragged and bragged about how smart and beautiful you've grown. Here I see she's correct. In fact, she is more than correct!"

I try to smile, but my legs feel unsteady; Auntie Gifty hasn't aged either, though her hair looks so unnaturally black that it must be dyed or a wig. Did she just say that my mother still attends Ghanaian Bible Study?

"And who is this young man?" Auntie Gifty turns to regard Wisdom, who's standing next to me but might as well have been in Timbuktu for the past few moments. He looks like he'd rather be in Timbuktu, the smile plastered to his face a demonstration of what I must look like when I'm feeling awkward around too many aunties and uncles sizing me up.

"This young man is Akosua's . . ." Auntie Fergie smiles and looks at me expectantly.

"My friend Wisdom," I say. "Um, not Daniel, Auntie Fergie. Not him."

"Oh, okay. I see. Daniel couldn't come, so you brought Wisdom in his place."

"No." I shake my head as emphatically as I can. "Not in Daniel's place. Wisdom's in his own place. This is his place. He's the one I brought," I stammer, and though my collection of aunties and uncles all cast puzzled looks in my direction, I know that Wisdom knows what I mean and values these words I've spoken.

"It is very nice to meet you all," Wisdom finally says, offering his hand to everyone, though Auntie Fergie insists on hugging him again. "Happy Thanksgiving, everyone."

Wisdom's words seem to wake everyone up into their proper roles: both uncles start in on Wisdom, asking him about his studies, whisking him away to the den. The aunties compliment my outfit and I compliment theirs, Auntie Gifty in a royal blue dress with silver trim, Auntie Fergie wrapped in a gold skirt and blouse that seems too much for this occasion and definitely too much for the kitchen, which is where we head to finish cooking the meal.

"Oh, delicious, a pie," Auntie Fergie coos when she sees Wisdom's pride and joy, but both aunties don't look at the pie for long.

Apple pie, I fear, will only interest Wisdom and me. Auntie Gifty has brought along her famous bread and Auntie Fergie has plans to make kele wele, spicy plantain fried with onions and ginger and pepper that has always struck me more as an appetizer or side dish than dessert but that everyone else will no doubt favor over boring old apple pie.

Standing in the kitchen feels like standing in the oven: the heat suffocates me, and the smell of various foods cooking churns the acid in my stomach. It's almost too much, every burner on the stove occupied by a bubbling pot, the oven stuffed with a turkey, a ham, and baked fish, the counters covered with bowls and trays of side dishes African and American.

"Okay, Akosua," Auntie Fergie says, pressing her palm against my shoulder. "The jollof rice will be done soon. We have all the meat in the oven. We have made the macaroni and cheese, the cranberry-whatever-that-is jelly is out of the cans, we made stuffed crabs, the beef and spinach stew, the fried yams and tatale, and the groundnut soup for the fufu. Do you know what we need now?"

"No, Auntie, I'm not sure. What do we need?"

She takes me by the shoulders and shakes me gently, though it's not really gentle enough for the uneven state I'm in. "The fufu itself, you silly girl. The last time you were here, you expressed an interest in learning how to make fufu. So come. I will teach you."

At Auntie Fergie's instruction, I wash my hands and slip an apron over my outfit. She has pulled off her blouse and stands ready to cook in her bra and an undershirt; Aunty Gifty slides an apron on, too, and begins to inspect the plantain she'll use for dessert.

"Really, my dear, here in an American kitchen, there is no point in making fufu the traditional way." Aunt Fergie pulls out a blue box of fufu powder, and I think that this isn't going to be any kind of lesson at all, just her showing me the easy way to prepare this West African staple: boil water, add the powder, stir over heat until the mixture thickens to the consistency of a giant dumpling. But she continues, "Powders like these are a shortcut. You know, if your Wisdom likes fufu once a week or more as my Fergie does, you need a fast way to prepare it."

"At home," Auntie Gifty jumps in, referring not to Michigan but to Ghana, "you cut cassava and plantain into chunks and boil it for a long time. Then the cooked cassava and plantains are added piece by piece into a big wooden mortar and pounded very carefully with a big stick, tall enough that you must stand on your feet to pound it."

"*Very* carefully," Auntie Fergie repeats. "One person cannot do it alone. Two people must do it. One to feed the chunks of food into the mortar, one to crush the cassava.

"You sweat. Oh, how you sweat," Gifty laughs. "And it goes right into the food."

"At first, all you hear is the sound of the pestle hitting the wood. Knock, knock. But as water is added, as the dough is turned and kneaded, there's a different sound. The person doing the pounding slows down, so that the pestle only touches the dough, the pestle going in and out of the food as it becomes thick and smooth, and instead of 'knock, knock,' it sings, 'fu-fu, fu-fu,' as the air trapped inside the dough tries to escape." Auntie Fergie claps her hands together with a flourish. "And when it is just smooth enough, no bumps or lumps, you are done. You add your soup or stew and you eat and while you eat, you sweat out the same sweat of the people who pounded the fufu in the first place.

"And maybe your mommy never told you, and perhaps you never learned in school, but when slaves came to this country from Africa, they brought with them this staple, fufu. And it became hoecakes, cornbread, grits. Black American Southern food, it all came from this history of preparing fufu, it is all the same idea but modified for different situations. It all came from our practice of pounding roots with care until they form something of such overwhelming sustenance that you must sleep after you eat it."

Auntie Fergie pauses, exhales deeply. She's never spoken to me for so long in English; she's usually speaking at me, around me, about me. She waves the box of blue powder in my face. "So even though this is not the traditional way of making it, it's okay! It's still authentic. And it still puts a smile on my Fergie's face." To my surprise, she stores the blue box in the cabinet again. "Now since today is a special occasion, we can indulge ourselves and make it from scratch with real roots."

It's still an American compromise. Instead of the mortar and pestle, we use a food processor. Instead of cassava and plantain, we use boiled potatoes and yams. Auntie Fergie shows me how to mash the roots with a wooden spoon, how to process the mixture long enough to remove lumps but fast enough to keep the fufu thick.

"Now you can teach your mommy the next time she comes to visit," Auntie Fergie says when we've formed the fufu into large balls and covered them until we're ready to eat.

"What?"

"Everybody knows your mommy can cook anything but fufu." Fergie shrugs. "Your grandmother never taught her. That's why she never taught you. Her mommy wanted her to be a modern girl, only time for books, no time for pounding fufu. But it's okay. Now the modern American girl can teach her modern Ghanaian mommy all about the tradition."

As I sidle up to Auntie Gifty, who offers to teach me how to make tatale, I'm feeling weak-limbed, but I'm also aware of the invigoration of blood coursing through my veins. Perhaps it's because I miss my mother: I feel weak because I wish she were here, yet I feel thrilled at the possibility that I'm having a good time without her, that I don't always need to hide behind her when I'm with these people, my family.

The crystal plates, bowls, and goblets lined up and down the Fergie's dining room table gleam, the sparkles dancing. I don't know if the heat from the kitchen's still affecting me. I wipe my brow.

Wisdom, seated at my left, discreetly presses his hand against my knee under the table. When I look at him, he nods in a way intended to offer reassurance, but the glassiness of his red eyes doesn't provide much comfort. I'm worried that my uncles, who pressured him into drinking akpeteshie while they flipped in between soccer and football in the den, might have gotten Wisdom drunk.

Uncle Akrofi, though, pours himself a shot of the very potent, distilled palm wine, even though my aunts have placed bottles of champagne on the table. He glances at me, a smile playing on his lips. "Akosua. Don't think you and your aunties should be excluded from this custom. Akosua, you're a big lady now. Try some."

My aunties laugh, but I don't move my glass when he pours me a shot with a fairly shaky hand.

"Oh, Uncle, I'm not so sure about that," Wisdom speaks up, smiling, though the crease in his forehead shows he's actually worried. "Your niece here is a lightweight."

"Uh-oh, I think the boy is worried that his lady might outdo him. Wisdom here is already under the table," Uncle Akrofi laughs, and everyone else joins him, except for me. I'm confused about whether I'm really expected to drink this rubbing alcohol he's placed before me.

"Of course you don't have to drink it if you don't want to," Uncle Akrofi says, as if he's read my mind. "I'm only teasing you."

"Yes, leave it to your uncles to take care of it if you can't," Auntie Gifty says, and she fills all of our glasses with champagne.

My aunties rise to their feet, reaching for the serving spoons. But before Auntie Fergie can gather some slices of turkey to heap on her husband's plate, Uncle Akrofi holds his hands up to stop her.

"Now, now. Madam Fergie, please. I must propose here that the women receive their food first."

Auntie Fergie chuckles, still poised to serve Uncle Fergie. "Oh, please, Akrofi. Gifty, why does your husband like such theatrics?"

"Yes, why the theatrics when I'm hungry?" Uncle Fergie adds good-naturedly, but one hand clutches the edge of his plate, the other grasps his fork, and he's trained his eyes on the turkey his wife's ready to spear for him.

"Sister Fergie, wasn't it you and Gifty and my little one who cooked all of this food for us?" Uncle takes the fork from her, waves her out of the way. "Sit. Go on. White meat or dark meat?"

"Well, if I'm to be treated like a queen today"—Auntie Fergie casts a glance at her husband—"why should I pick? I'll have both!"

Everyone laughs, except me; I am preoccupied with the warmth that rose to my cheeks as soon as Uncle Akrofi called me his little one. I open my mouth, wanting to ask him, *Do you adore me as I adore you, and is it because I remind you of him?* But everyone is moving while I'm thinking: now Uncle Fergie has risen to his feet, too, heaping ham onto Auntie Gifty's plate, and though he grumbles under his breath, I know his objections are mostly for show.

Wisdom looks at me and reaches for the serving spatula. "Want some fried fish?"

I shake my head, reach for another serving spoon, and scoop a small mound of turkey stuffing onto my plate. Wisdom picks a fat hunk of fish for himself and I am glad. It doesn't seem right for me to expect him to serve me food right now, given the many other things he's done for me. After all, he's here with me, with my family, despite the constant barrage of mixed signals he must perceive from me.

Wisdom, after all, is the hero of this act. He tried to beat Daniel to a pulp. He returned to my apartment to check on me. And once my uncles have placed mountains of food on the women's plates and their own, Wisdom also saves me from having to endure a conversation in a language I don't know.

Auntie Gifty says grace half in English and half in Ewe. I understand most of it, especially since it's nothing different from the sort of prayer my mother gives on any special occasion: we thank God for the food we're about to eat, we pray for peace, good health, and prosperity for all, we thank our ancestors, our fathers and mothers before us, for their unending guidance.

But after we say amen and dig in, Auntie Fergie says, "Sister Gifty, it is too bad that your Adoma and her husband could not join us for dinner."

"They are having Thanksgiving dinner with his friends and professors," Gifty says, shrugging his shoulders. "They will come and visit you tomorrow. We can have a second Thanksgiving tomorrow."

"Sure, I suppose. But what is this with kids not wanting to enjoy the holidays with their families, eh? If they were having dinner with his family, maybe I would excuse it, but a professor?" Auntie Fergie sucks her teeth. "Wisdom, *nukata mele akpedada ve aza dumu kple dziola wo o?*"

All heads at the table swivel toward Wisdom.

Mouth closed, he finishes chewing before answering, "My parents still live in Ghana. I'll probably go home to visit next summer."

"Next summer? *Tso! Nukata maayi afeme efedzi o?*"

Wisdom glances at me, then looks back at Auntie and answers in English, "Well, Auntie, because of my medical school schedule, I won't have as much time around Christmas this year. But—"

"Wait a minute, aren't you an Ewe? You don't speak Ewe?" Auntie Fergie cuts in.

Wisdom nods politely. "Yes, Auntie, I do." Again he lays his hand on my knee beneath the table. "I'm feeling rusty tonight. Maybe it's the akpeteshie. But as I was saying, I'm very pleased to spend the holiday with Akosua's family. It's almost like being at home with mine."

"Except yours won't get you drunk, right?" Uncle Akrofi quips.

"Shame on you, don't tease the boy," his wife says.

"Gifty, my love, he's not a boy, he's a man! Look at how he eats his fufu, just like a man. Our Akosua must be a good girl, because Wisdom has quite an appetite. You know what they say, if a woman were like fufu, a man could get to know her before he married her."

And everyone laughs again, of course, of course they do, because Uncle Akrofi has that effect on people. I can't laugh, partially because I'm not sure I comprehend the nuance of the proverb, partially because I think I do, but mostly because I'm thinking of something else. I try to place my father as he might look now at a seat at this table. I try to picture him throwing his head back and laughing at his best friend's dirty jokes. But I can conjure only his grinning mouthful of teeth, a flash of pink tongue. I try to hear the sound he makes, but it's not so much a sound as a vibration in my heart, which doesn't feel like a heart in this instant as much as it feels like a hole through which everyone slips, a hole that will widen the longer Uncle Akrofi sits in my presence.

Thanks to Wisdom's white lie, everyone speaks in English for me, but I cannot listen, I cannot hold onto the threads of conversation they weave. Because every conversation is a strip of kente cloth or a sprawling American quilt, isn't it? Auntie Fergie and her constant chatter make up the basic building blocks, the pattern most repeated, the swatches of fabric on which the entire quilt depends. Auntie Gifty's the rare patch of velvet, rarely speaking, speaking softly. Uncle Fergie, the red, gold, green, black star that makes this quilt authentic; though he says little, every word he speaks declares, *I am an African man*. Uncle Akrofi, of course, appears in bursts of bold colors, flashes of beauty across the cloth canvas, and Wisdom trims the edges, not quite in the pattern but still a part of the narrative.

I, however, am remote, am a book or a spoon or a piece of broken glass on a nearby chair, am an object that could never fit into a sturdy weave. I sit on the outside. I see, I envision, I revise. Won't I wrap myself in the memory of these moments and words, or better yet, unravel the story and reweave the fragments into another likeness, call it memory, call it history, even though it's nothing but an approximation?

Under the table, Wisdom nudges me with his toe. "Akosua, your uncle..."

"Oh!" I blurt, and automatically reach for the dish of food closest to me, the macaroni and cheese, but the Pyrex shoots sharp heat through my palms and I immediately let go of the bowl. The table jolts, knocking over the shot of akpeteshie Uncle Akrofi left for me on the table. "Sorry, sorry!" I wave my hands in the air to stop the pain, then press them against my cool glass of water.

Beginning to clean up my mess, Wisdom says, "It's okay. I startled you, huh? You didn't hear, your uncle was asking you something."

Uncle Akrofi smiles warmly at me. "I was just asking how school is going. Your mother says you're following in your daddy's footsteps and going into academia."

"Did she?" *My daddy's footsteps. Did she say it just like that, or did he add the part about my father?* I glance at Auntie Gifty, who talks to my mother more regularly than he probably does. She would know; she could tell me if my mother ever speaks about my father.

"History, right?" Uncle Akrofi asks. He looks at me, his eyes attentive despite the alcohol and large quantities of food. Everyone's on their second plate; I'm still picking at my first. "Tell me, Akosua, why did you choose to study history? Kofi was always such a history nut. I think he only did engineering because it was expected of him; he would have just studied world history if he had a chance."

I hold my breath, hands still gripping my glass for dear life, as if water could steady me. I'm expecting him to go on about my father, but he's looking at me, and I realize that he really wants to hear my answer to his question. I feel the light pressure of Wisdom's foot on mine. I want to cry, maybe because he's offering reassurance, maybe because Uncle Akrofi cares to hear from me, maybe because I wish Uncle Akrofi wanted to do nothing but babble on about my father.

"Well, I wanted to study history . . ." I shrug, too tired for spinning yarns. "To be honest, I just *enjoy* learning about history, and I didn't know what else to do. I'm not really a good academic, not a history scholar at all. Maybe a history enthusiast."

"I'm sure you underestimate yourself," Auntie Gifty says kindly.

At the same time, her husband chuckles. "Beautiful. It is nice to hear the honest truth. Kofi would be proud. At least the one I used to know. He's been out of touch, as you know . . . He did contact me when he returned to the States, but I haven't had the chance to call him to plan a visit before your Auntie Gifty and I return to Michigan. It is a difficult thing, to keep in touch with an errant friend. Ah, Kofi. But yes, he would be proud of a budding history scholar."

Do you really think so? Did he ask about me when he contacted you? But instead, I blurt, "Not that I won't necessarily get my PhD in history—"

"Don't get into that PhD business until you are certain," Uncle Fergie speaks up now, shaking his head. He raises his half-eaten turkey drumstick, wags it at me for emphasis. "I see too many students suffering. If you're not truly invested, it is not worth the effort. Wait until you are certain. And if you change your mind, that is okay. As they say, you change your steps according to the change in the rhythm of the drum."

"And don't forget to think about when to fit in your family. I know your mother wants grandchildren," Auntie Fergie says, glancing from me to Wisdom, "and so do I, so you must think about these things. It takes up so much time, doing your own research, grading papers. You should see, your uncles both have books and papers spread all over the place in the den. The work never ends. But you must put family first. Have you thought about these things?"

"Um . . ." I pick up my water glass, bring it to my lips, and drink as fast as I can. I think as fast as I can about how I can steer the conversation back to the topic of my father's possible pride in me.

"I read an article," Wisdom jumps in, "about the dilemma women face in terms of balancing marriage and career and family. Pressure from the older generation is a huge factor . . ."

The conversation continues without me. I realize I'm out of practice; I haven't spent time around large groups of people in a while. My brain tells my ears not to listen, just to hear the words and scan them for any mention of my father, my father who is so close (in the embodiment of Uncle Akrofi, in the city of New York) yet so far. He is nowhere, he is nothing but a word that clings to my tongue.

12

Wisdom and I get stuck washing the dishes. Rather, he offers to help my aunties wash the dishes and Auntie Fergie laughs and says that they planned to leave them in the sink until morning but that he can tackle them alone if he really feels the inclination. During dinner, both of my aunties gave in and had a shot or two of akpeteshie, and that in addition to the champagne has turned them especially festive. The last we saw, my aunties and uncles were in the living room dancing to highlife music and laughing. The scene reminds me of the old photos of the parties they used to have back when everyone lived in Michigan, back when everyone lived in Detroit, back when everyone was starting off humble in America.

But Wisdom and I don't fit into those pictures any more than we fit in with fifty-or-sixty-something-year-old drunk relatives, so we don't mind holing up in the kitchen and cleaning.

Wisdom dabs a puff of soap suds on the tip of my nose. "There. Now you look perfect."

I try to put my fingers in the sink—I want to cover his thick eyebrows with soap suds—but he knocks his hip against mine to thwart me. His action reminds me how liquid my legs feel, and I stumble away from him a bit.

"Whoa, whoa. Are you sure you didn't drink any of that alcohol?"

"Probably inhaling it was enough to get me intoxicated," I say. I stop and lean my elbows against the kitchen sink, but offer him a smile.

"I'm having a lot more fun than I expected. Your family's cool." Wisdom's mostly sober now, as he refused to touch any more alcohol.

His eyelids look heavy, though, and I can tell from the way he keeps stretching that he's feeling sated from all the food and drink.

"They are, aren't they?" I raise my head, and despite the dizzy, hazy way I feel, continue to dry the dishes Wisdom has washed by hand, the ones too fragile for the dishwasher.

"You're acting a little funny, though. Are you feeling okay?"

I don't look at him, I act like I care very much about making this crystal butter dish shine. "Yeah."

"It's your aunt and uncle from Michigan, huh?"

"He's my dad's best friend, that's all."

"Oh. I gathered that they meant something to each other, that he means a lot to you."

"Not really. I don't care. It's a little awkward, that's all."

Wisdom puts down his sponge, wipes his hands against his pants to dry them. "Sweets, you hugged the man for dear life. I don't know if anyone else noticed, but I did. I saw your eyes and how you almost cried." He touches my cheek. "You can tell me."

I let him keep his hand there, but only for a moment before I take his hand in mine and hold it, let it go. "Don't worry, I'm feeling tired, that's all."

A gust of air from Wisdom's nose blasts my face as he exhales. "I don't understand. Why can't you just admit you want to hear things about your father?"

I press my index finger over my lips. "Hush, I don't want the adults to hear."

"We *are* adults. You seem to forget."

"Well, what am I supposed to do, monopolize the conversation and bring him up at every chance? No one wants that, least of all me."

Uncle Akrofi's baritone filters into the kitchen; he's singing along to the music.

Wisdom turns my body around so that we stand and face each other. "You had so many chances, Akosua, it came up naturally in conversation, and you could have just asked. Anything about your father. Anything."

"Hush. I cannot talk about this anymore."

Wisdom remains silent. He leans over and kisses my forehead. Then he removes the dish towel from my hands. "Are you sure you're okay? It's not your head, is it? Maybe you need to take a break from the dishes."

"Of course not. Besides, I can take care of myself."

Softly he says, "I know you can. But when you can't, I want to help." He wipes the soap suds off my nose. "Is that okay, honey?"

I nod. "Yes, it's okay. Thank you, Wisdom. But. I can take care of myself enough to know I'm fine to wash the dishes."

We finish together, though once we're done, I know enough to ask the Fergies if I can lie down in their guest room, because I do feel like someone has drained all the water from my body, as if I am a wilting flower.

Wisdom hovers over me as my eyes flutter open; he has come to say goodnight. While I slept, he hung out in the living room with my aunties and uncles a bit more, sharing memories from Ghana.

"It was fun," Wisdom whispers, sliding his fingertips along the nape of my neck. "I wish you had been awake for it."

He tells me the Fergies have insisted that we spend the night, since it's so late and Wisdom's so exhausted, and, anyway, if we stay, we can meet Auntie Gifty and Uncle Akrofi's daughter the following day.

"I told your aunts and uncles I'll be sleeping on the floor in here, but I think they know I won't be."

"Who says you won't be?" I joke. Though I feel like I'm moving through water, I raise my arms and wrap them around his neck, pulling him down to me. He crawls in bed beside me and, like old times, falls asleep as soon as he's fit the curve of my body into his.

But I feel restless now as his chest rises and falls against my back. Take care of yourself, Akosua. That's what everyone says. So I will. I will go to the bathroom to find some Ibuprofen for my unending headache.

Once I remove myself from Wisdom's grasp and tiptoe out of the bedroom, I realize it's later than I thought; everyone's sleeping, the Fergies' bedroom door closed, Auntie Gifty and Uncle Akrofi presumably locked into the room where my mother stayed when I hit my head. As I pass the den, I peek in, and the digital display on the television's cable box says it's after three o'clock in the morning. Uncle Fergie's computer screen lights the room an eerie blue. The desk in the den is covered with Uncle Fergie's usual papers, and as Auntie Fergie mentioned earlier, Uncle Akrofi's work is added to the mix: I see an expensive-looking leather attaché case on the desk chair. I am compelled to walk into the room and run my hand across the leather, see how soft or rough it might feel against my fingertips, but instead I back out of the room and get the painkillers from the medicine cabinet. I take two tablets, chasing them down with cold water I gather in my palm.

On my way back to bed, the glow of the computer screen draws me back into the den. Maybe I will check my email, reply to the dean's assistant. I walk to the desk chair and bend over to remove what must be Uncle Akrofi's attaché case, but instead of removing it, I open it up and look inside. The bag overflows with what looks like a stack of midterm exams for a beginning calculus course. I strain to read the names scrawled on each test, wondering what his students think of him. I wonder what my father's students think of him. Professor Agbe.

I find my hands feeling along the inside pockets of his attaché case; I find my hands stumbling upon his tablet, which isn't password protected. Now I am shamelessly caught up in this; now I am poking through his virtual address book. Here I can find my father's number; here I can find something I can use. But because I don't know what I'm doing or where to look, I end up in Uncle Akrofi's email inbox. I scroll up and down the menu, aware of the rapid rhythm of my heart. I can feel everything in this moment, each nerve in my body has awakened. The emails are mostly work related, from department heads and fellow professors, from students requesting extra help or grade changes, from his daughter.

And then I see his name: Kofi Agbe. My father sent my uncle a message only a handful of hours ago, early Thanksgiving morning.

> *Akrofi,*
>
> *Your Thanksgiving plans sound pleasant. If you do see my daughter, send her my love. Send the Fergusons my best as well. Hope to see you before you and Gifty return to Michigan. Will be out of the office for the holiday, so please call my home phone number. By the way, I saw your Adoma last month when she attended a service in Brooklyn.*
>
> *K.*

I press the email to my heart as though I can transfuse those words into my blood if I try hard enough. My father. My father. My father attends church? Since returning to the United States, he has seen Auntie Gifty's daughter, but he hasn't seen his own. I copy down his email address and begin to scroll through the inbox to see what other correspondence they might have had—am I searching for that home phone number my father mentioned? Maybe, maybe I am, how can I not, wouldn't anybody?—but I feel a presence at the door.

"Daddy?" I whirl around to greet him.

"Akosua, it's me."

Wisdom shakes his head, fast, though I cannot see his expression in the dim light of the room. "Mercy Akosua. Baby, what are you doing?"

"Nothing," I say, but he rushes over to me and sees that I'm looking at Uncle Akrofi's email, and that says it all.

"How can you tell me you're not interested in your father when here you are, snooping around for stuff about him, when it's not necessary? Ask the Fergusons. Ask your Uncle Akrofi."

"It's not that easy—"

"Ask the internet, for goodness sakes, he's a professor. I'm sure he's listed. You know how easy this could be."

"You don't get it, it's complicated, I have my mom to think about, and what other people might say . . ." I clutch the back of the desk chair, my knees feeling as if they could crumble any moment.

"You're twenty-four, Akosua. Your mother will accept that if you force her to. This isn't about her. It's about you. You don't have to hide. All you have to do is ask."

Above the noise of my heart pounding I hear the creak of a bedroom door.

"Who is there?" A voice asks softly: Uncle Fergie.

"Oh, Wisdom," I hear my voice say, and I sound so far away from myself. "I don't feel so well, I feel so, so not well."

"Come on, let's go," Wisdom beckons to me in a whisper.

But as I try to step forward, I know that I can't. I can't move my legs, and before me, Wisdom holds out his arms expectantly, his face shocked in the blue computer screen light. Rubber burns in my nostrils, stars burst and bleed against the inside of my eyelids. My brain shuts down the world. My leg muscles buckle, I cry out, I see the floor rushing up to meet me as I make my final fall.

I suppose you'd like to know where you go when you die, but I can't tell you much about where you will end up, I can only narrate my own experience, so here's where I am: a place that is presumably heaven, except the air is dark purple like God's angry fist has smashed a bruise into the sky, except I'm not sure if it's a sky or not because I can't breathe, except I'm not sure whether I can't breathe because there's no air or that

I can't breathe because I literally cannot breathe: possibly I have no nose, no mouth, no lungs. I'd presume I have no body at all, that I am just a collection of the thoughts and words that once existed in the confines of my skull; finally, I am free, free floating, I am a billion motes swirling in the dark violet of heaven, of wherever and whenever I am.

A voice descends unto me from the firmament. I sense its words more than I hear them:

—I've given up on my brain.

—What?—I try to ask the voice, but I forgot, I no longer have a mouth with which to speak, and maybe the voice didn't even descend *upon me since I'm up here with it, I'm in the firmament, I am the firmament, because when you have died, are you not one with God?*

—I've given up on my brain / I've torn the cloth to shreds / and thrown it away.

—What? Who is that?

—If you're not completely naked / wrap your beautiful robe of words / around you / and sleep.

Okay. Okay. Heaven, I think, or wherever I am, is a place of lyrical beauty. Heaven is where the poets go. They are singing to me. I am overwhelmed by a flood of understanding.

—This all makes sense to me now—I try to speak, but all that remains of my voice is a low hum.

—Sweetheart, don't think, just sleep. Be still.

Heaven must also be a place of wisdom. Not just wisdom, but Wisdom. Because he's here with me: for a moment, the purple blackness clears and a fluorescent light illuminates the plaintive wrinkles over the contours of his face.

"Be still," he says, and I feel his warm palm on my cheek, and I know now that I am not yet dead. "Go to sleep, but come back, okay? Because we want you here. *Xeyi na gbor.* Do you know what that means?"

Xeyi na gbor. Yes, Wisdom, of course, of course I know what that means. *Go and come.* A way of bidding someone "safe journey." An expression of faith, my mother once told me, because the words empower you to go, but trust that you will come back. Go and come back. Leave so that you may return. Sleep so that you may finally, truly, wake up.

∽o∽

When I wake up in the hospital, I'm alone, no one's with me. My eyes blink away the fluorescent lights overhead. I touch my arms so that they exist, I wiggle my toes so that they are real. I speak a word and immediately forget what I have said.

The final test is this: can I process what has happened? My mind recalls Wisdom standing in the dark den waving me closer to him, and then my mind recalls Wisdom touching my cheek as he stands over my hospital bed. The moments in between have broken and scattered in my mind. Maybe I could put the puzzle pieces together if I had the energy, but I do not. The muscles in my legs refuse to contract. It's like they are resting from a marathon I didn't know I'd been running.

Somewhere nearby, a toilet flushes. The bathroom door opens and Wisdom emerges. He strides over to the bed and takes my hand in one of his, massaging my knuckles.

"There she is," he says. "You're okay." He cups my face in his palms. His touch is warm. This is the final test, and I have passed it. Because he is touching me, I know I am alive.

I look at Wisdom, regarding his watery eyes.

"It was your voice that was there when I didn't have a body. You were in the firmament."

He nods, as if he really understands the nonsense I've just spoken. He says he wants to leave, to find the doctor, to find my family, but first he needs to stand here for a moment and look at me.

Chronic subdural hematoma.

My stomach lurches at the words the doctor speaks. This doctor's not at all like the one I saw at the hospital near my school, the one who diagnosed my possible post-concussion syndrome. Though he smiles, everything about this doctor's face is serious. He's letting me know I have every reason to be scared. So I am scared.

My new diagnosis feels much more concrete than the one I received when I first hit my head. I'm suffering from a subdural hematoma, or a hemorrhage. Small veins in my brain have burst and blood has built up between my brain and its outermost protective layer. The blood threatens to compress my brain, a dangerous condition. This doctor, too, shows my family, Wisdom, and me a diagram of a brain. I shudder as he takes his pen and scribbles a dark spot into the paper brain's folds. He describes the spot in a way that sounds almost quaint: a collection of old blood on the brain.

"This is my fault," I murmur, staring at the pattern of tiny blue squares that covers my hospital gown. "I didn't feel well. All those headaches. I should have done something."

"You can't blame yourself," the doctor says. "You've been having headaches, feeling weak and tired, but there was no reason to believe it was something serious. That's the dangerous part of a mild head injury. The warning signs are very subtle, sometimes undetectable. In a way, the fact that you had a seizure is a good thing, because it put up a huge red flag. Hopefully we've found the hematoma before it's gotten too critical, and we can monitor you and protect your brain from any further damage."

All of my aunties and uncles take turns holding my hand as I sleep in the hours after my seizure. I wake up only for tests and to eat. Wisdom continues to read me poetry from a book he bought at the hospital gift shop, poetry that soothes me in my sleep. He and my family wear strong faces, their grip on my hand firm and reassuring, but when the doctor says that he might have to drill a hole in my head to drain the blood and relieve the pressure, Auntie Fergie begins to cry.

"I'm sorry for crying, my baby," she says.

I manage to smile. "I don't blame you. I feel like crying, too."

Strangely, though, I don't actually feel like crying right now. I'm scared and tired, but mostly my body feels frosted, like I am half buried in a pile of snow. Uncle Fergie keeps asking me if I'm all right, jiggling my arm gently, his eyebrow furrowed in a way that tells me he's irritated, which tells me he's scared. Auntie Gifty and Auntie Fergie dab their eyes with tissue, and Uncle Akrofi continues to say things like, "Doctors. You cannot always trust these doctors," and "I have a friend at NYU's medical center, I should call him. If anyone's going to perform any procedures on you, he will know the right doctor to do it."

Finally I suggest that everyone go home and get some rest. It is too tiring for me, worrying about their sad faces, especially given that they seem to be feeling much more than I am. Auntie Fergie and Wisdom refuse to leave, though, and they take turns passing the indistinguishable hours by my bedside.

I only realize how much time has passed when Auntie Fergie enters the room to announce that Uncle Akrofi and Auntie Gifty have come to say goodbye.

"Goodbye?" I lift my head from the pillow in an attempt to sit up, but I feel myself sinking back into the bed again. It's still too much work to move.

"Yes, Akosua. They're leaving tomorrow morning to return to Michigan." Auntie Fergie explains that it is Saturday afternoon; they were supposed to leave New Jersey late Friday night, but they decided to stay a little longer, at least until my mother arrives to take their place watching awkwardly over my bed.

Auntie Gifty tiptoes into my hospital room, bearing a stuffed teddy bear that makes me cry because it's such a sweet, unexpected gesture.

"I spoke to your mother. She will be here soon, okay? You must get better. And when you visit her in Windsor, you must come and visit your uncle and me too, okay?"

Uncle Akrofi strides into the room then. He places a purple vase filled with a rainbow of flowers on the table next to my bed. He nods his head and squeezes my hand, and I think that this way he's saying goodbye is much worse than any somber words the doctor has spoken: Uncle Akrofi, the entertainer, is finally floored. His slow-moving smile doesn't move at all, his mouth remains a grave crease in his face. He turns away to leave, but then stops, turns back to look at me.

"I must tell you," he clasps one hand, palm up, against the palm of another, asking my forgiveness. "I am sorry if I should not have done so, but I told your father that you are in the hospital. I couldn't help it. He didn't want me to tell you in case it would upset you, but these flowers are from him."

I snort. "Are you sure that you're not just trying to be nice? Practically every gift my mother gave me in childhood she said was from him. And they weren't."

Uncle Akrofi nods. "That is a fair doubt to have. But these really came from him." He kisses my forehead and leaves me alone with the tulips and daisies.

◦◦◦

At some point after he leaves, I sleep the way I normally do: under the burden of a dream or remembrance. I fall asleep wondering, in the numb way that has become my trademark since the seizure wore my body out, what it will feel like if the doctors decide to drill a hole into my head. I picture my brain as a slab of raw hamburger, and for a moment, I fear I might vomit. The doctors could find anything, lay it out on a table before me, and try to make meaning. At least *try*: the doctors wouldn't know what to do with all the refuse they might uncover.

Maybe, then, it'd be better if the task of excavation rested in the hands of people who know me better. My mother, for instance, who hates to think of me as a messy woman, would definitely charge herself with the responsibility of cleaning out my head. Auntie Fergie, too, would hustle and bustle her way into the mix.

My mother and aunt shrink themselves down to the size of my pinky finger; they become lost in the maze of black grass that is my hair.

"This won't hurt," Auntie Fergie calls into my ear. "It is tradition."

She hands my mother a long wooden stick—I can see this all because I am both spectator and patient lying in a hospital bed—that I recognize as a fufu pestle.

Auntie Fergie nods her head encouragingly. "Go on, Enyo. Pound the pestle right at that spot."

My mother raises the pestle and slams it down into a spot above my ear, to the right of my temple. She repeats the action, once, once more, and begins to gain momentum.

"Good, now you're finally learning how," Auntie Fergie says, laughing, her feet padding against my scalp.

None of this hurts, not my mother pounding into my head, not my auntie's shrill shouts of encouragement, not the tearing of their toenails into my skin as they take tiny steps. When my mother finally cracks a hole into my thick skull, a river of blood flows out, rusted brown like sludge from an old pipe, but the blood gives way to dry soil that spills and piles on a table beside my head. My auntie roots around in the mounds of soil while my mother pokes through the hole in my head.

"What are you looking for?" I hear myself ask.

"Anything," my auntie says. At the same time, my mother says, "We'll know it when we see it."

They continue to excavate. I can't feel anything, I can only hear the sound of soil hitting the table, the sound of my mother's hands making movements inside my cavernous skull. Auntie Fergie has no luck with the pile of soil. But something vivid, the color of an apricot in the sun, peaks out of the hole my mother has made. With her elbow, my mother nudges it a little, until from the corner of my eye I see the tip of a green leaf sprouting from my ear. The two ladies hunker down: they pull and pull until one whole leaf emerges, until I feel the velvet of a lush tulip petal brushing against my ear canal.

"We got it," my mother cries, her voice echoing in my ear as she peeks inside the holes in my head one final time.

Since it stands taller than they do, it takes both women to hold up the golden sunrise tulip.

"The roots didn't break from the stem," my mother says. "We can transplant this flower into a pot and watch it bloom."

Everyone assumes I am sleeping all the time, but I'm not. I'm awake now, but the lack of light filtering through the window blinds, as well as the fact that someone has turned off the lamp in my room, lets me know that it's late at night. I should be asleep. The hushed voices outside my door also let me know that my family thinks I am sleeping; I hear Wisdom speak my name every so often, I hear a foreign female voice—I assume a doctor or nurse—discussing my condition.

"She's in good condition; there's no danger as long as she stays calm and thinks positively . . ."

"Which is exactly why he shouldn't be here," Wisdom hisses.

"How dare he," a different female voice adds, and it is not the nurse this time, it is the most beautiful sound I have heard in days: my mother has arrived. "How dare he come and intrude upon our family."

So, I think, placing my hands over my heart to still it. *He must be here.* Or he was here. In the waiting room, sitting in a chair, maybe he sat next to Wisdom at some point, or even my mother, his former wife. And how sweet: Wisdom and my mother are attempting to defend me, to protect me from the emotional shock of my father finally being here.

But I feel sick of it, their worrying, and sick of thinking about myself, too. Nothing is such a big deal, is it, when you're faced with the notion that your brain might literally collapse under the pressure of old blood? I run a fingernail along one of the flowers' green stems.

I am not surprised when my mother comes into the room, because I hear her negotiating with the nurse: "I know that visiting hours have ended, but I just arrived from Canada. I promise not to wake her."

Opening my eyes wide, I try to appear as awake as possible so that my mother won't feel guilty about coming into my room so late. But the first thing my mother says as she strides into the room, the scent of her musky perfume unsettling the sterile air of this space, is *I'm sorry.*

"For what?" I reach my hands out to her to beckon her closer, and when we embrace, I shudder, finally feeling my body melt into awareness, because her presence reminds me that there's an emergency happening, and I am frightened for my health.

My mother sits on my bed, her hands holding onto my forearms. She won't let me go. "Well, the last thing you heard me say to you before your—seizure—was that it was a blessing that I hadn't talked to you in days. But that was so wrong. *You* are a blessing. That was so very wrong."

"It's okay. I was being disrespectful."

"It's because of your head injury," my mother says, smoothing down my unruly hair.

"No, I think that was just me."

I watch her watch me: she remains unreadable, her face unchanging as she examines my face. I wonder what she sees. I want to use her as a mirror; if she looks alarmed, then I'm in bad shape, but of course she doesn't look like anything but my heavily armored mother.

"Your daddy is here."

"I know."

"He wants to see you."

"I know."

My mother gently takes my chin in her hand, turns my head so I'm looking her in the eye. "Oh, really? How do you know?"

"Well, why would he come here, if he didn't want to see me?"

"True." My mother sighs. "Perhaps you should see him. He's come all the way from Long Island, after all. I hope that he has come here for the right reasons, and not to clear a bad conscience. That is my only reservation."

I don't know how to respond, so I don't. Finally I say, "Long Island, huh?"

My mother seems relieved to have something to say now. "He lives there. He teaches at a community college in Brooklyn. He's a visiting professor."

"Wow, how do you know all of this?"

My mother laughs at me. "We talked in the waiting room."

"You talked?"

"Yes, of course. Silly girl. You can't really be in a room, worried about the health of your daughter, and not speak to your daughter's mother."

I have to refrain from rolling my eyes at the haughty way my mother often speaks. "Well, did he say he was sorry?"

She laughs again. "For what?"

"You know. For everything. Everything he did."

"What did he do?" My mother sucks her teeth, the corners of her mouth turned up, bemused. "Do you know how long ago that was? I don't even want him to say a word to me about all of that. It would be like putting a bandage on a scar."

I look at her closely, trying to watch for any tears that might spring up, but the only thing I notice is the dark circles under her eyes.

I clear my throat. "Was it good to see him?"

My mother shrugs, and finally I detect a change: her face flickers and I don't know if it's annoyance, sadness, anger, everything or nothing at all, but finally she settles on a firm set of her face that might represent diplomacy, or truth, or both.

"It does not make up for all the years," she says, "but it was good to see that he came for his daughter."

In the morning, I wake up before Wisdom, my mother, or the Fergies have arrived to visit me. I reach for the remote control to turn on the television for the first time but think better of it: maybe the flickering images of the screen will somehow upset my brain signals and send me into a convulsing frenzy. I think about what I overheard the nurse saying, that if I stay calm and think positively, I should be fine. Happy thoughts might keep my brain safe.

So I close my eyes, the inside of their lids are my movie screen. I'm not sure what scene to play against them. Because what in life causes the sort of unadulterated delight you see on a baby's face? I picture a baby's face, any baby, no, I need a specific baby, one cute brown baby from a recent diaper ad, and yes, maybe it's working, picturing the infant's toothless grin is definitely a happy sight. But ultimately, I'm not really happy myself, I'm just observing the happiness of someone who can achieve the kind of pure joy I desire. This baby, this imagined little creature, is so precious and adored by me—and the rest of society—because he knows how to take pleasure from simple things. A soft blanket, the jangle of car keys, warm milk, his own foot—something simple evokes in babies a sense of contentment—no, elation—that nothing can sully. I try to think of the last time I've been happy without anything else getting in the way, and I come up blank. To make matters worse, the baby's gone: I couldn't sustain the image, the joy has faded. I think of what I do for fun, who I spend time with when I'm free. When I spend time with Ella, though we laugh a lot, though I feel grateful to know someone as witty and insightful and caring as she is, I'm also usually thinking of something else: will I ever seem as pulled together as she does, would she rather be with Roger or one of her cooler friends right now, how long will she tolerate me as her best friend? Worries of whether they will last, or whether I deserve them, always seem to taint my happy moments.

But then I remember a time about a year ago when I lazed in the middle of campus—around the same spot where I fainted over two weeks ago after hitting my head. I'd finished from the library on a Friday and laid down on a bench in the middle of campus to wait for Wisdom to meet me for dinner. The crisp late November air crept in through the collar of my coat, but I didn't mind; I'd felt stuffy in my office at work. I liked the clearness of the sky even though I knew that if it were cloudier, the air wouldn't be so cold. I liked that I could see straight through to the blueness. I closed my eyes, feeling weightless. I tried to make myself think about Wisdom. Our relationship felt established yet fresh; recently, one drowsy morning, Wisdom had declared that he loved me. Everything felt like summer instead of almost winter; everything felt green instead of fading to the brown of late, late fall. Since he'd said I love you, I'd spent a lot of time daydreaming about him, bringing him up in conversations where he didn't belong. Lying on the bench, I tried to think of him, to get myself worked up about the marvelous situation in which I'd found myself, but I couldn't get my mind to focus on anything, not even romance. Instead I thought of nothing, my mind completely evaporated—kind of like that feeling I had after my seizure when I thought I was dead, in fact, except that as I lay on the bench, I knew I wasn't dead, so it was okay to feel so detached from the world. It was like the first whiff of Novocain at the dentist, except that there was no discernible cause of the buoyancy I felt.

Back in my hospital bed, I shut my eyes tightly as I struggle to get that feeling back. Just as I'm about to drift off, I feel the presence of someone else in the room. Maybe it's a doctor or nurse, maybe it's my mother, so I keep my eyes closed, hoping that whoever enters the room will promptly leave me alone.

But then I hear someone clearing his throat—a man, I can tell, I can tell it is a man and that it's not Wisdom and that it's not a doctor, it is not a stranger at all, it is someone that I know—and I have to fight to keep my eyes shut because almost everything in me wants to open them up and behold this person that I know right away is my father.

"Mercy Akosua." He speaks in a quiet voice that is not quite a whisper. His voice sounds hoarse as if he has a cold—or as if he's been crying. He's silent for such a long time that I would think he left the room were it not for the fact that I can sense him, I can detect the way the air particles respond to his presence.

"You are a very pretty young lady. You look the same as when I last saw you, except that now you are a woman."

I am attuned to every noise in the room; I can hear him take a step closer to my bed.

"I am sorry."

I hold my breath now, finding it difficult to keep my eyes closed; a moment passes in which I think I might open my eyes and reveal that I'm awake.

"I'm sorry that I didn't contact you sooner. When I heard that you fell and hit your head, I should have contacted you, but I didn't want to bother you."

My muscles unclench and my heartbeat slows, nervous energy dissipating, because he's not apologizing for what I thought he would. Even though he thinks I'm asleep and can't hear him, even though this is the perfect opportunity for him to say anything he wants, he's content to say nothing at all.

"I am still teaching, my daughter. It is very rewarding and I plan to stay for a while, but Ghana could really use some engineers."

"I may start to work with Engineers Without Borders."

Every time he says an incongruous thought, he pauses as if to give me a chance to speak, as if he knows I'm awake or wishes I were.

"I am very impressed to hear that you have been educated at an Ivy League school, both for undergraduate and graduate school. You must be a very smart young woman."

"One thing I'll never quite get used to, even after living in Michigan all those years, is the weather here. I miss the heat of Ghana."

Finally he falls silent. I wait for him to say more. I feel literally beside myself: I do not inhabit my own skin and bones, I am hovering on the outside of this experience. He's here, a whole person before me, no longer in my fantasies or daydreams, no longer bits and pieces of himself. Yet he adds up to nothing. I want him to say something meaningful, please, Daddy, I beg.

But in the end, someone else does. My doctor strides into the room, saying, "Are you Miss Agbe's father? I'd like to talk to someone about her discharge procedure."

I hear the man stammer. "Yes, I'm—I'm her father. But her mother's in the waiting room. I'm not the appropriate person . . ."

"Okay. Let's go talk to her. I think your daughter is about ready to go home."

13

At the same time that an orderly arrives with my breakfast of rubber pancakes and graying sausage links, my mother and the doctor enter the room to tell me news that I overheard earlier this morning. Soon I'll be released. I take the convergence of events as a good sign.

"The positive news is that we believe the hematoma can heal on its own. We'll give you medication that should help your body reabsorb the blood," the doctor says.

My mother, though, is literally biting her nails, something I've never seen her do. "Akosua, I have asked him repeatedly, and he assures me that this treatment should be okay. So don't worry."

"I'm not," I lie.

"There's no need to risk procedures or surgeries yet," the doctor explains. "We've determined it's safer to simply monitor you and make sure you stay rested."

"Oh, okay." Though I'm glad that no one will drill my head open for now, somehow, I wish a doctor would *do* something instead of diagnosing me with things that they can barely treat. Maybe if someone took some kind of action, went into my head to fix something palpable, I wouldn't have to worry about myself anymore.

"We also need to put you on anticonvulsant medication to prevent anymore seizure activity," the doctor says, and he explains that seizures come in many different forms. The one I had, from the way Wisdom described my fall, involved muscle convulsions in my legs, but not all seizures manifest themselves so obviously. I might simply blank out or feel a tingle in one of my limbs. I might lose my memory or have strange dream sequences.

"If you notice any of this behavior or anything else out of the ordinary, you're to call me immediately," the doctor says. "Don't worry that you're overreacting. Just call or if it seems urgent, come to the hospital."

"But I live in Manhattan. I was just visiting—"

"No, it will be fine," my mother interrupts. "I'll be staying in the area indefinitely, so you can continue to see Dr. Warner here."

"Well, I have to go back to school," I start, but my mom gives me a look that lets me know to drop the conversation until later.

"Either way, you need to stay in close contact with a doctor. If need be, we can have your chart forwarded." He peeks down at the pager clipped to his lab coat pocket. "Excuse me, I need to make a call."

As soon as the doctor leaves, I begin to protest. "Mom, you have to go back to Windsor. You need to work. Your life's there."

My mother snorts. "I didn't say I'm moving here permanently now, did I? Either I stay here while you recuperate, or you come home to Windsor with me. We've already decided."

"Who's 'we'?"

"All of us. Your auntie and uncle, your friend Wisdom, and myself. Your auntie and uncle have gone home to prepare for long-term visitors, and Wisdom went to return his rental car. He will come back here by train with some clothes and toiletries you will need while you stay . . ."

I listen to her speak, let her words wash over me. Decisions and plans happening to me and for me. How easy it is to fall into this pattern.

When we arrive at their apartment, new flowers line the room that the Fergies now call my bedroom. They're beautiful and in solid colors, unlike the pastel, Easter-like colors of the daisies and tulips my father had his best friend Akrofi bring to me in the hospital. A dozen red roses, a dozen white roses, and multiple pots filled with the deepest purple African violets I've ever seen. The scent overwhelms me as I lie in bed with the bouquets and potted plants lining the dressers, bookshelves, and tables around me, but when Uncle Fergie asks me how I like my new room, I nod and say that I love the flowers. He barely looks at me as he smiles, so I know that he was the one in charge of buying them.

"Welcome home," he says in a gruff voice. "Take a nap, eh?"

My mother is already napping in the other guest room, the one that will be hers "indefinitely," as everyone keeps saying. I bury myself in the fluffy white comforter on the bed that's indefinitely mine. I feel uneasy, not at all relaxed the way I felt when my mother and I stayed with the Fergies when I hit my head. Back then everyone thought I'd just bumped my noggin, no big deal, and then my mother had stayed for five whole days. Now that I've had a seizure, now that doctors have discovered a spot of old blood on my brain, I can't imagine how long my mother might stay in New Jersey.

"I don't live in New Jersey," I say aloud, sighing into the empty room.

Of course no one answers; the Fergies are elsewhere in the apartment, my mother so exhausted that her snores carry down the hall.

"I live in New York," I say, and though I don't expect an answer, I get one, a faint scratching against my door.

"Hey, it's me, can I come in?" Wisdom whispers, and though he can't see my nod through the door, he turns the handle and enters the room, shutting the door behind him. He drags in a large suitcase—not a duffel bag or carry-on suitcase on wheels. "Do you mind where I put this?"

"Um, yes, I'd prefer you put it back in New York." I reach my arms out to him from my spot in bed, but this action makes me feel like an infant reaching out for a parent. I get out of bed and go to him, hold him.

"Your mom specifically asked me to pack your biggest suitcase full of clothes," he says apologetically. When he pulls back from the embrace, he looks at my face carefully, the way he did in the hospital. "But maybe it's not so bad that you are here with your family. You don't look so good. Your pretty brown eyes are sad."

"Oh, I'm fine."

"Yeah. That's the thing that scared me most when you were in the hospital, when you first woke up. Your eyes looked sick. Have you ever seen anyone's eyes look sick, I mean really sick, like they're not themselves anymore?" He's holding my head in his hands still, his face inches from mine. He smells, as usual, like the mint tea he doesn't let many people know he drinks incessantly; he smells like fresh soap and aftershave. His eyes gleam beneath his glasses, and though I feel many things at once, the emotion overriding everything in this moment is remorse.

"I'm sorry," I begin to say, but he shakes his head.

"Not you, me, okay? I have to go now. I don't know when I'll get to see you again."

"What does that mean?"

He takes my hand, leads me to the bed, and begins to tuck me in. "Well, you're staying here with your mom. I sadly have to get back to the city. I need to get back to school." Wisdom bundles the edge of the comforter under my chin. "Don't look so worried, I'll come back to visit on the weekends or something. But it might be a couple of weeks, because next weekend I'm going to this conference at Harvard..."

"What? A couple of weeks?"

"I'll call every day, though."

"No, not that. I mean, I will miss you, but I mean—do you really think I'm going to be here in Jersey for more than a couple of weeks?" Despite myself, I feel my tear ducts kicking in. "Wisdom, I can't just stay here. I want to go back to school—or I want to—I don't know what I want to do, but I want to do it, not just lie here."

"Well." He kisses me lightly. "Rest for a couple days like you're supposed to. And then: tell your mother what you want."

"It's not that simple."

"Yes, it is."

He makes it sound so simple, even though I don't quite believe him. I love him for his belief in the words he speaks, for his attempt to make me feel like everything will end up okay. I kiss him. I open his mouth with mine. It is easy; us, Wisdom and me, we are the simple thing that I haven't recognized all along and now, finally, I do. I will let him as close as I can, as close as he wants to come. His mouth is warm, his body, as we pull his sweater and undershirt over his head, is warm. He reaches for the hem of my pajama top but stops, studying my face in that same careful way.

"It's okay," I whisper.

He burrows into the sheets and blankets, he burrows against me. I remember all of this, the smoothness of his shoulders, the soft kisses he plants on my collarbone. Part of me considers mentally reliving moments we shared in the past: picnic lunches, Friday nights in the movie theater, car trips gone wrong. But mostly it seems ridiculous of me to think of thinking so much when all I want is to do the very thing that this man, Wisdom, and I are so close to doing. I shut my brain off the best I can. His hands slide against the flannel of my pajamas and eventually, my skin.

At first, because of the sound of blood pounding in my ears, I don't hear the knocking. But when Wisdom puts his finger over his lips, I hear again the sound of a fist against the wooden door.

"Akosua! Where are you?" My mother's sleepy voice carries through the door. Next to me, Wisdom's muscles tense. We lie as still as we can, breathing into each other's necks.

"I'm in here. I'm fine."

"Come and sit with me in the den. Aren't you hungry? What are you doing?"

"Nothing. Coming out in a sec, okay?"

I hear my mother's feet padding against the hardwood floor, away from the door and down the hall. Wisdom and I exhale, collapsing against each other; it is over before it's begun.

He mumbles something against my shoulder, something I know must be his declaration that he should leave. I ask him the one thing I've wanted to ask the most but didn't think I could voice until this moment when I'm hearing myself speak:

"We're back, right? Together?"

Wisdom rolls his eyes, a smile playing across his lips as he pulls on his sweater. He extends his hands and helps me out of bed. "What do you think?"

At night, in bed, it's not Wisdom but my mother sleeping beside me. She stays on her side of the bed, though her fingers lightly hold onto my forearm. I think of moving my arm, of shaking her shoulder and telling her to go back to her own guest room. I will tell her that I don't need her to be so close, that I'll be okay without her. But in the next moment, when I feel the way my mother grips my arm, I remind myself that sometimes it's she who needs me, and that maybe one of those times is now.

I tried to take Wisdom's advice and tell my mother, plain and simple, that I need to get back to my life in the city. But my nagging her has had an undesired effect; after nearly a week of resting at the Fergies' under my mother's watchful gaze, I am returning to my campus, but with my mother leading the way. In fact, she is dragging me. She insists that if I'm so worried about my life in the city, she'll escort me to the graduate studies office and help me figure out how to get some extra time to catch up on work that I've missed.

"This is what you wanted, right?" she says as she eases her rental car out of the Fergies' parking garage. "You keep saying that you need to straighten out your life. Well, that is why we will return to your school and fix things there. Then we will come back to the Fergies' and you will continue to recuperate."

"But you don't have to worry yourself with my problems. You need to get back to Windsor. And we're wearing out our welcome with Auntie and Uncle."

"That's not true. We're family. We can never wear out our welcome." My mother laughs. "Besides, I think they're better off with us around."

I don't want to admit it, but it's true: the Fergies seem to enjoy our company, even Uncle Fergie. The day after I left the hospital, my mother decided to rent a car of her own so that she could go grocery shopping and pick up my prescriptions and whatever else she needed to do without having to wait for Uncle Fergie to return from work and chauffeur her around. My mother has also used her free time to cook everything from spinach stew and plantains to fettuccini alfredo. Uncle Fergie has been thanking my mother nonstop for keeping his wife company, saying, "Sister Enyo, since you arrived, you women bring only cheer to my apartment," which is another way of saying, "Thanks to you, I've been eating like a king and my wife's no longer bored." The rental car has liberated Auntie Fergie: she and my mother have been shopping for clothes for me and for themselves, my mom drives Auntie Fergie to visit her friends, and now Auntie Fergie says she might buy a car of her own—that is, if she can pass a road test.

"Sister Fergie, I can teach you how to drive," my mother keeps saying, and the notion, though cute, worries me, because it's as if my mother won't ever leave New Jersey, as if I'll never leave either.

But now my mother eases the car through the Lincoln Tunnel. We have left New Jersey; we have returned to Manhattan. I crack open the car window and breathe in the cold air.

"Akosua, it is nearly wintertime. Close the window so that you don't catch the flu on top of everything else."

I inhale once more, but eventually close the window as she requested. "You know, the offices at school might be closed today."

"It's Friday, Akosua."

"Really, a lot of offices aren't open on Friday," I mumble, but I know there's no use. She's determined to save my graduate career.

"When we go in there, you should be firm, tell them you are absolutely interested in continuing your studies, but that your health comes first. If they offer you extra credit opportunities, take them. If they offer you extra time, take it. You need to earn strong marks so that you can apply for your PhD."

"Okay, Mom, I hear you." I rest my head against the back of the seat and stare at, not through, the glass of the windshield. If I look hard enough, I can almost see myself. I want to see my eyes, to see if they're still sad the way Wisdom described them, though I'm not sure I know what would make my eyes look happy or sad, anyway. It's irrelevant—mostly all I see is the blue sedan in front of us.

"Akosua. Are you okay?" My mother waves her right hand in front of my face. "You're not blacked out, are you? Are you having a seizure?"

I take her hand from my face and hold it in my lap. I know she's been scared, watching the tilt of my head as I lounge in the Fergies' apartment, studying the movement of my legs as I walk across their living room. She's looking for a vacant gaze, a twitch or a shudder; she's looking to catch me if I should start to fall again. "No. I was just thinking."

"About what?" She squeezes my hand and quickly lets go, gripping the steering wheel again, as if her moment of panic never happened.

And then—because even though I wasn't really thinking about him, wasn't I really thinking about him?—I reply, "About Daddy. Have you heard from him?"

She laughs. "Of course not. Why would I?"

"I dunno, you talked in the hospital, so I figured . . . I mean I expected . . ."

"I hope you didn't expect him to come around more frequently. That's not the kind of man your father is. You know he is not the kind of man who will make it easy for you. Tso! He will not help you to justify going to him for anything, he won't give you one bit of reason to. You have to want to go to him on your own." She sucks her teeth. "This is exactly what I've always warned you about. That he might disappoint you. Don't think about him now, you will aggravate your head injury."

"I wasn't thinking about him, Mom. I was really just staring into space."

My mother looks at me carefully. She doesn't know what to say. So she turns on the radio, and we listen to golden oldies all the way to my school.

I haven't had a seizure since the first one, not anything more than the faintest headaches, but the one side effect of the medication is severe drowsiness. I'm dozing as we pull up to my dorm, and she helps me up to my room, and she tucks me into bed, saying that I need to rest and she'll visit the graduate studies office without me. Since we came all this way, she doesn't want to leave without at least talking to someone about my situation.

"Don't, Mom, I'll take care of it myself," I say, but then I fall into a dreamless sleep.

I awaken with a start. I don't know how much time has passed, but my mother's still gone. In no time, she'll return, and she'll know that I'm only enrolled in one course, that I'm losing my financial aid, that I'm failing. I sigh, stretch my arms to the ceiling. Maybe it's better for me to stop hiding the truth from her.

Maybe it's time for me to stop hiding, period. I think of my father, how he referred the doctor to my mother, his voice sounding as though he'd swallowed a cactus whole. I didn't open my eyes to see his face. I pretended to sleep, hiding behind the guise of unconsciousness. After seventeen years of not seeing my father, he appeared in plain sight, but I still didn't have the courage to see him.

But then I think about him, my father, and the limited ways he's been in my life. I think about the way his presence made me feel as a little girl. I loved him. But he was less a person than a force acting upon us. You could either bask in the sunshine of his admiration or drown in his sea of expectation. He drank all the air. He took up all the space in our home, and then he left a void that took up all the space in my heart.

I won't let him happen to me again.

I climb out of bed and shuffle over to my desk, bleary-eyed but somehow more focused; I've fixed my gaze into a deep fog, waiting to see whatever will be there when it clears. I sit down in front of my computer, place my hands on the keyboard. Wisdom's right: now that my father is in the country, it is easy to contact him. I've always known that, right? I don't need information from Daniel Cobblah and his cousin. I don't need to sneak through Uncle Akrofi's email. I don't need to find out through so-and-so who knows so-and-so who lives next door to Kofi Agbe.

I just need to finally want to do it.

I search for his name on the internet; I know that his name and possibly email address and phone number will be in some online directory for a college in Brooklyn.

Sure enough, his school provides a work phone number, a fax, a university email address, and a link to his personal website. There's no picture, like some school websites have, only his name: Dr. Kofi Agbe, Visiting Professor of Civil Engineering. I click the link to his website. It's simple, one page. There's a picture of the Ghanaian flag—red, gold, green, black star—juxtaposed with the stars and stripes of the US flag. Below is his name, Kofi Agbe, and a link to Ghana's official website, next to a link back to his university's website. Then there's a link to a PDF file of his résumé, but I am not at all interested in his past accomplishments. I am interested in the fact that at the top of his résumé he has typed his home address. Duncan Road, Hempstead, New York. My mother was right: he lives on Long Island.

I open a new page on the internet, type his address into a search engine that helps me find directions. Driving directions to his house. I learn that it would take under an hour to drive there from my apartment. I like how neat and straightforward the internet makes it seem to get from me to him. I like the numbered steps. Street by street, it is simple. I stare for more than an hour at those words on the screen; I memorize them; I imagine what those streets might look like.

One foot in front of the other, Akosua. If I'm not careful, I'll trip over my feet.

I will call his work number.

After three rings, when no one picks up, I will myself not to hang up, which is precisely what I want to do. I hang on. Hang on, Akosua, hang on.

The phone clicks as though someone is answering, but it is only the voicemail message. Maybe, I think, I will at least hear what he sounds like now, his non-hoarse voice, but I am disappointed that it's an automated voice, not his, who tells me,

"Extension 5-9646 is not available at this time. This mailbox is full. Please try your call later."

Right when I'm about to hang up, I hear another click, and then that same voice I heard in the hospital, the one that sounds sick with strep throat, amends, "Professor Kofi Agbe. I am out of my office through December 1. For emergencies, please call my home phone at . . ."

I scramble for a paper and pen but have to settle for writing the number on the back of my hand with a black permanent marker. Does he have a cold? The flu? Is that why he's taking off so many days from work? Thanksgiving is a week old; he should be back to work already. I have sudden flashes of him devouring cranberry sauce during Thanksgiving dinner, the only type of sweet he really loved.

Now I have his number on the back of my hand, indelibly.

I am giddy and subdued, euphoric and devastated. There is nothing left to do but what I've been avoiding, what I've been struggling not to do, what I'm pretty sure I desperately want to do.

I dial the number that I've written on the back of my hand.

My heart, as I wait, beats so forcefully that I feel it in my throat. Each time the phone rings, I catch my breath, afraid that if I breathe fully I will choke my own heart to death.

Someone picks up after the fourth ring.

But no one says anything for a while, at least not to me. I hear the sound of someone fumbling for the phone, the sound of small feet pitter pattering nearby, a sweet baby voice saying something I can't hear. And then the same voice I heard on the office voicemail.

"Oh, be careful baby."

And then a wail, the wail of a small child.

"Oh, baby, did you hit your head?"

And he must be holding the baby in his arms now because I can hear the crying very close to my ear as the voice that is my father's finally says, "Hello? Hello? . . . Sorry, o, we had a bit of an accident over here. Hello?"

I'm sure he can hear me breathing; I'm practically gasping for air.

"Hello? *Hello?*" And then, "Akosua?"

I hang up the phone.

Blood rushes to the surface of my body; suddenly I am hot and tingly as if I have run through a steam room. On the other end of the line, my father. But not just my father: my father and a girl baby, his girl baby, his new family. No wonder he's had no time to contact me. Maybe there's a wife, too. Maybe a boy in elementary school. Maybe his house is teeming with children who, when they fall down, are enveloped by my father's arms and the gentle question, "Oh, baby, did you hit your head?"

Not for me, though. Not for me. This was all a mistake. No matter what I do, my father will be saying no to me. He has been saying no since he left when I was seven, no letters, no phone calls, no gifts, no how are you doings, just no, no, no, all over again, and I knew this would happen if I tried to reach him, a disappointment, utter humiliation. I was expecting nothing yet everything at once because no matter how many times he says no I am waiting, waiting, waiting with my heart between my teeth.

When my mother returns a few minutes later, I'm still sitting with the room phone on my lap, listening to my own breath, hearing his raspy tone play in my head. Saying my name over and over. Except in real life he only said it once. It's just my head playing tricks on me as usual.

"Akosua, aren't you supposed to be sleeping?" She bustles into the room, carrying, of course, two bags full of groceries, because her goal always seems to be to feed me. "This is why you need your mommy around. You don't take care of yourself."

"I'm fine, promise." I look at her face. That it's not contorted in anger is a good sign; either the dean didn't tell her how badly I'm doing in grad school, or she's realized all on her own that I'm no scholar. "What did my dean tell you?"

"Your dean?" My mother has already made her way to the kitchen and begins to unpack cereal, cans of soup, and granola bars. "I couldn't speak with any dean. I was told I needed an appointment. But I did explain your situation to the assistant there in the office, and she kindly explained the types of leave you can take."

She stuffs the plastic grocery bags under the sink, strides back into the living room, and pulls a folder out of her purse. She waves the papers in my face. "These are very important. The woman made it clear that if you do not take the appropriate action, you will lose your spot in the program."

"Oh."

"Your education is important. There are some parts of this paperwork that I'd like you to get started on filling out now, if you're not feeling sleepy anymore. I am going to start cooking dinner."

"It's about five hours from dinnertime," I point out.

"I thought I could have it ready in advance."

I can't help it; I burst into laughter not unlike the kind my mother's always unleashing on me. "Mom! Don't you see? There's not even that much for you to do here, you know? I swear, I really am fine. Or at least I'm going to be. You should go home to Windsor."

"I know, I know. I will, soon. Once I know your school situation's straightened out."

"I'll be fine, I swear," I continue, as if she hasn't spoken, "even if the school stuff never got straightened out, I'd be fine."

"What does that mean?" My mother's already in the kitchen warming up soup that I don't want but will eat anyway, because it's chicken noodle and she's adding fresh vegetables and my favorite spices, because she loves me, that's all that her actions say, over and over, yes, yes, and yes, to me. "Of course the school situation will be fixed. You don't even have to read everything. The first option is the best."

I sit down on my bed with the paperwork. It looks like the dean's assistant just printed pages from the university website. I shake my head as I imagine the woman directing my mother to the internet and my mother insisting on hard copies. She's nothing if not predictable; she still thinks of hard copies as the only official way to do business.

And it turns out she's predictable in another way. I skim the options and I see that the first option, the one she thinks is the best, involves taking a personal leave for a whole semester.

"Mom," I say, "what about the medical/mental health leave?"

She doesn't look up from stirring the pot in the kitchen. "Oh, that one requires you to give medical records, talk about diagnoses. It is too much. You don't want your school to be involved in your personal matters."

"But the personal leave is only a semester at a time." I explain to her how the medical/mental health leave is more flexible, allowing me to ease back in with a couple of classes at a time. If I do this personal leave, it might take me a whole additional year to graduate.

"Well, that might actually be a good thing. More time to bring up your marks, do some special projects that will bolster your PhD application." My mother puts her spoon down, leaves the kitchenette and joins me on my bed. "Listen, I talked to Auntie Gifty. Did you know that her son-in-law also had some struggles before entering his PhD program? She and Uncle Akrofi said that all you need to do is—"

"Mom, I don't want to do a PhD program," I finally say.

"What?"

"I just want to finish my MA and figure out what to do after that. I don't want extra time to bolster my application. I just want to finish and move onto something else."

And as I say the words, I know they are true. They've been waiting in my mind, in my throat, on the tip of my tongue, and now they are free.

I must have spoken more firmly than I realized, because my mother has been shocked into silence. She's looking at me, and I'm holding her gaze. It's uncomfortable, and part of me wants to look away, but I know that I can't. We're hashing it out in our eyes. We're having a conversation for which we don't have words. Telepathically, I can tell her that I need to take control, that being independent doesn't mean I'm not still a part of her. Telepathically, she can tell me that she wants me to have all that she once wanted for herself, that she wants every good thing for me.

Finally, she speaks aloud. "Okay. Medical leave. And then no PhD. Unless you change your mind."

I wrap my arms around her, squeezing her close, breathing her in. My sweet mother. I keep hugging her so I don't have to look at her as I say, "Medical *and* mental health leave. It's not just for my physical health. The blood will get reabsorbed in my brain, but my mental health will still need attention. My emotional well-being."

She stiffens a little bit in my arms. "You are not going to write that on the form, are you?"

"No."

She breathes a sigh of relief, pulls away from me. "Good girl."

"I'm going to type it into the form. Who does paperwork anymore?" And she unleashes her wild laugh. "Naughty girl."

After our talk, my mom's wiping copious tears from her eyes. She blames the onions, and when I point out that she didn't add onions to the soup, she revises her answer and blames the tears on laughter.

But I know the truth, and I decide to leave the apartment for a few moments so that she can collect herself in private.

I head downstairs to check my mailbox in the lobby. I rarely get any mail except for campus advertisements, so I expect nothing. But when I turn the key in the lock, the door doesn't open. After I jiggle the key for a while and the box opens, I see why: my tiny mailbox is stuffed with enough papers and envelopes to jam the door.

Flyers for parties and cultural dinners on campus, credit card offers, coupons to restaurants and grocery stores. Some of the flyers advertise events that happened a month ago. I separate the junk mail into piles right here in the lobby, leaning against the rows of mailboxes, the open door of mine poking me in the back. It's not all junk, though: a cell phone bill. Another cell phone bill. A notice for a past due credit card account. Two envelopes marked urgent, return address, the dean's office. Two envelopes from the hospital. I rip them open; one's a laundry list of charges from my first hospital stay—who knew they charge you for every single blood test—and the other's the bill from the first ambulance trip. The pace of my heartbeat begins to pick up as I peruse the dean's letter and read again of my "impending ineligibility for federal aid," as well as the fact that my change to part-time student has all but voided my school medical insurance. Oh. Okay. On the outside, I am shaking, but in my head, I am laughing at myself. This is not mail that has gathered over the week. This is mail from the past month. *So this is what happens when you neglect the practicalities of daily living, huh, Akosua?*

Now I am laughing out loud, or crying. Or maybe I'm laughing so hard that I'm crying. All I know is that the laughter sound issues forth from my mouth, tears prickle at my eyes, and my shoulders shudder. I gather up all these bills and papers; I hold them in my arms and clasp them to my chest and inhale the papery scent. This mess I'm embracing could be the unraveling of me, yet I'm still holding it close. Somehow this action liberates me, even though there's nothing remarkable about this moment of chaos. Everyone's life is unraveling, everywhere, all the time. Life is constantly falling apart and then finding a way to weave the threads together again.

The next morning, I discover that I have a message on my cell phone from my father. I listen to it in the bathroom while my mother sleeps in a cot that someone from the Housing Department delivered to us last night when my mother announced it was too late to drive back to Jersey City; I filled out the request form online, and someone other than Daniel Cobblah or Pete knocked on my door and set up the cot in between my bed and desk.

"Akosua, hello. Eh, this is your father, Kofi."

No, really? Not my father Robert, or my father Steve?

"Eh, according to my caller ID system, I, eh, received a phone call from a New York cell phone area code. It was a number I did not recognize. I thought perhaps it might be you? If so, you called during a bit of a hectic time. My sister, your Aunty Comfort, is here for the holidays with her children, your cousins. The baby girl is two. The twin daughters are six. We are truly blessed. I am sure they would love to meet their big cousin sometime soon. Akosua . . ."

He pauses, and for a moment, I'm filled with the promise of his saying something I want to hear him say, whatever that might be.

He clears his throat. "They were hoping to see their first snow, but as you might know, the weather has been relatively mild.

"Well. Do call me back, if you would like. Please get well soon. Warm regards."

That's the end. That's all he has to say.

Immediately, I think of who I might share this message with. Not my mother, because she might laugh, or worse, complain about how useless he's proven himself. Ella's still down in Atlanta visiting Roger's family. I forward the voicemail to Wisdom, following it with a text message: "Heartwarming, huh?"

I listen to my father's message again. His voice strains, grating against my ears, and I think, maybe he's not even suffering from a sore throat. Maybe that is the way his voice sounds, now, weak and unconvincing, as if it lacks the strength to convey anything important. The words he speaks might never be enough.

Before I leave the bathroom, the phone vibrates in my hands.

"Wisdom, did you listen to it?" I answer.

"Hey, Akosua my sweet, I miss you. How do you feel?"

"Wisdom, are you still in Boston? Did you hear my father's message?"

"What message? No."

"Then why are you calling?" Through the shut door, I hear the squeak of my mother repositioning herself in the cot.

"Because I wanted to, silly. I'm back in my apartment. I took the train instead of the bus on my way back from Boston. Because I want to see you. Do you think your family will mind if I come to Jersey?"

He's here, right now. A short subway or bus ride away. I tell him to come here, to me, to my apartment.

"Your mom's gone?"

"No. She's sleeping right here. She's like my bodyguard."

Wisdom laughs a little. "Okay. Well, get ready. I'll come over and we'll go get bagels and coffee. We can all have breakfast together or something. I want to win her over."

Oh, Wisdom, so earnest. If my mother could hear him now, she might say something like, "It's going to take a lot more than bagels to win me over, especially since you are a man." But I know that her words would be all, or mostly, talk.

I'm on my way out the door before he calls; though he gives no warning, I can sense that Wisdom's nearing my apartment. It's the bond of our love. Or maybe it's just that I've timed how long it usually takes him to ride the bus from his place to mine. I scrawl a note for my mom: be back soon. I slip into her wool coat and Ella's red scarf and tiptoe out of the apartment, shutting the door behind me with a gentle click. The good thing about my mother's presence, apparently, is this: I enjoy the thrill of sneaking out to see my boyfriend, the element of danger should we get caught. *I'm twenty-four.* Wisdom embraces me, presses his hand to the back of my head as if to hold it intact.

"You okay?" he asks.

"Mm-hmm."

"You sure?" Wisdom pulls away and pats me near my right hip, near the pocket. "Hey, you're poking me."

He reaches into the pocket of my mother's coat and unearths her very heavy set of keys; suitcase keys, keys to the front and side doors of her condo, keys to her car, keys to her office and the trunk in her basement and her mailbox and a file cabinet by her bed, and now, since the start of her stint in New Jersey, keys to the Fergies' apartment, my apartment, and her rental car.

"This is perfect," Wisdom says, holding the keys up to the sunlight as if they are covered in jewels. "Forget bagels. When your mom wakes up, can we ask her permission to drive to that bakery up in Inwood, the one with the carrot cake muffins? Or maybe we can all drive to my favorite diner in Brooklyn."

"Oh, we don't need to ask her permission," I say. "She's not going to care." She's not going to *know.* "Let's go to Inwood. It won't even take that long."

"Are you sure?"

"Yes, I'm sure. She even let me drive her and Auntie Fergie to the mall the other day. She says the car's as much hers as mine." I am not exactly telling the truth, or maybe not at all. I am thinking of how nice it would feel to be on a road to somewhere. "I've never driven in this city, Wisdom. I'm always walking and running and riding the train. Can I drive?"

After a moment's consideration, he places the keys in my open palm. "Take us wherever you want to go."

At first, in the car I am scared. The streets are much narrower here than in Michigan, where I'm used to driving; there are more pedestrians to watch for, bike riders to accidentally maim. But I get the hang of things. I take the surface streets uptown, pass by Wisdom's apartment, then drive past the intersection where last week I went looking for Ella to give her the scarf I'm now wearing around my neck.

"Are we doing the tour of Harlem?" he asks. He is gripping the dashboard but leaning back in his seat. He is trying to appear cool and calm and in control, because it's clear that he thinks I am not.

I am in control. I know exactly where we are.

"Do you know how to get to Inwood?" Wisdom asks. His fingers touch the black rectangle frames of his glasses. "Are you okay?"

"I'm fine, I promise. Relax."

But I am not exactly relaxed because tiny flakes of snow have begun to fall. The first snow of the season. I know I'm from Michigan, but that doesn't mean I particularly like the snow. Well, I do like the snow. Just not driving in it. I might slip. The car might slip. I might crash.

"Do you want me to take over?" Wisdom asks me at the next red light.

I shake my head no and guide us onward.

"Wait, what are we doing? You know we're getting on the bridge, right?" Now his voice rises to a panicked pitch. "Are you okay? Are you even supposed to be driving right now?"

No, of course not, not with the medication I'm on, not until I'm used to the drowsy way I feel on it, but I'm not going to tell him that. He won't understand that even though I'm not supposed to be, I am clear on where we're headed.

Though I can't leave him hanging forever, I don't know if I can vocalize what it is I've decided we're going to do. Where it is we're going. I ask him to listen to the most recent message on his phone. The volume on his phone is loud enough that I can hear the gravelly sound of my father speaking, though I can't make out his words. I don't need to make out his words. I know them by heart; they are saying, drive, drive, drive, because there's nothing left to lose.

Wisdom pockets his phone. He sighs, nudges my cheek with his knuckle. I feel his eyes on me for a long time, but he doesn't say anything. Finally he says, "Need a navigator?" It is an attempt at levity, but I know he's not truly asking. No one in this vehicle knows the way except for me.

This is the only history I know clearly: the very literal steps of how I got to where I almost am. I memorized each numbered line from the computer screen. I lived those words; I pictured the route before I even knew I would come here, before I knew I would take the chance. The numbered streets, the avenues, the Triborough Bridge, the highway clogged with passengers, most traveling to places they planned to go, but some, I'm sure, winding up where they least expected. I am driving without thinking; I am moving myself to this resting place; I am following the street signs I have internalized.

Wisdom sits back and watches. As I turn the car onto Duncan Road, he reaches over and squeezes my knee. But he doesn't say a word. He knows he shouldn't say a word because words will only clutter up my mind, my mind which is as clear and as cold as the highway I have taken here.

I am here. I am holding Wisdom's hand now as I pull into the driveway, as I prepare to raise my head and see what is in front of me. I'm shaking, then calm, then shaking, one extreme to another in a split second, oscillation and indecision personified, the only way I know to be.

And in this state, dear daddy, I bring myself to your door.

ACKNOWLEDGMENTS

I'll take it way back and thank the teachers who stoked my love of reading and writing, including Mrs. Hill, Mr. Onickle, Mr. Castellani, Mr. Dave Wilson, Dr. K, Dr. Lovasz, Mrs. Hannett-Price, and Mr. Fremuth. My deepest appreciation to my writing instructors over the years: Matthew Sharpe, the late great Leslie Woodard, Carolyn Ferrell, Eduardo Santiago, Simone Dalton, and Jennifer Crystal. Special thanks to Mary Morris and David Hollander for guiding me as I worked on this book in its earliest iterations, and to Taylor Larsen, whose incisive feedback and generosity of time and attention helped elevate this project into a novel--just in the nick of time.

Too many amazing fellow writers at SLC to name, but in particular, I have to thank Sarah Morgan for her friendship, as well as Mike and Molly, for our novel-writing trio.

No words for you, Andrew Colom. You are a singular artist and genuine friend and I don't think of good music, books, or flicks without thinking of you (ok, I did manage a few words).

Thank you, friends I don't deserve (but I will keep trying to): Madeline Leung, Erin Usmen, Anna Levitt, Stefanie Kopchick, Alicia Delisser-Nuttall, JLR (no matter what); Jennifer Brown, Vanessa Prescott, Khaliah Williams, Amanda Finigan (the love is there). Thank you to all the students who taught me.

Thank you, Christina, Marissa, Kathya, Lena, Parul, Bruna, Lynn, Jessie, May Zhee, Thierry, and Poets & Writers, for helping me Get the Word Out.

I can't thank the Red Hen team enough, so professional and kind and dedicated. Rebeccah Sanhueza, Monica Fernandez, Shelby Wallace, Piper Gourley, Kate Gale, Tobi Harper Petrie, Mark E. Cull, Em Villaverde for the beautiful cover, and all the other people behind the scenes who made this book possible. Thank you, Deesha Philyaw, for your beautiful writing and for seeing what you saw in this book. Thank you, Itoro Bassey, for embodying the idea of women lifting each other up. You've been so generous in the short time I've known you.

I truly appreciate you, Cassie Mannes Murray, for your warmth, creativity, and insight in promoting this book. Your support means more than I can say.

Thank you, Deys, Bediakos, and Kirstens far and wide. I'm fortunate to have the family I do. And thank you, Ewe fam, for excusing my inexact transliterations of our language. *Babanawo.*

So much gratitude and love to my creative, smart, kind, hilarious boys, Edem and Isaac, who weren't yet around when I started writing this but who were there for the end, cheering me on without even knowing it.

And last but not least: Mr. Sun, Moon, and Stars, Super Dad to our super sons, the person who encouraged me to revise and submit this novel in the first place, the best of all the good eggs. I joke, but please know that I know I'm lucky to have you in my corner. A toast: to Jonny!

BIOGRAPHICAL NOTE

Esinam Bediako is a Ghanaian American writer from Detroit. She holds a BA in English from Columbia University, an MFA in Fiction from Sarah Lawrence College, and an MAT in Secondary English from University of Southern California. A finalist for the *Porter House Review* Editor's Prize, the Frontier Global Poetry Prize, and *North American Review*'s Terry Tempest Williams Prize, Esinam taught high school English for nearly a decade and currently writes and edits for a health nonprofit. Her most important job is editing the masterpieces of her two young sons, who create stories, poems, and videos with enviable speed and imagination. Esinam lives in Claremont, California, with her family.

Printed in the USA
CPSIA information can be obtained
at www.ICGtesting.com
JSHW021123270724
67102JS00002B/2